LAYOVERLAND

A NOVEL BY

GABBY NOONE

RAZORBILL

In loving memory of my friend Stephen Costello (1994–2016).
I hope there are no granite countertops in Heaven.

RAZORBILL

An imprint of Penguin Random House LLC, New York

First published in the United States of America by Razorbill,
an imprint of Penguin Random House LLC, 2020

Visit us online at penguinrandomhouse.com

Library of Congress Cataloging-in-Publication Data
Names: Noone, Gabby, author.
Title: Layoverland : a novel / by Gabby Noone.
Description: New York : Razorbill, 2020. | Audience: Ages 14+ |
Summary: When seventeen-year-old Beatrice arrives in Purgatory and is chosen to
help others reach Heaven, the last thing she expects is to fall in love with Caleb, with
whom she shares a tragic history.
Identifiers: LCCN 2019036469 | ISBN 9781984836120 (hardcover) |
ISBN 9781984836137 (ebook)
Subjects: CYAC: Purgatory—Fiction. | Future life—Fiction. | Love—Fiction.
Classification: LCC PZ7.1.N64 Lay 2020 | DDC [Fic]—dc23
LC record available at https://lccn.loc.gov/2019036469

ISBN 9781984836120

Book manufactured in Canada; jacket printed in the USA

10 9 8 7 6 5 4 3 2 1

Design by Kelley Brady. Text set in Tiempos text.

PROLOGUE

You know the kind of crying where you're crying over one thing and then you think about a slightly less upsetting but still definitely upsetting thing and it makes you cry even more? And then you think about every bad thing that's ever happened to you in your whole life and everything you think is unfair in the world? And it's like you're taking part in some Guinness World Record competition to see who can fit the most toppings on a single pizza and your face is the pizza and your tears are the toppings? The pepperoni of your mistakes, the black olives of not being pretty enough, the mushrooms of rejection, and, for good measure, a few chunks of pineapple to represent how bees are dying at an alarming rate and you have no idea how to stop it?

No?

Me neither.

I'm not usually someone who cries. I wasn't familiar with this kind of crying until today, but it's the kind of crying I'm doing as I drive around in my used Honda Civic. My car was manufactured in 1999, which is three years before I was born, four years before my little sister was born, and twenty years before today, when I accidentally ruined her life.

I mean, I don't think her *whole* life will be ruined, but her life *right now* is ruined, and isn't that really the same thing?

I'm too ashamed to make my way home and face her, but I've been crying so much that I'm afraid of showing my red puffy face anywhere in public. I don't have a best friend's house to seek refuge in because, to be honest, my sister was my best (and only) friend. So I've just been driving aimlessly around town for the last five hours.

The slightly less upsetting thing that's making me cry even more is the realization that there aren't enough songs about having a fight with your best friend. And there are possibly zero songs about having a fight with your best friend who also happens to be your sister. There are definitely zero songs about having a fight with your best friend who also happens to be your sister, because you've just ruined her life.

But after hours of driving around in circles in total silence, I decide I need to find something to listen to. Maybe music will make things better or, at least, drown out the sound of the ragged sobs that are somehow coming out of my own mouth and not that of some wild animal. At a stoplight I scroll through my phone and try to pick something, but nothing feels right. I look at the Top 50 Songs in America playlist. Every track is either about people who are having sex or wish they were having sex. I can't believe that I've ruined my sister's life and there isn't even an appropriate soundtrack for me to feel bad about it over.

The light turns green. I stop scrolling.

"Hey, Siri," I sob into my phone. "Play a song about missing your sister."

I think talking to the virtual assistant feature on any phone or TV is so deeply idiotic, but I use it sometimes while I'm driving because the only thing *more* idiotic is being the teenage girl who actually gets in a car accident while looking down at her phone. I refuse to be a useful statistic for local nagging parents.

"Playing 'Hey, Soul Sister' by Train," the robotic female voice says back to me.

"What? No! Play a song about *missing your sister*!"

"Playing 'Hey, Soul Sister' by Train," it repeats.

The opening notes blare out of my phone speaker.

Heyyyy, hey huh ayyyy, hey huh ayyyy.

"Siri, shut this off!" I yell.

But the song keeps going. The singer says something about a girl's lipstick stains on his head or something. It's definitely a song about people who wish they were having sex and *not* about actual sisters.

"That doesn't even make any *sense*!" I half yell-sob as I throw the phone onto the passenger seat.

But before I can ask Siri to change the song again, I see a silver SUV driving on the wrong side of the road, speeding straight toward me. I blink back my tears, hoping it's a hallucination or just some kind of optical illusion created by the makeup pooling under my eyes. Just as I frantically try to hit the brakes, we collide. Then it all happens so fast, yet so, so slowly.

Our cars make an awful squeaking, crunching noise, like someone dragging a million pairs of long acrylic nails over a chalkboard and crushing a million soda cans all at once. Then it's like I can see my own body rise up into the air and my head smashing into the glass of the front window. For a quarter of a second, the other driver and I make panicked eye contact, then his head slumps forward. Somehow, though, the music from my phone keeps playing.

Heyyyyy hey huh heyyyyy.

With shards of glass covering my neck, and my spine cracking in multiple places, all I can think is: *I'm going to be so pissed if I die while this song is playing.*

1

When I try to open my eyes, I'm blinded by fluorescent white light. I feel a gust of cold air directly above my head, and a chill runs down my spine. A smell lingers in the air—a combination of bathroom cleaner and vegetable soup. I'm strapped upright into what feels like a hard yet lumpy bed. Beside me, I hear the sickly sound of someone gagging followed by the unmistakable plop of vomit.

All awful elements individually, but combined, my brain processes them as one thing: hospital.

Somehow it makes sense to me that I'm here, but the exact reason *why* I'm here sits at the farthest edges of my brain where I can't quite grasp at it.

I'm squinting away from the light, attempting to go to sleep, when I feel the nudge of someone else's elbow against mine. My eyes burst open again and I bolt upright.

I look down at the offending limb where it sits on an armrest to my right. My eyes wander up to its owner, a sunburned man with bleached-blond spiked hair who is wearing a Hawaiian shirt and currently hurling the contents of his stomach into a paper barf bag.

But hospital beds don't have armrests, right? Why would they? One thing I know for certain is that patients aren't meant to share hospital beds, especially when one of those patients is a Guy Fieri look-alike who seems like he's coming back from a bad trip to Flavortown.

I look to my left. There's another armrest and another elbow, this one as wrinkly as a dried apricot. Its owner is a sleeping white-haired old woman wearing a pastel nightgown, her hands clasped serenely on her lap.

I look behind me and realize I'm not strapped to a bed, but to a seat upholstered in battered orange vinyl. All around me, in front and behind, side to side, are more of these seats. And they're full of people. We're in a long, narrow room with low ceilings and walls made of plastic and tiny windows with a view of nothing but pitch-black darkness and . . . it hits me—I'm not in a hospital. I'm on an airplane.

"Where are we flying to?" I ask the man next to me, my voice sounding like it's coming out of someone else's mouth.

He looks up from his barf bag and stares at me like he's also just noticed there are other people around him, then shrugs.

Suddenly a crackling noise projects out of an overhead speaker.

"We are now *skrshskrsh*," a woman's voice says. "Arriving *skrshskrsh* our destination *skrshskrsh* please *skrshskrsh* seated *skrshskrsh* . . ."

"Where?" yells a scattered chorus of other passengers.

I turn again to my neighbor.

"Did you catch that?"

He frantically shakes his head.

"Absolutely useless," I mutter, rolling my eyes.

I'm about to desperately nudge the old woman to see if she knows what's going on, but a jolt of turbulence forces me back against the seat. I clap my hands over my ears to muffle the grating sound of an engine revving up somewhere beneath my feet.

As if controlled by a light switch, the pitch-black darkness outside the tiny windows turns into daylight. There's a loud popping noise like opening a can of refrigerated Pillsbury biscuit dough. With a thud, we touch down onto the tarmac. I'm no expert on aviation, but this can't be normal. The one time I've been on an airplane, a disappointingly Disney World–less visit with my grandma in Florida, we circled the city of Orlando for twenty minutes before we landed.

"We have now *skrshrshskrsh* at our destination," the voice booms from the speakers. "You may *skrshskrsh* the plane. Please line up *skrshskrshskrsh* orderly fashion *skrshskrshskrsh* collect all belongings *skrshskrsh* brought *skrsh* on your journey *skrshskrshskrsh*. We hope *skrshskrsh* have a wonderful time here at *skrshskrsh*. Goodbye!"

A door drops open in the middle section of the plane, letting in a burst of natural light. There are a few gasps, one or two screams, and the old woman next to me suddenly grunts awake, but mostly everyone looks over their seats in amazed silence at the open door.

I expect a flight attendant or *someone* to give us more directions—or rather, *any* directions—but nothing happens.

One man in an aisle seat wearing a business suit unlocks his seat belt and stands. Everyone cranes their necks to stare at him. He takes one big deep breath then walks out the door.

Others stare at one another, then toward the door, then at

one another again. Slowly, they begin to stand and follow the man outside.

I undo my seat belt and feel around for my belongings, only to realize I haven't brought any with me other than the clothes on my back: a fuzzy cropped black sweater and a pair of mom jeans—my least favorite pair of jeans. I'm never absolutely certain that they make me look cool and not like an actual frumpy mom, no matter how many times my sister reassures me they don't.

It seems no one else brought anything either because when they open the overhead bins, they're empty.

The guy to my right stands, dropping his barf bag onto the floor.

"Hey, don't just leave that for someone else to clean up," I protest.

He looks at me helplessly, like there's truly no alternative but to dump his sopping wet bag of stomach acid and likely chunks of partially digested jalapeno poppers right in my path.

"What's wrong with you? Just because you're sick doesn't mean you have a pass to treat this like your personal trash can. There are other people on this plane."

Before I can berate him any more, he pushes his way into the aisle, not waiting his turn as people begin to exit in an orderly fashion.

Looking around at the rest of the passengers, I can't figure out where we could possibly be going. No one seems to be dressed for the same kind of weather. There's a woman in a heavy down parka. Another woman in a straight-up bathing suit. A handful of people wearing nightgowns like the old lady next to me. Everyone appears to be of different races, genders, and ages—well, actually, mostly everyone looks to be at least over fifty. There are a handful of younger people, but none as young as I am.

As I finally walk out of my row and into the aisle, I notice one teenage boy. Something about him strikes me as familiar, but I can't pinpoint it. I stare at him for a second, but when he makes eye contact with me, I look away immediately, which is what I always do when I make eye contact with a boy I don't know. It's a mistake to ever let boys think you're even remotely interested in their existence. He probably only looks familiar because he's just wearing, oh, the most common (and most boring) boy outfit in the world: basketball shorts and black slide sandals with white socks. It's just the uncanny valley of boyness that's tripping me up.

I shuffle along to the door, then down a temporary flight of stairs onto the tarmac. The plane has let us off directly in front of a wide fenced path that leads only to a massive glass-and-concrete structure resembling a giant pair of wings. A thick layer of fog obscures the view behind the plane, but ahead of me, the sky is clear. Another plane takes off from the other side of the building and disappears into thin air.

Without thinking I gasp loudly at the sight, then look around to make sure no one heard me. You should never show signs of weakness around a new group of people, especially when you're not entirely certain whether or not you've all just landed in the Bermuda Triangle, or even know where you've landed at all.

But it doesn't matter. No one notices me gasping because they're too distracted by the enormous sign at the end of the path that says ARRIVALS hanging above a revolving door that must be able to fit at least twenty people at a time. The passengers ahead of me push and elbow their way in. *Like pigs to a slaughter*, I think, but there's nowhere else to turn, so I reluctantly follow their lead.

Inside, it looks like everyone from the plane is already splitting off into survival alliances, but then I realize they're actually flocking to different placards that read LAST NAMES A–C, LAST NAMES D–F, and so on. Yet right in the middle of all of them is one person holding up a giant sign that covers half their body. And on that sign is my name.

In glitter.

"Beatrice Fox?" a Valley Girl voice that sounds straight out of an eighties movie shouts from behind the sign to everyone who passes by. "Be-uh-trice Faaaahx?"

I stop in my tracks and swallow back another gasp. Everyone around me stares at the sign. I contemplate making a beeline for one of the other placards and just assuming a totally new identity from here on out, but my need for an answer as to where and how I'm here propels me to walk forward.

"Uh, hi," I say.

The sign drops, revealing a girl who looks to be only a few years older than I am, with friendly eyes covered in pearlescent blue eye shadow and warm brown skin contoured with neon fuchsia blush. On top of her curly hair sits a pillbox hat that's the same shade of orange as her dress. The same shade of orange as the gross seats on the airplane. A shade of orange that is suspiciously similar to the color of a prison uniform.

"That's me," I say, pointing to my name on the sign. Her face lights up immediately.

"Beatrice! Oh my god, I am so, so happy to see you!" she

says, frantically dropping the glittered sign to the ground. She pulls me into a tight hug and my whole body stiffens.

"Um, you too. I think," I say.

"Sorry, where are my manners? I'm Sadie."

She pulls back from the hug and reaches out a white-gloved hand toward me. I give it a limp shake.

"I'm Beatrice, but I guess you already know that," I say, eyeing the glittered sign on the floor. "I go by Bea, actually."

"Aw, Bea? So cute!" Sadie replies, tenderly clutching her chest.

"So are you picking me up? Like, to drive me somewhere?"

"Mmm, nope! Right here is where you're supposed to be."

"And that is?"

"Great question, Bea," she says, blinking once.

I expect her to say something more, but we just stand in awkward silence.

"So are you going to answer it or . . . ?"

"You're funny!"

"I'm serious."

"Okay, okay . . . We're at the airport," Sadie says matter-of-factly.

"But, like, *where*? You know, are we in, say, Ohio?"

She doesn't answer me, but just gets this funny look on her face.

"Japan? New Zealand?" I press, my heart pounding in my chest and my mind spiraling with possibilities. "Am I getting hotter?"

"Pressing me for more specific information? Oh my god, you are going to be, like, totally perfect for the job."

"For *what* job?" I beg.

"I'm getting ahead of myself. C'mon, your flight was the last to arrive and we're running late," she says, putting her arm around my shoulders and steering me away.

"Late for what?" I ask, elbowing her off me. "I'm not going anywhere until you tell me where I am and who you are and why you know my name."

"Bea," Sadie says, gripping me again, tighter this time. "I promise if you just come with me, you'll find out everything you need to know. Unless, of course," she adds, her voice lowering an octave, "you want to stand around out here completely helpless with the rest of these losers who also have no idea where they are and can't help you at all."

I look around at the clueless groups of people. The distinct smell of hot dogs wafts into my face, and when I look over the heads of the crowd, I spot a cart selling them in the distance. Suddenly I feel just like the barfing man on the plane who I'd been judging so hard a few minutes before.

"You lead the way," I say, narrowing my eyes.

Sadie takes us from the entry hall and down a long, winding wing of the airport. Even though it's full of people, the whole place has the vibe of those abandoned malls you'd see online with some annoying headline like "15 Pictures of Ghost Malls That Look Haunted AF."

We pass a counter with a neon sign that says REFRESH-MENTS (half the lights are busted, so you can only read SHMENTS) a newsstand selling magazines that look more like props than actual publications, and a bar with a poster on its door that reads IT'S FIVE O'CLOCK ANYWHERE!

Finally we turn down a narrow hallway then stop at a door with a RESTRICTED sign on it. Sadie knocks on the door three times in a row at three different spots, like she's communicating in some kind of code. The door opens the tiniest bit, only enough to see a sliver of a pair of eyeglasses.

"What's the password?" a nasally voice asks.

"C'mon, Todd, it's Sadie. I already did the secret door knocking. You know it's me."

"What's the password?" the voice insists.

Sadie looks up at the ceiling and sighs deeply.

"Toddcanrunasevenminutemile," she sputters.

"I'm sorry, what was that?"

"Todd. Can. Run. A. Seven. Minute. Mile."

The door opens fully, revealing a sweaty white guy who has the thick foggy glasses and combed-over red hair of a nerd, yet also the beefy physique of a bodybuilder. He's wearing a vest and pants in the same color as Sadie's dress.

"Welcome," he says, glancing at me.

"What's your deal?" I say, my eyes darting between these two uniformed freaks. "I'm not going in some closet with complete strangers. Why won't you people tell me what's going on?"

"Oh, she'll be great," the guy whose name is apparently Todd says to Sadie, raising his eyebrows.

"I know!"

"Great at what?" I say, heat rushing to my face and my heart pounding in my chest. "What are you gonna do to me?"

"C'mon, Bea. Don't worry. I was in your . . . tennis shoes once," she says, squinting down at my feet. "It's all very disorienting at first, but I promise you'll be fine," she adds, pushing me through the door.

I fear that behind it I'll find some kind of cult initiation or freaky sex party or a combination of both, but there's just a small space that looks like a neglected high school classroom with three long folding tables in a row facing a projector screen at the front. Behind the first two of the tables sits a handful of people, some in orange uniforms, others in plain clothes. Sadie leads us to the back row and we take a seat.

Todd flicks on a dinosaur of a projector behind us and walks back to the front of the room to turn out the lights.

"I know you newcomers probably have a lot of questions," he says, throwing his voice too loud for the tiny room. "Save them until the *end,* okay? Without further ado, please enjoy this short informational film."

A video crackles to life on the wall. Staticky instrumental music begins to play as WELCOME ABOARD flashes onto the screen. Then there's a montage of people in orange uniforms walking and eating and laughing all around a shinier, newer version of the airport.

The camera cuts to one man in uniform riding down a moving walkway by himself.

"*Hello,*" a vaguely familiar-looking man says.

"*My name is Todd, and I'll be guiding you through this next chapter of your journey.*"

I look over at the wall where the Todd who answered the door and turned on this very video leans. He's mouthing along to the words of the narrator and I realize . . . they're the same exact person. The video looks about forty years old, but somehow Todd hasn't aged a day.

"*If you're watching this,*" he continues on the screen, "*that means you've been chosen out of millions of people to join a very elite team known as the Memory Experience Department.*"

He hops off the moving walkway, tripping over its almost flat edge, and continues to slowly pace through the airport.

"It also means you are, unfortunately, dead."

Spit pools in my mouth like I'm about to vomit.

You are . . . dead.

"Excu—" I manage to garble out.

"Save your questions for the end," Sadie whispers, placing a hand on my arm in a way that I'm not sure is supposed to comfort me or restrain me.

"You may be wondering, 'Well, if I'm dead, then where the heck am I?'" Todd continues on-screen. *"Well, the answer is, 'Where aren't you?' And the answer to that is . . . you aren't in Heaven."*

My stomach feels like it's falling through my butt, straight down to the floor, as my brain deduces where this is going.

I'm in Hell.

That's what this is. I should've known Hell would be me trapped in a room with some egomaniac dude taking forever to explain to me that I'm in Hell.

"But the good news is . . . you aren't in Hell either!"

"Then where the *HELL* ARE WE?" someone at the front of the room calls out.

"Shh!" Present-day Todd places a finger to his mouth.

"You're in . . . the airport," Todd from the video says, splaying his arms as the words THE AIRPORT flash across the screen, like us viewers are supposed to find this information revealing and satisfying.

"When bad people die, they're sent to Hell. When good people die, they're sent to Heaven. When mostly good people who are harboring secrets, fatal mistakes, and/or emotional

hang-ups die, they have a layover here at the airport on their way to Heaven.

"*Take Rod here for example,*" he continues, the video cutting to footage of a man who is clearly just Todd without his glasses and wearing plain clothes exiting a plane, a look of confusion on his face.

"*Rod was a good guy on Earth. He was committed to his job as a regional manager of a low- to mid-level audiovisual supply company and to his relationship with a human woman. Sometimes he would bag groceries for other people at the supermarket because he just felt like it. He couldn't seem to figure out what in the world could be holding him back from moving on to Heaven.*"

Now Rod sits in a waiting area, looking bored out of his mind.

"*That's where we, the Memory Experience Department, come in,*" Todd narrates. "*When each person arrives here, they're given a number.*"

A voice calls a number over a PA system. "Rod" looks down at an orange passport in his hands and then jumps up out of his seat in exultation.

"*When their number is called from a lottery system, an attendant from our team is assigned to assist them in revisiting memories from their lifetime using advanced technology.*"

The words ADVANCED TECHNOLOGY appear on the screen.

A smiling woman in an orange uniform waves at Rod and the shot expands to show that she is standing next to an enormous machine that looks like two hair-dryer chairs with a clunky computer in between them. Rod sits in one of the chairs and the woman lowers its plastic helmet onto his head; then she sits in the second chair and does the same to herself.

"Through this device, which we call the Memstractor 3000, Rod and this attendant are able to screen his memories and sort through them. It is the attendant's job to ask, well, the tough questions, and to help Rod become more honest about himself and his life on Earth. After one to thirty sessions with his Memory Experience attendant, Rod finally confronts the truth of whatever it was that was holding him back. The Memstractor is then able to detect when a neural pathway of self-realization has formed."

A green light begins flashing on Rod's helmet. He and the attendant high-five.

"Rod is free to continue his travels on to Heaven!"

The video cuts to him boarding an airplane while the attendant robotically waves goodbye. Then it cuts back to Todd, addressing us head-on again.

"Now, remember what I've said: You're an elite group. You're not here to confront your own memories. You're here to confront the memories of others. You're here to help. And when you help enough people move on to Heaven, you'll be able to move on too."

He winks then turns, riding away very, very slowly on the moving walkway. The shot fades out as instrumental music plays again, then abruptly stops with a scratch.

Present Todd flicks on the overhead lights.

"If you have any questions," he says, with much less enthusiasm than his on-screen self, "please direct them to the attendant who picked you up at arrivals. They will be providing you with hands-on training for your job. Now, let's get everyone measured for uniforms."

He pulls a tape measure out of his pocket and stretches it between his hands.

I gasp for air and it fills my lungs, making me feel way too present, too aware of this moment than I'd expect for being dead.

God, I wish I'd just been sent to Hell.

2

They say you should "live every day like it's your last," but I
have no idea who "they" is, other than a robot who works on a
Pinterest content-making farm or the person who's in charge
of picking out the inspirational home decor sold at T.J.Maxx.
So I didn't live my last day on Earth like it was my last. I lived it
like I lived every day: by just trying to get it over with.

I woke up twenty minutes before school started, which
I know sounds bad, but when you consider the starting bell
rings at 7:55 a.m., I almost woke up *too* early. Still, that didn't
stop my showered-and-fully-dressed little sister from yelling
at me, like she did every morning.

"Get up, Bea! You're going to make me late," she said,
standing in front of the mirror and wrapping a floral circle
scarf around her neck.

"I never make you late," I groaned from the bottom bunk
of our shared bed, most of my body submerged in the purple
unicorn-print comforter that I'd outgrown a decade ago.

"That's exactly what you said last Thursday when you
made me late."

"If you don't like my driving schedule," I said, forcing my
body upright, "then take the bus! Or why don't you get a ride

with Skyler? Are you too afraid of him finding out you live on the wrong side of the tracks?"

Emmy squinted her eyes into the mirror. My characterization of where we lived was a bit harsh, but technically correct given there was an actual regional rail line that cut through the neighborhood at the end of our street. Our school was huge, with hundreds of kids in each class. A handful of them lived in McMansions, some of them lived in normal-size split-level homes, but most of them lived in tiny houses (not to be confused with capital-*T* tiny houses that people buy when they decide they're sick of having too much space) like ours, which was squat with a brown roof and brown shutters and a brown lawn. The only distinguishing part of it was the rusty pink Cadillac that sat out front, a hulking relic that belonged to my elderly neighbor, who we shared the driveway with.

"Skyler knows where we live. I *like* driving to school with you. Although it would be better for the environment if *all of us* took the bus."

"Ugh, but the bus comes at 6:50!" I said, finally sitting up. "Even *you* couldn't be ready by 6:50. Don't blame climate change on my driving. Blame it on the Northwood School District and their completely fascist scheduling system."

"I wasn't," Emmy said, rolling her eyes. "But it's important to remember how all the little choices we make every day can add up to make a big impact."

"You're too good for this trash planet, Emmy," I said, rubbing an eye booger off my face.

She turned and smiled at me, glowing like some kind of Glossier model even though all she did was apply ChapStick.

We looked alike, but everything about Emmy was softer.

We both had dark brown hair, but while mine was bone straight and couldn't hold a curl, hers was soft and wavy. My eyes were flat brown, while hers had a hazely sparkle. We both had heart-shaped faces, but hers looked noticeably comparable to a cartoon heart, while mine just registered as a normal face. Well, maybe not normal; I had one of those intense faces that made teachers ask me if I was "doing okay" when all I was doing was thinking about what I wanted to eat for lunch.

"And *you're* forgetting what day it is, Bea."

"Thursday?"

Emmy slumped her shoulders forward and sighed.

"Friday?" I asked. "Oh, thank god."

"Yes, it's Friday, but it's also . . ."

She gestured vaguely to the velvet mini dress hanging on our closet door that I had helped her pick out at Forever 21 to wear to the . . .

"Snow Ball? That's tonight?"

"Yes," Emmy said through gritted teeth. "And, in case you forgot, anyone who arrives late to school today isn't allowed to attend, so . . ."

She motioned for me to hurry up.

"Right! Ahh! Okay," I said, jumping out of bed and rummaging through a pile of my clothes on the floor. "Have you seen my jeans?"

"Which jeans?"

"My favorite jeans! The black ones that make my butt look semi-good."

"Bea, please don't freak out," Emmy said, biting her lip, "but I think I saw Monica grab them while you were still asleep and she was in morning-cleaning panic mode."

I shook my dirty-underwear-filled fists toward the ceiling and groaned.

Monica was technically my stepmom, but you would never know it by reading the bio of her pathetic, lifestyle-blogger-wannabe Instagram account ("Wife to Tommy. Mom to Grayson. Lover of candles, cookies, and cuddles. Amen. <3"). She never posted photos of me or Emmy, just our two-year-old demon half brother. Not that I'd ever want to be associated with her, online or IRL.

"Can you just wear another pair today?" Emmy pleaded. "Please, just this once—"

"Monica!" I yelled, storming out of our room, down the short hallway, and into the kitchen. "Did you put my jeans in the wash without asking? I was going to wear them today!"

"Of course." She shrugged, pouring Cheerios into a bowl and setting it on Grayson's high chair. He immediately pushed it away, showering the linoleum floor with tiny o's. "*Someone* had to do your laundry. I figured it might as well be me."

"You know I'm perfectly capable of doing my own laundry on *my own* schedule," I said, pulling open the closet where our washer and dryer sat stacked on top of each other. Inside the washer, my poor favorite jeans were pushed up against the window during the rinse cycle, like they were drowning and begging me to rescue them.

"Gosh," she said, cracking open her morning can of Diet Coke. "I was just trying to do one nice thing for you."

Monica's "one nice thing"s are never actually nice things. It's like, she'll come home from Walmart with some body spray for me that smells like coconut-flavored vodka, not because she thinks I'll like it, but because she thinks I smell and need to cover it up. The worst was when she watched some TV show on the "life-changing magic" of getting rid of crap, and then Emmy and I came home to find her digging through all of our stuff and deciding what should go to Goodwill without asking us.

"You know what, Monica? You're a hypocrite."

"Excuse me?"

"Your nightgown," I said.

She looked down at her chest, where it said BUT FIRST, COFFEE in big bold letters.

"You don't even drink coffee. You just guzzle Diet Coke."

"So?"

"So, you're living a lie. Everything about you is one big lie, even your stupid nightie."

"Bea!" Emmy interjected as she walked into the kitchen. "We're going to be really, really late if you don't get dressed right now."

"Fine."

So I stalked off to my room, grabbed a sweater and my least favorite pair of jeans, and got changed, certainly not dressed for the last day of my life.

3

—

"So, I hope that was helpful for you!" Sadie says, freeing my arm from her grasp. "Do you still have questions?"

"No," I say, giving her a death glare, literally. "I don't have any. That was so, *so* helpful. I feel really satisfied with all the information I was just provided."

"Good!"

"Of course I have questions! Are you insane? I just found out I'm dead via an infomercial!" I scream at her, jumping up from my chair.

"Beatrice," Sadie says like she's my mother. "Where are you going?"

"Anywhere!" I say, pushing through the line of people waiting to be measured for uniforms and toward the door.

"Todd, stop her!" Sadie calls.

"Meh," he says, not looking up from the waist he's measuring. "She won't get very far without her passport."

I open the door and run into the hall.

"Bea, did you hear that?" Sadie says, calling after me. "You won't get very far without your passport!"

"I'm sure I'll figure something out," I call back, the door slamming shut.

I'm running away and down the hall, but then, almost without a sound, Sadie is suddenly next to me again.

"They won't let you check into your hotel room without it," she says calmly.

"I'll sleep on the floor."

"You won't be allowed into the continental breakfast."

"Oh god, *how ever* will I go on without some mini-muffins?" I say sarcastically, but the mere thought of food makes my already churning stomach feel worse.

At the end of the hall, I see a sign for a women's restroom, push through its swinging door, and lock myself into one of three stalls.

"Fine," Sadie says, her voice following me inside. "Your date of birth was June 1, 2002. Your date of death was December 12, 2019, 9:19 p.m. Eastern Standard Time. Location of death? That's easy! It was the intersection of Huntingdon Pike and Susquehanna Road, Northwood, Pennsyl—"

"What? How do you—" I call out.

"Cause of death: blunt-force trauma," she continues. "Broken spine, and internal bleeding caused by car accident."

Instinctively, I feel for my neck with my hands, then look for blood on my fingers. The car swerving into my lane, the awful song, my head crashing through the glass—it all comes back to me and, without thinking, a strangled scream comes out of my mouth.

I open the stall door. Sadie is standing on the other side, reading from an orange-covered passport like the one Todd was holding in the video.

"It's all in here," she says.

"Give me that," I say, reaching out. She hands me the passport, her face serene.

On the inside cover, my name is printed in white block letters below a cropped photo of my face that I don't remember having taken. Based on the orange background and my half-asleep expression, I realize it must've been taken when I was on the plane. I turn to the first page. Sadie's right. There's my life and death tidily summarized like it's a daily weather report or something. *Blunt-force trauma* and *internal bleeding* look as commonplace as *10 percent chance of rain.*

"If that's what happened to me then . . . why aren't I, like . . . more . . ."

"Mangled? Grossly deformed?" Sadie asks. "When people die and come here, they arrive in the physical shape they were right before their deaths. So if anyone dies in, like, some traumatic way, they don't bleed all over everything forever."

I look up over her shoulder into the mirror above the sink. I may not be bleeding, but I'm a mess.

My hair lies exactly the same as it did the night of the crash, oily at the roots and in desperate need of some dry shampoo. My pale white skin looks ghostly under the fluorescent lights. A ring of berry-colored lipstick lines my lips and faint black remnants of smudged eyeliner and mascara still linger on my cheeks.

I walk over to the sink, drop my passport onto the ground, and splash cold water in my face, but the makeup doesn't budge. I take a squeeze of industrial pink hand soap out of the wall dispenser and rub it around my eyes. It stings, but still none of the dried-up mascara moves. I know waterproof makeup technology has improved over time, but I really doubt

Maybelline makes products that last through several dimensions of space, time, and mortality.

I keep violently rubbing my eyes until they feel raw, but they look exactly the same.

"Hey, hey, calm down," Sadie says, reaching out her hands. "Your makeup can't move no matter how much you touch it. It's like a tattoo."

"Um . . . how?"

"Well," she begins, twirling one of her curls around her finger, "from here on out you don't age. Your hair won't grow either. Everything about you, down to every detail, gets preserved like you're a jar of pickles."

"You mean to say the makeup I hastily applied while I was half asleep before school is now a permanent fixture on my face? Forever?" I ask, gripping the sink.

"Not forever. Only until you move on to Heaven."

"Why does your makeup look so perfect then?" I say, pointing at her flawless blush and eye shadow in the mirror.

"Oh, I died while competing in a beauty pageant," she says, like this is the most natural sentence in the world. "It's not as bad as it sounds. My nail polish hasn't chipped for decades. So convenient."

She pulls a white glove off her left hand, revealing five perfectly oval, mauve-colored fingernails.

I look down at my own. They're short, uneven, and covered in three-week-old specks of dark red polish that I'd been meaning to remove.

I grip the sink even harder. It's the worst kind, like the ones they have at public parks with a faucet you have to press down that releases super-cold water for only, like, seven seconds.

"If I'm dead, then why do I feel like I'm gonna be sick?"

"Your internal organs aren't aging, but they're functioning. You still need to eat and go to the bathroom."

I look at her in the mirror like she has to be kidding me.

"What?" Sadie presses. "You thought God would let us off that easy?"

"What's the point of all this?" I ask. "Assuming God is real, like, what is he doing by putting people here?"

"Or *she* . . ." Sadie interjects. "God could be a woman!"

"No," I say, shaking my head and pushing myself away from the sink. "Only a man could be stupid enough to create a place like this. I mean, it's not that hard. People are good or bad. They have their whole lifetime to be judged. Just pick one and make up your mind already, sadist!"

I don't believe in a lot of things, but I do believe most people are bad until they prove they're not and, for most of my life, this has been a useful skill. I pride myself on my ability to accurately predict the worst in people. I can determine who the killer is within the first five minutes of any *Law & Order* episode. I can tell other girls when their boyfriend will cheat on them to the exact date, regardless of whether they ask me for that information or not. Most people are bad. When you accept this like I have, you're rarely disappointed. Just majorly annoyed. All the time.

One time I was sent to my school's psychologist after a teacher, probably my gym teacher who once gave me detention for calling PE "state-sanctioned violence," tipped her off that I seemed "disturbed." The psychologist told me my glass-half-empty outlook can probably be pinpointed to the fact that my mom was killed by a drunk driver when I was five.

To which I was like, *Well, yeah, duh*. But I would cast an even wider net to include the fact that I've come of age in a world where a man with a meatloaf for a brain was elected President of the United States, the climate is transforming the polar caps into a water park, and the only way to make a decent living if you come from nothing like me is to be beautiful and hawk laxative teas to your Instagram followers.

Really, my "all people are bad until proven not guilty" philosophy is a completely logical response to an increasingly awful society.

"Well, not everything is so black-and-white all the time," Sadie explains, crossing her arms and leaning against the bathroom stall divider. "Lots of good people die with words left unsaid to people they loved. Apologies to people they hurt, either intentionally or by accident, that they never got around to giving. Loose ends they never got to tie up and make peace with before dying. General regrets in life. That kind of thing."

"But doesn't everyone have those things when they die?"

"Sure," Sadie says. "But this is stuff that would weigh so much on people's hearts, they'd never know peace without confronting it."

I mull this over for a moment.

"So . . . it's sort of like when people on reality shows go on and on about how they need 'closure'?"

"Reality shows?" Sadie asks.

"You know . . ." I say, hesitant if I should reveal the depth of knowledge I have about my guilty pleasure of choice. "*Real Housewives, The Bachelor* . . ."

She squints at me.

"Like, *Keeping Up with the Kardashians*? Shows like that?"

"I don't watch a lot of TV these days," she explains apologetically. "I'm always working. And, as of tomorrow morning, you will be too! So we better go get you checked into your room. You'll need a good night's sleep!"

"Yeah, about that . . . I noticed Todd didn't say anything about how much I would be getting paid as a member of his 'elite team.' I'm not really into performing unpaid labor for, like, eternity—"

"Beatrice!" Sadie snaps. "Money doesn't even exist here. You're getting paid in *atonement*. Do you not get it? You weren't chosen to be on our team because you're so much better than everyone else. You were chosen because you were *almost* sent to Hell. And you still could be . . . if you don't cooperate."

"What?"

"We're not actually 'elite.' That's just what Todd calls our team to make him feel better about himself. People like him and you and me . . . we were all really good at manipulating other people in our lives. We could spot everyone else's weaknesses and insecurities and use them against them. I had it down to an art. I mean, I went from a likely runner-up to Miss Teen Tri-State Area all because I whispered to my top competitor that she had spinach stuck between her teeth right before she went onstage, when she didn't even really."

Sadie's eyes go glassy and she stares off into the distance for a second.

"Anyway," she continues. "The point is that instead of being damned, the powers that be decided we could atone by using our bad qualities for good. We help people look at their memories and we quickly spot their weaknesses so they can confront them and move on to Heaven."

I lean against the bathroom stall and press my face to its cool metal door.

"But what if I don't want to help people?"

"It's not a question of what *you* want. Other people are counting on you. Including me! You're my replacement. Once I've successfully trained you for the job, I finally get to leave."

A low wailing noise comes from behind the bathroom door and then it opens. I jump at the sight of its source: an old woman in a tattered nightgown with long, matted gray hair down to her waist.

"Hi, Gladys!" Sadie says in a sudden saccharine-sweet voice, with a smile. "How are you?"

Gladys ignores her completely and shuffles her slipper-covered feet into one of the stalls, slamming the door behind her. Her wailing gets even louder. Sadie's face falls and she glares toward the sound.

"Who's that?" I whisper.

"She's been having a layover longer than I've been here. Her lottery number has been called dozens of times, but she's just . . . It's like talking to a wall. I've been stuck with her twice. She gives you nothing and wastes a whole month of your time, only to be shot back into the lottery. No memories. No recall. She just walks the halls and cries. She's, like, the void."

"How long do I have to stay here?" I ask, my stomach churning each time Gladys moans.

"That depends on how many souls you have to help move

on. It's different for each of us, kinda like a prison sentence. The number should be in your passport."

I pick it up from the ground and open it.

"Five thousand people? How long will that take me?"

"Well, the lottery draws one person for you to help each day, but you can get backlogged. And each session only lasts four hours. My average is 1.4 sessions per person. Of course, it went up significantly the times I got stuck with *that one*," she says, nodding toward the stall.

"Some people take a few days, even weeks, before they finally come to a conclusion and are ready to go to Heaven. If someone can't be helped within thirty sessions, they're pushed back into the lottery and have to wait to be called on again. All the work you do in those cases still won't count toward your quota."

I do the mental math. Even if I help one person a day, it will still take almost fifteen years to complete my quota. I put my youthful head in my youthful hands, feeling the weight of my youthful skin.

"I'm gonna be. So. Old," I cry.

"Don't worry about that," Sadie says, putting her hand on my shoulder. "You won't age, remember? You'll be seventeen forever. Just like I'm forever twenty-one."

"Oh god," I moan. "Like the store."

"Like what?" Sadie asks.

"You know, Forever 21?"

She stares at me blankly.

"The store with extremely cheap and flammable crop tops?" I add, distracted from my existential dread for one half of a second.

"Is that like Contempo Casuals?"

I stare back at her just as blankly.

"Wait, what year did you die?"

"1989," she says nonchalantly.

For some reason, this . . . this is what gets me. The next thing I know, I'm kneeling over the toilet, vomit and tears pouring out of my face in equal measure.

THE HOTEL LOBBY is enormous, but there's nothing grand about it. Orange patterned carpet that's falling apart in the highly foot-trafficked areas. Imitation wood paneling on the walls. People waiting to check in with one of the clerks behind the counter stand in a winding maze of a line separated by rope dividers. The sight of it makes my already exhausted body feel like it could collapse right onto the lint-covered floor.

"I need to lie down, Sadie," I say, hunched over. "I won't make it out alive if I have to wait in this line."

"Mm, well, technically you won't make it out alive if you *don't* wait in this line. . . ."

I just stare up at her, hoping that my eyes are shooting daggers but knowing I'm too weak to accurately pull it off.

"Still too early for death jokes? Sorry! You'll get there. Hold on," Sadie says, eyeing the line. "I know someone who can help us."

She leads me around the line and up to the side of the counter.

"Belinda!" she calls, leaning over the counter and waving, putting on a voice like the one she used when I first arrived and in the bathroom with Gladys. I can now confidently say after approximately one hour of knowing Sadie that this is her Fake Nice voice.

A middle-aged blond lady with a haircut that looks like it could walk right off her head and speak to a manager itself turns from the person she's checking in and looks at us.

"Sadie!" she calls back in a voice possibly even faker than Sadie's.

"Think you could fetch the room keys for my new friend here?"

"Sure thing," she says, flashing a smile and exposing a pair of teeth with blotches of pink lipstick on them.

"Let me just borrow your passport for a second, sweetie."

I hand it to her and she goes off to rifle through a file cabinet.

"How'd she get this job?" I whisper to Sadie. "Why didn't I just get assigned to manning some desk? Seems a lot more chill than whatever it is I'm about to do."

"People who did a lot of good deeds but were extremely rude to service workers in their lifetimes get sentenced to all the operational jobs here."

"So you mean . . . bad people," I say. "You know, this whole airport concept is stupid and probably counts as cruel and unusual punishment and I'm really annoyed that I'm here, but it's nice to know that some kind of karmic payback exists. I used to work as a barista after school at this coffee shop in a strip mall that—"

"What's a barista?" Sadie interrupts.

"Oh my god, you *are* ancient. It's, like, um, a person who make coffee drinks."

"So you mean . . . a waitress."

I roll my eyes.

"As I was saying, I got fired last month because I snapped at this lady who would always come in and order complicated drinks and would never tip or say thank you. I poured her non-fat latte with two-percent foam on her fake Louis Vuitton bag. It was amazing," I say, smiling to myself.

"I'm sure it was," Sadie says, nodding vaguely.

"Here you go!" Belinda says, returning with a key attached to a plastic fob. "Room 315."

"You guys don't use those room keys that look like credit cards?" I ask.

Both women just stare at me.

"Of course you don't."

"Thanks so much, Belinda!" Sadie says, smiling so hard that her cheeks must be cramping.

"Oh, anytime!"

"Oh, Belinda?" Sadie asks. "One more thing."

"Anything, sweetie."

"You've got some lipstick on your teeth," Sadie says in a stage whisper, gesturing to her own front teeth with a finger.

Belinda's eyes narrow.

"I know, Sadie. As you might recall, I was putting on lip-stick right before my stroke and . . . well, I'm sure I've told you this story before," she answers, her voice strained, and her tight smile threatening to crack her face in half.

"Oh, of course! How could I forget?" Sadie says, rolling her eyes at herself. "Well, thanks again! Have a great day!

"Tacky bitch," she whispers to me as we walk away.

The hotel has four elevators in the lobby, but two have

pieces of paper with *Out of Order* scribbled on them taped to the doors.

We wait for what feels like an hour but is probably more like seven minutes until the metal doors of one creak open with the same level of effort as a dead body trying to escape from a coffin. Sadie and I and about fifteen other people squeeze inside the elevator and it feels exactly how I imagine a coffin to feel, except less accommodating. I stick my hand through a maze of other people's body parts and press 3. The elevator moves up and up about an inch at a time until it stops at the third floor with a thud that makes my heart jump.

"Third floor?" an old lady wearing an oxygen tube with no tank attached says to another old lady. "Has somebody never heard of the stairs?"

"It's her first day," Sadie explains apologetically, following behind me.

The women gasp as their heads turn toward us.

"So young!"

"Yeah, I was robbed of my adulthood, so the least you can do is let me take the elevator in peace," I say, pushing my way out.

The doors clatter shut behind me and Sadie and it's completely silent. Only now that it's gone do I notice the absence of the constant, undecipherable noise of a bunch of people all talking at once that filters through the rest of the airport. It's just me and Sadie in the carpeted hallway with dark walls that feel at once claustrophobic and never-ending.

A plastic sign stuck to the wall instructs me that rooms 300–349 are to my left, 350–399 to my right.

"Um, I'm gonna go then," I say to Sadie, gesturing down the hall.

"Sure," she replies.

But as I walk, she continues right behind me.

"Sadie," I say when I get to my room, about to turn the key. "I don't know how to say this politely, but can you just leave me the hell alone now?"

All I would like to do is lie down face-first on a bed by myself and pretend nothing that's happening is really happening.

"All right," she says, hands up in surrender and an amused smile on her face. "You know, you're doing great. Aside from the vomiting and the crying and the cursing and the screaming . . . I'd say you're taking this all in like a pro."

"All I've done today is vomit and cry and curse and scream."

"Hey, that's still four things!" she says, counting them out on her fingers. "Most people don't get that many things done in a day."

"If you tell anyone you saw me crying today, I swear I will—"

"You'll what? Kill me? Ha!"

"Goodbye," I grumble.

"If you need anything, I'm upstairs in room 689. I'll be back bright and early to pick you up tomorrow so we can grab some breakfast before your very first day of work!"

"Oh, I'm so totally looking forward to it," I deadpan, opening the door and then slamming it shut in her face.

4

"What is *that*?" I said to Emmy as she placed a lidded mason jar full of green goop in my car's cup holder.

"Green smoothie," she said, zipping up her backpack.

"Since when do you drink green smoothies?"

Junk food had always been a sacred pastime Emmy and I shared. Totino's Pepperoni Pizza Rolls. Boxes of Kraft Easy Mac eaten together over the stove. Ben & Jerry's eaten out of the pint. The generic versions of these items when they weren't on sale. Fistfuls of off-brand cheese balls that came by the plastic tub, regardless of whether or not the name brand ones were on sale, because we thought they actually tasted better. Few things made me as happy in life as the Friday nights when Emmy would shrug off her homework and binge-watch TV with me while we chowed down on our perfectly optimized snack assortment.

"I drink them sometimes. I'm just usually already digesting all of its nutrients by the time you wake up," she said. "You know, green smoothies help you focus and give you sustained energy until lunchtime."

"Did Skyler tell you that?"

I was never a big fan of my sister's boyfriend just by virtue of him being the boy my little sister dated. But I tolerated Skyler because he made Emmy happy. And Emmy was the only person whose happiness I cared about. Still, everything Skyler said and did and wore fell under my scrutiny. I didn't like how he analyzed every joke I made aloud after I made it, as if I myself had no idea why it was funny to begin with. I didn't like the way he corrected me for using the word *aesthetic* incorrectly even when I was just informally pointing to something, like a picture of a pastel-colored geode I saw on Instagram, and proclaiming it "my new aesthetic." I didn't like the way he consciously pushed his thick glasses up his nose when he was making a point, like he wasn't an actual nerd but just playing the role of one in a movie.

At this point, what I didn't like most of all was that he was convincing my sister to become vegan. It wasn't that I was personally against veganism like some annoying guy whose entire counterargument against it is "But bacon though!" It was just that somehow Emmy's decision felt symbolic, like the beginning of a major change in our relationship.

"No, Skyler did not tell me that!" Emmy protested, twisting off the lid of the jar. "I learned it on my own. He drinks them for breakfast because *I* introduced them to him. You can have some if you want. It's got kale and banana and peanut butter. I know it's green, but you can barely even taste the kale!"

She dangled the open jar in front of the steering wheel. I grimaced and shook my head.

"I'm good," I said, looking my own breakfast: a can of Diet

Coke and a bacon, egg, and cheese Hot Pocket stuck in its paper sleeve, both nudged into my cup holder.

"You know . . ." she started to say, eyeing my meal, but then stopped and bit her lip.

"What? I know my breakfast is trash, okay? You don't have to tell me."

"No, it's not that," Emmy said, staring out the window like the strip mall we were driving past suddenly had deep significance to her. "It's nothing."

"Tell meeee," I begged.

"Okay," she said, turning to look at me. "You were really hard on Monica back there."

"Oh," I say, taken aback. "She took my pants against my will! Of course I was hard on her."

"Well, that and the Diet Coke thing. I mean, you drink it too. Why snap at her like that?"

"It's not about the Diet Coke itself. Obviously, I couldn't care less if Monica also wants to fill her body with carbonated cancer juice. It's about the *principle*. It's representative of her whole phony lifestyle. Acting like she has this picture-perfect, latte-art-loving life when she doesn't," I said, slamming on the brakes as we approached a red light. "Can you reach into my backpack and get my makeup bag?"

Emmy moved her hand behind my seat, but paused.

"Not if it means you're going to do your eyeliner while you drive. If I'm going to be late to school, I would at least like to make it there in one piece."

"I swear, I will get you there on time and with all your limbs."

"You know, Bea, you're so pretty," she said in a singsong voice. "You don't need a smidge of makeup!"

"Oh really?" I asked. "Well, I'm just gonna put on some lip balm."

"Then why don't I just get your lip balm out of the bag so you don't have to dig through—"

"*Emmy,*" I said, staring straight ahead.

Wordlessly, she placed the makeup bag on my lap. The light turned green and I kept driving.

"I know Monica is corny," Emmy continued. "But I don't think she's as awful as you make her out to be sometimes."

"She acts like we're her evil stepdaughters. You know she can't wait for us to graduate and move out so she can finally have her dream family. She wants to pretend we don't exist. That's why she told Dad it was a good idea to fix up this piece of junk for me," I said, banging my hand on the plastic steering wheel. "So she doesn't have to drive me around. The one *actual* nice thing she's done for me."

"You don't think she told Dad to surprise you with a car because she just . . . cares? And, like, *gets* that you want a little independence?"

"No!" I said, grimacing at Emmy. "Since when are you Monica's biggest fan? Did I miss something?"

"No!" she blurted back to me, weirdly defensive. "You didn't."

"Yeah, I know I didn't, because I don't miss anything in your life. I don't miss any time you talk about Skyler in your sleep. I don't miss a single fart—"

"Bea!"

"What? I'm not blaming you. This is all because *Monica* forced us to bunk together so that her ugly spawn can have his own room."

"Grayson is our brother, Bea!"

"*Half* brother. You know that time he spit up in my boots? I swear he made eye contact with me while he did it."

"You always say that," Emmy said, cracking a smile even though she was clearly trying not to.

We came to another stoplight. In one rapid motion, I unzipped my makeup bag, pulled out my eyeliner, and flipped down the sun visor mirror. The light turned green and I put my foot to the pedal while drawing on a wing.

"Bea. Please," Emmy moaned, staring up at the car ceiling.

"I have my eyes on the road! It's fine."

"I just think that maybe you should consider how this is all maybe weird for Monica too. She annoys you, but I'm sure she gets annoyed that she inherited two teenage girls, including one who has the cranky attitude of an old lady, I might add, before she could even have kids of her own."

I squinted into the mirror as I moved on to my right eye.

"Um, I have an amazing attitude! And she's not responsible for me at all and I never asked her to be. If she didn't want this, then maybe she shouldn't have married Dad. In my opinion, me and you are honestly the best part of the deal. What else did she get out of it? A prematurely balding car mechanic for a husband? A house with one bathroom for five people? She should be *grateful* for *us*. We make her small life interesting. We give it some *spice*."

I capped my eyeliner shut with one hand and used the other to turn into the entrance of our high school.

"Slow down!" Emmy said.

"I'm just trying to get you to school on time! It's Snow Ball, remember?"

Our school parking lot was basically a public safety hazard. The school sat at the very top of a hill, and the parking lot fell behind it with each row of cars on an incline, meaning rear-end accidents between people pulling out of the lot at the end of the day were a weekly occurrence.

There was a direct correlation between the quality of cars in the parking lot and the slope of the hill. The top of the hill was full of shiny Audis and hand-me-down Volvos driven by honor students who arrived early and had moms who I imagined made them homemade cinnamon buns and freshly squeezed orange juice every morning. The lower part of the hill was full of banged-up used cars driven by slackers who arrived late because they overslept, stopped at McDonald's on the way, and/or were busy smoking weed in the woods next to the high school.

When we arrived, there were only spots available in the very bottom row.

I pulled into one, just narrowly avoiding the hatchback belonging to Dominic Reed, a repeat junior who tried hard to look like a young Eminem but really just looked like buzz-cut-era Justin Bieber, hanging out of the side of his car and sipping a Monster Energy drink. I never understood why slacker boys always drink those, harnessing all that artificial energy to do absolutely nothing.

The two-minute warning bell rang through the parking lot. Emmy opened her door to get out before I'd managed to take the keys out of the ignition.

"Good morning, baby girl," Dominic said, blocking Emmy as she tried to get out of the car. She stared down at the ground, holding a textbook close to her chest, and slithered her way past him.

"What?" he bellowed. "You and your tight ass can't stop and say hello to me?"

Emmy's cheeks reddened. I grabbed all my stuff and got out of the car, kicking my door and slamming it hard.

"What did you just say to her?" I barked. Dominic gave me an amused grin. Emmy just kept walking with her head down.

"I swear to god," he said into the window of his car where his buddy was smoking, "I stay the same age, but they keep getting younger."

"It's 'I get older, they stay the same age,' you . . . *idiot*!" I screamed. "Trying to sexually harass us and you can't even get the stupid movie quote right!"

"Chiiiill. I was talking about your sister, not you," he said, taking a swig of his Monster. "You look like a raggedy-ass witch."

"Oh yeah?" I said, walking around the front of my car, closer to him.

"Bea!" Emmy hissed through her teeth, about four feet ahead of me. "C'mon! Please don't do this."

I didn't take my eyes off Dominic.

"Well, you look like an illiterate motherfucker whose only reason for coming to school is to get off by staring at girls who are way too young for him."

Before I could think twice about it, I knocked the Monster can out of his hand using the Diet Coke can in my own, the two beverages pouring down his shirt as one disgusting cocktail.

And then, just because I could, I squeezed the Hot Pocket I was holding toward him, its innards flying out like it was a miniature scrambled-egg-filled squirt gun.

"Yo, what the *hell*?" he yelled, stepping back and shaking off the bits of egg like a wet dog. "Bro, I swear to god this bitch just got . . . Hot Pocket on me?"

From inside the car, I heard a laugh, but then the door opened and Dominic's way more muscular, way more tattooed counterpart was stumbling toward me.

"Bea!" Emmy yelled, turning around and stopping in her tracks even though the final morning bell was ringing. "Run!"

5

The hotel room, which I guess is now technically *my* room, has the same ambiance as the lobby and hallway (i.e., zero ambiance), plus a super-low ceiling the exact texture of cottage cheese and two queen-size beds covered in peach-colored bedspreads. When I flop onto the first bed, it feels how you would imagine flopping face-first onto a mattress somebody had left out on the side of the road would feel. I get up and fall onto the second one, but it feels exactly the same except that it also makes a pronounced squeaking sound. Home sweet home.

I roll over and notice a television. It's the kind with antennas, which I've never actually seen in real life. On the bedside table between my two beds, there's a remote the size of a graphing calculator. I pick it up and press the power button. The TV comes to life with a staticky clicking sound.

Elevator music begins to hum out of the speakers and a weather report calendar floats on the screen. I scoot up to the edge of the bed to read it. The graphic only lists the days of the week, but not the exact date or month. It claims that the next week is going to be fifty-three degrees every day, mostly cloudy with a drizzle of rain. Weather that's just bad enough to be a little annoying, but not totally awful. This place is nothing if not consistent in its mediocrity.

As I stare into the TV, I realize the music playing from it sounds vaguely familiar. It's a jazz cover of "Hey, Soul Sister" by Train—the song playing in the car when I died. Without thinking, I jump to my feet on the bed and hold out the remote toward the TV like I'm wielding a sword.

"This has got to be a sick joke," I mutter, pushing a button to change the channel, but nothing happens. There is no other channel. I press the power button again and shut the whole thing off.

Before I can do anything else, a wave of exhaustion, even deeper than the one earlier, rolls through my body. I always assumed jet lag was just some problem rich people invented as an excuse to hide being hungover, but in this moment, where the thought of even lifting one of my fingers sounds like the equivalent of bench-pressing a ton, I finally get it.

I pass out horizontally on the worse of the two beds.

I'M AWOKEN BY a noise that sounds like someone jack-hammering through my door.

For a second I forget where I am and everything that's happened to me. I reach around for my phone, which I usually sleep with under my pillow even though my sister has sent me several news articles that claim it's giving off radiation and slowly transforming my brain into a bowl of pea soup. My hand grasps the TV remote instead. I stare at it for a second as if it will provide me with an answer as to who I am and how I got here. When it doesn't, I try the next best thing and hit its power button.

The TV turns on. The song it plays is the same, as cursed to me as ever, and brings yesterday's events trickling back into my head.

Now instead of the weather, a stock footage montage of breakfast foods plays across the screen. A spinning plate of pancakes with thick maple syrup slowly being poured on top. Bacon sizzling on a griddle. A mug of coffee with steam rising up from the top. Text flashes across the bottom of the screen:

FREE breakfast served 7 a.m.–9 a.m. every day outside the hotel lobby! "WHEN YOU'RE HERE, YOU'RE HERE!"

My stomach makes an audible rumble. I realize that for the past day I've only been subsisting on fumes and desperately need to eat.

The jackhammer noise continues.

"Beatrice!" a voice calls. "Beatrice, are you up yet?"

Sadie.

I look over at the analog alarm clock sitting on the bedside table. It's 6:50 a.m.

"Beatrice is still sleeping!" I yell toward the door. "You can leave a message for her though."

"Okay!" she replies cheerily. "Well, tell Beatrice if she doesn't get her butt out of bed, Sadie will come in there and take it out for her, because her entire future is riding on training Beatrice to replace her on the Memory Experience team, and if she doesn't, there will be literal Hell to pay."

I get up and trudge over to the door. Slowly.

"I'm up," I say, opening it halfway. "Just give me a few minutes."

"Good morning, Bea," Sadie says, pushing herself fully through the door before I can stop her. "I brought a special welcome gift for you."

She plops a heavy white garment bag in my arms.

"Please don't tell me this is what I think it is," I groan.

Sadie just smiles maniacally at me.

When I unzip the bag, my worst fear is confirmed: there are seven identical orange dresses, like I'm staring into the closet of a cartoon character.

"How? I didn't get measured."

"Oh, well, they're standard-issue, not custom-made. There's really no reason Todd has to measure every single person. He just likes the near-human contact."

I cringe, although I'm not sure if it's at the ugly dresses or the thought of Todd or both.

"I only wear black and black-adjacent colors," I explain.

"What's black-adjacent?"

"It's like when you buy a shirt thinking it's black, but then take it home and hold it up to the light and realize it's just a super-dark purple."

"Well, *here* we consider orange a neutral! Oh, and don't forget your accessories," Sadie says, handing me a cardboard hatbox. "Get changed and I'll meet you in the lobby for breakfast."

"Must we do everything together?"

"Bea, you're new here. You need me! Look, at least I'm not making you change right here in front of me. I'm learning how to give you *space*," she says, backing away and out the door.

I lock myself in the bathroom, which itself is so tiny that it barely fits me, like it's meant for an airplane and not an airport hotel. I brush my teeth with the flimsy plastic travel tooth-brush on the counter, and take a shower, even though I know it's futile now. I hope the hot water will soothe me anyway, but, not surprising me in the least, it never even gets close to warm. And even when I stand directly under the showerhead, some-how my hair doesn't get wet, refusing to let the water wash away its three-day-old grime.

When I get out, I wrap myself in a towel and stare down at the uniform like we're two cowboys in a shoot-out. But I'm way too hungry to put up a fight any longer, so I just slip it on.

Inside the hatbox there's a pair of low-heeled white patent pumps mysteriously in my exact size, white gloves, an orange pillbox hat, and a white train case. I put on the accessories and take another look at myself in the mirror, which is just slightly too short for me to see my full body in without awkwardly tilt-ing backward.

The contrast between my mascara-stained face and the cheery outfit is awful. It looks like I'm the lead singer of some kind of airplane-themed emo band. I fold up my fuzzy sweater and my least favorite pair of jeans and put them in a drawer underneath the TV, not knowing if I'll ever wear them again.

I DON'T SEE Sadie in the lobby, but I don't make a great effort to look for her either. I take this miscommunication as a gift and make my way to the breakfast area alone. When I get there, I'm shocked to find that it's all there. The pancakes. The bacon. The coffee. Except everything is encased in assorted shapes and flavors of Jell-O.

The breakfast buffet looks like it's straight out of a page from a cookbook you'd find at a yard sale and laugh at for a second but never expect anyone to actually cook from. There are three kinds of eggs, scrambled, boiled, and even fried, all suspended in clear gel. The coffee isn't steaming, but cold and cut into cubes to be chewed rather than sipped. Mini blueberry muffins sit inside an elaborately shaped blue mold atop a cake pedestal. All of the food looks like it's trapped behind glass, begging to escape. The only thing that actually looks comfortable with itself inside of Jell-O is the fruit salad, but even so, I don't trust it.

But my stomach grumbles violently. I don't have room to be picky. So I grab a plastic tray and fill it up, quietly accepting that my diet for the foreseeable future will mainly be defined as *wobbly*.

The giant seating area looks like a hospital cafeteria, mostly full of people eating alone, but there are a few groups having lively conversations like they're just in a normal restaurant with normal food, catching up with their normal friends. I feel a pang of anxiety like it's the first day of school and I have no friends to sit with in my lunch period. But I steel myself and remember that I'm not here to make friends; I'm here to . . . well, I'm here to help everyone move on to Heaven?

I take a seat at an empty two-person table near the wall of floor-to-ceiling windows and dig into my pathetic feast. I wolf down what I am about 50 percent sure is a cherry Danish, followed by what I am only 10 percent sure are hash browns.

"Anyone sitting here?" a deep but friendly voice says as I proceed to scrape Jell-O off of a hard-boiled egg.

I look up. It's the boy in basketball shorts from my flight.

I swallow hard and shake my head in response, but it's not exactly an invitation for him to join me.

"Mind if I join you?" he asks.

Sigh.

"Go ahead," I say.

He places his tray on the table. It's full of pancakes suspended in a brown gel that I hope tastes like maple syrup.

"I'm Caleb," he says. "Caleb Smith."

"Bea . . . Fox," I say, unclear why we're exchanging last names.

"You were on my flight, weren't you?"

"Oh. I don't know." I shrug, knowing full well I saw him on my plane. "Did you come in yesterday morning?"

"Yeah."

"I guess I was then."

I feign disinterest in him by continuing to pick apart my egg with laser-sharp focus.

"This place is weird, huh?" he prods, poking at his pancakes with a fork.

"Yeah. *Weird* is definitely one way to put it."

"I mean, airports are liminal spaces to begin with, but this is literally a liminal space between life and death, right? It all just feels too on the nose."

I drop my fork and knife and look up, still avoiding eye contact with him.

"You know what I mean by 'liminal spaces'?" he asks, but doesn't pause to let me answer. "Airports, rest stops, waiting rooms—places that feel like they don't really exist because they're just passageways to the things we're actually heading toward. When you're in them, reality feels altered because they weren't designed for people to spend extended amounts of time in and—"

"Yeah," I say, putting my fingers up for him to stop talking. "I know what they are. I read that really long Tumblr post about liminal spaces too. Okay, Mr. Neil deGrasse Tyson? Over here trying to explain the universe to me . . ."

I spear a cube of coffee with my fork and dramatically swallow it, only to then cough it back up because it's gross. I'd assumed it'd be sweet, like actual Jell-O, but somehow it really just tastes like cold, burnt black coffee.

"But I agree," I say, humbled by the awful taste. "This whole thing is a little too on the nose."

He grins at me.

"Like a minute ago," I continue, "I earnestly thought to myself, *What's the deal with airline food?* like I'm some kind of bad stand-up comic. This place is making me think exclusively in clichés.

"I mean, look," I say, holding up a long slab of Jell-O enveloping a once-crispy piece of bacon. "The food is literally suspended in time, just like we are."

Caleb chuckles and, reluctantly, so do I. While I'm at it, I properly look at his face for the first time.

It's a nice face. His eyes look red around the rims and have bags underneath like he hasn't slept a wink, but the eyes themselves are brown with golden flecks. He has olive skin and thick eyebrows and wavy brown hair that's short on the sides but floppy in the front so that one small tendril hangs above his forehead just . . . so. I didn't even know boys had haircuts like this in real life.

But the longer I stare, there's something that bothers me

about his face. And it's not his slightly uneven chin that juts out a little in an admittedly cute way while he smiles. It's that it's the kind of face I don't trust. The kind of face that is only nice to me when it wants a favor, like the faces of the boys at school who only acknowledged my existence when I was at work because they thought it would get them a free caramel macchiato.

"So," Caleb says as my smile fades and I look back down at my tray. "You're one of the agents who gets people through to Heaven?"

My face falls further.

"How do you know that?" I mumble.

"Because your, um, dress says so." He points to the small embroidered text on the left side of my chest that reads *Beatrice* and then, in smaller text below it, *Memory Experience*, which I only notice right now.

"Oh," I say, looking down. I'm basically wearing a neon sign announcing my job. "Right."

"Which, might I add, looks great!" he says. "Orange really suits you."

"Oh, screw you," I blurt out, knowing I'll think of a better comeback than "Oh, screw you" in approximately three hours.

Caleb laughs again. It's a really nice laugh. Ugh. I just want to shove a disgusting gelatinous pancake into his mouth and make him stop.

"Um, but seriously, is there anything I could do to, you know," he says, lowering his voice so only I can hear. "Get my number called sooner?"

And there it is.

"Are you propositioning me?" I say loudly enough for the other tables to hear. "So you can move on to Heaven ahead of everyone else who is waiting *ever so patiently*?"

"No, I'm just—"

"'Just'? Just what? What do you even have to offer me in exchange for doing something like that? We don't have money here. We don't have anything except these useless meat sacks that, I guess, carry our souls around," I say, gesturing to our bodies. "What are you gonna do? Offer me *your* useless meat sack?"

Words . . . they are . . . just coming out of my mouth today.

"I don't know! Maybe." He shrugs.

"Ew," I say, grimacing.

"Wait, no!" he exclaims. "That's not what I meant. That was gross. Sorry, but honestly, who says *meat sack*? You set me up."

"Look, my point is," I say, setting my hands down on the table matter-of-factly, "it seems the one good quality about this place is that everyone is treated equally. Everyone has to wait around for a mind-numbingly long amount of time and no one gets a special pass. Maybe your male privilege got you ahead on Earth, but it's not going to get you ahead here!"

"Okay, okay," he says, looking around self-consciously. "I wasn't trying to bribe you. I was just, you know, making polite conversation . . . asking for a favor from a friend."

"A friend?" I ask. I turn my head around, pretending to look for someone. "Your friend is around? Do they work here too? I must've missed them."

He plops his fork down.

"Ohhh. You meant me?" I ask sarcastically. "Well, Caleb

Smith, I don't know what it was like where you flew in from, but where I flew in from, partaking in half of one terrible meal together does not make us friends."

"Yet!" he says, his eyes widening and staring up into my own. I look away quickly, feeling myself blush again even though I am a sworn non-blusher, skilled at making my body resist any impulses that could betray my emotions.

"Anyway," I say. "Even if you did bribe me, it's not within my power to pick who gets called. The numbers are randomly generated. It's all part of the great equalization."

"Well, that's too bad. I was all ready to bribe you," he says, wiggling his eyebrows just slightly.

"All right, that's it!" I say, pushing my chair back. "Actually, I'll make sure your number never gets called. Have fun eating wet slop and wearing socks with sandals for the rest of eternity."

He looks under the table at his feet.

"Hey, how'd you know I'm wearing—"

"I saw you getting off the plane," I say.

His jaw goes slack.

"So you *did* notice me on the plane," he says.

"No, I just noticed your shoes. Not *you*."

I stand and pick up my tray. As I do it, my spoon falls off and onto the floor, under the table. When I reach down to grab it, I notice a passport lying near Caleb's foot. Quickly, without thinking too much about why I'm doing it, I grab the passport along with my spoon and place them both back onto my tray, underneath a napkin.

"Beatrice!" I hear a familiar voice call. I decide to stay low to the ground. "Beatrice Faaaahx!"

"I think someone's looking for you," Caleb says, eyeing me under the table.

"Pretend I'm not here," I bark.

He just nods, surprising me with his cooperation.

"You!" Sadie yells, closer now. "What are you looking at?"

"Me?" Caleb asks. "Nothing."

"No, down there."

"Uh, I don't know, a, um . . ." he stammers, his inability to lie rendering his cooperation absolutely useless.

"Hiya, Bea," Sadie says, her face suddenly inches from mine. "I've been looking all over for you!"

"Would you believe me if I said I got lost?" I ask, staring away from her and down at the minuscule bits of dried food stuck to the carpet instead.

"No."

"Well, I got lost."

"We're running late," she says, motioning for me to get up. I clutch my tray and stand.

"It was nice meeting you, Bea," Caleb says.

"It was . . . completely average meeting you," I say, staring into his eyes.

"Maybe I'll see you around?" he asks, smiling and raising his perfectly imperfect eyebrows.

"Hopefully not," I answer.

"Okay, enough with the chitchat! Let's go," Sadie says, pulling my arm.

"Beatrice, were you flirting with that boy?" she asks me once we're barely out of earshot of Caleb.

"Ew. Of course not," I say, looking back to make sure Caleb didn't hear.

"Good. I wouldn't recommend getting close to people who are only just passing through because, before you know it . . . poof!" Sadie says, snapping her manicured fingers. "They're gone."

"Sounds like you know from experience," I say.

"No!"

I give her a sidelong glance.

"Fine. Yes, I've had a few flings, but not in, like . . . a decade . . . ish. I've learned my lesson, okay?"

"Sure."

Out of the corner of my eye, I spot a row of trash cans and remember the dirty tray in my hands and the passport sitting on it that's not mine.

"I have to throw this out," I say, turning toward the trash.

"Of course," Sadie says, following right behind me.

I clear my throat, loudly.

"What?" she asks.

"I think I can manage to throw away my own trash without your help."

"Really? Because you got soooo lost before . . ."

I roll my eyes.

"Fine," she says. "I'll be right here. And I'll be watching you."

The trash cans are like the ones McDonald's uses that look like cabinets with little floppy doors you can dump your trash into without ever having to stare into the abyss of half-eaten McNuggets and fries. Except instead of having the words THANK YOU inscribed on the little door, it says YOU'RE WELCOME.

I snatch the passport off my orange plastic tray, slide the remainder of my breakfast into the trash, and discreetly slip Caleb's passport inside my stupid new train case.

Should I have alerted him that his passport fell onto the ground and then given it back to him? Yes.

Did I keep it because something inside me that I can't explain desperately wants to know more about him but is too ashamed to ask? Also yes.

Plus, having the passport gives me an excuse to talk to him again. An excuse that conveys "I'm just being a good person and returning a found object," not "I find you interesting and maybe extremely attractive even though I typically find boys to be sexist, thumb-like creatures who are incapable of having thoughtful opinions."

"Bea?" Sadie calls, interrupting my thought spiral. "Forget something?"

"Huh?" I say, in what I hope is a sweetly innocent tone. "Oh, that? I just . . ."

"Your gloves," she says, her face serious. "You're not wearing your gloves. You *need* to be wearing your gloves. They are an essential part of your uniform."

"Right," I say, rolling my eyes. I reach into my case and grab the white gloves, brushing against the passport and wondering how many hours it will be before I can take it back to my room and read exactly when, where, and how Caleb died.

6

___

My first day of work begins as I've always imagined most adult workdays begin: with a pointless meeting.

"Todd!" Sadie says, knocking on the door of the same room she took me to the day before.

"What's the password?" he calls from behind the door.

"Not this again," I mutter.

"Toddcanrunasevenminutemile," Sadie sputters.

"I changed it, remember?" Todd calls back, indignant. "For security reasons!"

"Of course," Sadie says, pursing her lips. "It's, uh, Toddcanbenchpressonehundredandfiftypounds."

"I didn't catch that," he says, a note of amusement in his voice.

"Todd. Can. Bench. Press. One. Hundred. And. Fifty. Pounds."

The door creaks open.

"Thank you for joining us, ladies," Todd says.

The room is packed with people. Today everyone is wearing orange uniforms and looking supremely bored. Sadie and I file in, standing near the back wall.

"Good morning," he says, pushing his glasses to the top

of his nose. "We have a few newcomers to the MX team this morning, but there is no time for introductions, so if you see a new face, please say hello! Now, for the meat of today's meeting . . ."

He begins to dramatically pace back and forth.

"Numbers are *down*, people! Okay? Our rate of sending souls to Heaven has dropped by over forty percent this month. I don't want to point fingers at *them*," he says, gesturing toward the door. "I don't want to point fingers at *us*, but, folks, listen, I gotta point my finger somewhere."

To emphasize this, Todd points his finger out, closes his eyes, and spins around, but nearly falls into a group of people clustered at the front of the room. They have to catch him and hold him upright.

I can't believe *this* is my boss, yet given the general unfair order of the universe, I can believe this is my boss.

"Ahem," he says, clearing his throat. "What I'm saying is . . . we have to point a finger at each and every one of ourselves. No matter how uncooperative people out there might be, no matter how long they take to reveal their truths, it is ultimately up to every individual in this room to get one soul to Heaven at a time."

He pauses, as if expecting a round of applause, but no one reacts.

"Okay then. Just a heads-up for all you new agents: you will be working in rotating four-hour shifts that start at eight a.m., twelve p.m., and four p.m. It can be hard to keep track of time during your shift, so you will know it's over when you hear me make an announcement over the PA system. I know. I know. 'But, Todd, why can't I work all day long?' Because there aren't enough Memstractor 3000s to go around and everyone needs to get their chance with them. 'But, but, Todd, why can't we just get more Memstractors?'"

The more times he says *Memstractor* the more I notice it sounds like *menstruation*.

"The answer? I don't know, people. All I can say is, Memstractors don't grow on trees," Todd continues. "Any other questions?"

I raise my hand.

"Yes, Beauregard?" Todd asks.

"*Beatrice*," I correct, squinting at him. "Yeah, just wondering, do we get any days off?"

I want to get out of here ASAP, but I don't think I can handle working every single day without a break.

"Days off?" Todd scoffs. "Ha! That's cute."

Sadie and some of the other agents in the room smirk at one another.

"No, Beatrice," Todd says, shaking his head. "There are zero days off at the airport. We are working toward our individual and team goals, each and every day. Actually, that's the perfect segue to congratulate the team member who moved the most souls this week. For the, well, what feels like millionth week in a row . . ."

Todd pauses and smirks.

"Sadie Robinson! With a whopping seven souls!"

Next to me, Sadie puts her hands to her chest and puts on a face of faux shock, like she's just been crowned Miss America. All around us, people reluctantly clap while some just roll their eyes at one another.

Great. I got paired with the airport's biggest ass-kisser.

But I guess if I can move people along as fast as she can, then maybe I can get myself out of here sometime this century.

"May I have your attention, please?" a woman's robotic-sounding voice suddenly calls from over the intercom. "We will now announce today's Memory Lottery recipients. Please have your passports ready. Recipient number one: number 09745, number 09745, I repeat, number 09745. . . ."

"All right, you know what that means. Let's rock 'n' roll, people!"

Todd opens the door and waves his hand, motioning for everyone to leave.

"Are you ready?" Sadie asks, smiling wide.

"No," I say, glowering.

"Okay, well, before we head out there, you're going to need to, like, stand up straight," she says, pushing my shoulders back. "Most people just don't trust a slouch. Oh, and always, always smile."

I stare at her.

"Can you just give me one smile, Bea?"

"No. I can't smile on command."

"Of course you can!"

"No . . . I . . . I don't know how."

I can smile when I want something from someone, but anytime I try to smile when someone tells me to, it looks all wrong. Maybe it's some deep, unnameable force of darkness that has been inside me since I was born, but I look like an animal baring its teeth in every school picture I've had taken.

"Fine," Sadie says. "Put your tongue behind your front teeth."

Reluctantly, I do, like an idiot.

"And lift your cheek muscles like so . . ." she says, reaching out to pull up the sides of my face with her fingers. "There. You're smiling!"

"Okay!" I say, pushing her hands away. "Can you stop pageant-mom-ing me?

As we file out of the room, Todd hands Sadie a ticket, then skips me.

"Why don't I get one?" I ask.

"It's our assignment for the day," Sadie explains, pulling me into the hall. "You'll get your own after I've trained you. We'll work together until we get this soul through to Heaven, then you'll be on your own.

"I don't want to put too much pressure on you," she says as we're about to turn the corner back to the public airport atrium. "But this is the last soul of my quota. Once we move this person along, I'm free. Well, technically, after we move this person and then you move two more people on your own, for a grand total of three souls that prove I sufficiently trained you for the job, I'm free."

"Right, got it. Don't mess this up or you never get to Heaven. Sounds easy enough."

But as we come upon the sight of an enormous waiting area, I'm not so sure it is easy enough. Hundreds of people sit around listlessly on rows of connected orange plastic seats, staring at a departures board covered in teeny, tiny letters. It's just an overwhelming mass of bodies desperately waiting for their chance to move on.

Behind the board are floor-to-ceiling windows that show off an expansive view of the side of the airport I landed on. A voice continues to call numbers out of the PA system, and every minute or so someone jumps out of their seat and runs to a desk below the departures board to check in and verify their number has been called. To the side of the desk, a bunch of people stand in line in a roped-off area, clutching their passports tight.

"Good morning!" Sadie says to the group. "I'm looking for a number . . ."

She glances at her ticket.

"08744? Anyone?"

A gray-haired woman wearing a denim jacket embroidered with tiny autumn leaves and matching pants steps forward. I wonder which is worse: wearing my uniform or having to dress like it's harvest season forever.

"Hello! My name is Sadie and this is Beatrice. I hope you don't mind if she joins us today? I'm just giving her some training so she can take over my job after me. See, today is a very special day. You are my last and final soul I have to guide before I hit my quota. Which means once you reach an emotional conclusion, not only do you get to move on to Heaven, but so do I!"

The woman makes nervous eye contact with us. If she had a purse, I'm almost certain she'd be clutching it for fear that we were about to rob her.

"What's your name?" Sadie asks, gesturing for the woman's passport.

"Wendy," she mutters.

"So lovely to meet you, Wendy. Let's all head out to the hangar, shall we?"

Sadie unlocks a door leading to the tarmac. We follow her outside and to a row of parked golf carts underneath a covered walkway. The weather report wasn't wrong; it's just cold enough out here to make me uncomfortable.

Sadie hops into the driver's seat of a cart and beckons for us to join her. Somehow Wendy beats me to the passenger's side, so I slide into the back seat that faces the opposite direction.

"All set?" Sadie asks us both, as if we're about to embark on a trip to the mall and not some existential reckoning. Before I can respond, she's speeding away and I'm clutching on to the cart for dear life, or dear whatever stage of existence it is that I'm in right now.

She pulls up in front of a huge airplane hangar and screeches the tires to a halt.

"Here we are! My second home," she jokes, waving her hand out toward the ugly, boxlike structure. "Stay put for a minute."

We sit in the cart while Sadie unlocks a normal-size door within the garage-size door, walks through, then shuts it behind her. The next thing I know, the entire garage door is lifting itself with a creaking noise.

"Ta-da!" she calls out from under it. "Come in!"

Wendy and I both reluctantly slide out of the cart and walk on the tarmac to the hangar.

In the middle of the huge concrete-floored room sits the Memstractor 3000 boasted about in my training video. It looks even more underwhelming in person. A clunky white machine that's caked with dust sits on a table between three chairs with attached helmets.

"This is it?" I ask.

"Yep," Sadie says, tenderly patting the machine.

"Why does it need this whole building? Why not just, like, an office?"

"The Memstractor is far too powerful. It'd blow out the airport's generator. Anyway, enough with the boring stuff. Wendy!" she exclaims. "How long have you been here, Wendy?"

"Oh. I dunno. I've lost count of the days," she says in a heavy Midwest accent.

Sadie walks over and hands me Wendy's passport. I look over the little information it offers.

Name: Wendy Thomas
Date of Birth: 3/6/1935
Date of Death: 10/20/2019
Time of Death: 11:38 a.m. CDT
Location of Death: Harmon's Pumpkin Farm, Bismarck, North Dakota, United States
Cause of Death: Heart Attack

"Almost two months," Sadie says, like this is for some reason impressive. "How about we all take a seat and get comfortable? Wendy, you take the seat with the red helmet."

As I settle in, "comfortable" feels impossible. Below me, some kind of spring creaks and the old vinyl covering the chair makes a squeaking noise.

"Next, let's all lower our helmets," Sadie instructs, taking off her pillbox hat and placing it on the table, then pulling the dome of plastic over her head. I do the same.

"In a moment I'm going to turn on a switch, and when I do, we will all be inside Wendy's brain."

"Hm. Seems fake, but okay," I say.

Sadie stares at me with wide eyes, then nods at Wendy. I sigh, push back my shoulders, and plaster on another fake smile.

"Now, Wendy," Sadie continues. "Have you given any thought to what might be holding you back from Heaven?"

"I don't know," she answers defensively. "What kind of question is that?"

"Ohhhhkay," Sadie says. "Why don't we start from the day you died and work backward then? Everyone ready?"

Wendy just nods once.

"I'll keep my left hand on this switch, so if you start to feel uncomfortable, just let me know and I'll turn off the machine and we'll be back to reality. Sound good?" Sadie asks, but doesn't wait for a response. "Here we go!"

I'm looking at her hand turning the switch and then, suddenly, I'm not.

There's no helmet, no chair, no airplane hangar. I'm in the open air of a pumpkin patch and my body is free. It smells like hay, and I see small children running through the tangle of pale-colored vines on the ground around me.

"Whaaaat?" I gasp. "Sadie, why didn't you just tell me that it's a virtual reality machine?"

"Because it's not," she says, suddenly standing next to me, Wendy right next to her. "And . . . because I don't know what that is."

I reach out to pick up a pumpkin on the ground, but when I do, my fingers pixelate and disappear before my eyes. I yank my hand back.

"We can't touch or interact with anything or anyone. It's just a memory," Sadie explains. "We can only watch."

"So we're just floating around and showing people their past lives like . . . like . . . the Ghosts of Christmas Past?"

"I'm not sure what you mean."

"Okay, you don't get a pass for that. Charles Dickens's *A Christmas Carol* was written *and* turned into a movie way before either of us were born."

Wendy waves for our attention and points across the patch, where there's another version of her in the same exact outfit. She lifts a pumpkin from the ground and then drops it, falling over and clutching her chest.

"Grandma!" a woman holding a child's hand calls over to her.

Then we're in complete darkness, floating in absolutely nothing. Without thinking, I clutch on to Sadie's arm, which, like the pumpkin, is just thin air.

"What?" she says, smiling. "Afraid of the dark?"

"No."

"Okay," Sadie says. "Wendy, that was your death? Can you show us some of your life? What did you do for a living?"

In the blink of an eye, we're in the back of a classroom full of children. A slightly younger version of Wendy sits at the front, taking attendance.

"A teacher?"

"More or less," she says.

"*Substitute* teacher?" I interject.

She nods.

"I'm sure teaching was so rewarding," Sadie says. "Do you

have any strong memories of helping to change students' lives? Or if not . . . maybe some regrets of . . . *not* changing students' lives?"

The room changes just slightly a few times in a row, Wendy becoming slightly younger each time. But in every version, all Wendy can conjure is the memory of taking attendance.

"What about your love life?" Sadie presses. "You had a granddaughter, so I'm guessing you had kids. Did you have a husband? Or boyfriend? Or . . ."

Now we're all huddled in a tiny kitchen that smells like Palmolive dish soap and coffee. At the table, a skinny old man in a blue bathrobe sits reading the paper. The microwave on the counter dings.

A younger Wendy emerges into the kitchen, opens the microwave, takes out a bowl of instant oatmeal, and places it on the table in front of the old man. He grunts in what I guess is his form of thanks.

"This is your husband?" Sadie presses.

Wendy nods.

"Were you happy in your marriage? Did you two ever have any arguments?"

Wendy just shrugs again, totally uncaring, her face a closed book.

"Well, what was your passion in life?" I interject.

The room shifts just slightly. The old man is gone. A few plates on the drying rack move around, there are fewer pieces of paper taped to the fridge, and the color of the kettle on the stove switches from blue to red, but otherwise everything remains the same. Now Wendy stands mopping her floors and listening to some doo-wop music on the radio, looking livelier than we've seen her this whole time.

"Are you kidding me?" I ask. "Your passion in life was *cleaning your house*? What is the point of us using this machine if all you're going to show us are memories that are as interesting as watching paint dry?"

"Bea," Sadie interjects sternly.

Wendy just stares down at the floor.

"Hold on," I say, putting my hand out and turning to Wendy. "Look, you gotta give us something. You and I both know you were sent here for a reason. The longer you drag us through the mud, the longer it will take for you to get to Heaven. And don't you want that? To go to Heaven? Think about it. Once you're there, I bet you'll have your pick of all the coordinating seasonal separates you want. Easter egg–covered jumpers. Christmas tree turtlenecks. Maybe even a T-shirt that commemorates a fifth season that doesn't even exist for us mortals. You're hiding something from us. I can tell. It's why you're being all cagey and showing us this filler memory of you Swiffering around."

"Okay," she grunts finally, crossing her leaf-covered arms. "Fine."

Her memory switches. Now we're all squished into the back of a car driving down a long stretch of desert highway. The dashboard of the car looks old, like it's from the 1950s or '60s, but new for its time. Past Wendy's hands are young and unwrinkled. A doo-wop song, like the one she was listening to in her kitchen, where a bunch of girls are singing about being in love with their mailman or something, plays out of the staticky radio.

As she drives on, two figures come into her vision standing on the side of road. Unlike everything else in her memory, they are blurry and indistinct blobs of color.

"Who are they?" Sadie asks.

Wendy just stares down at her lap.

"They look like ghosts or something," I say.

"Can you, like, stop bringing up ghosts?" Sadie whispers almost inaudibly in my ear. "It freaks people out.

"Sometimes, Wendy," she continues, in her Fake Nice voice at a normal volume, "when you can't remember someone or something or don't *want* to remember someone or something, it appears in your memories as a blur. Now, you're showing us this memory for a reason, remember? I need you to focus, Wendy!"

Wendy tightens her lips into a hard line, breathes once through her nose, then closes her eyes. Our point of view shifts just slightly. We're back about a quarter mile in the road, where the memory started.

What were fuzzy blobs before are now clearly a teenage boy and girl. The girl wears a poufy pink dress and the boy is in a suit. It looks like maybe their car broke down on the way to a dance, but as Wendy drives closer and closer to them it becomes clear that the girl is running from the boy. And she's running from the boy because he's wielding a knife.

Before I can even pause to comprehend this, young Wendy is swerving onto the side of the road. She drives directly toward the boy. His eyes go wide, but before he can do anything else, his body is being crunched by her tires.

"Holy crap!" I gasp.

Wendy and Sadie just sit there, taking this in like it's normal.

"Why aren't you freaking out?" I whisper to Sadie through my teeth.

"I can't even begin to count the number of times I've seen people kill someone in their memories," she mutters.

Wendy puts her car in reverse and then throws open her passenger door.

"Get in!" she calls to the girl, who does, her whole body shaking. Wendy's voice sounds young. Maybe as young as the girl's.

"So there," Wendy exclaims, making sarcastic jazz hands. "My big secret. The thing that was weighing on me.

"Neither of us ever told a soul about what happened that night," she continues, more serious. "We just pretended that her date had car trouble and while he was flagging down help, there was a hit-and-run, and that I just happened to come upon her and rescue her in a moment of distress. We didn't know each other, but after that, me and Mabel became best friends for life. I was the maid of honor at her wedding. Never told anyone I killed a man."

"I mean, would I tell the authorities if it had happened nowadays? Just claim self-defense?" she wonders aloud. "Mmm . . . probably not. I'm sorry I killed him, but I don't regret saving my best friend."

Suddenly an alarm blares, and in the blink of an eye, I'm back in my seat in the airport hangar, the plastic helmet on my head. I look over at Wendy. The noise is coming from her helmet, which is now flashing green.

I let out a breath, realizing I'd been holding it for the last few seconds.

"Well, all right, Wendy!" Sadie says. "That signal means you've successfully confronted what was holding you back. Time to get you moving on to Heaven."

"THAT WAS AMAZING," I say to Sadie once we're back inside the airport, standing at the departures desk while Todd fills out the paperwork that will get Wendy her ticket to Heaven. "Who knew that little old lady had it in her?"

"Yeah. What she did was wrong, but . . . it *was* pretty cool to watch."

"It wasn't wrong! She totally did the right thing. Do you know how many assholes I wish I could just run over with my car? She's, like, my hero."

"Didn't you die in a car accident?" Todd asks, without looking up from his paperwork.

"Yeah, but that was different," I protest. "And none of your business! How did you even know that?"

"I'm Todd. I know everything."

"Well, you did an amazing job, Bea," Sadie interjects. "The seasonal clothing . . . you spotted her weakness from a mile away and you pounced on it. I have complete faith that you'll get the next two souls moving along in no time. Until then, I'll be watching your every move to make sure you're giving it your all and not making me wait here longer than I absolutely have to."

She smiles and stares into my eyes a little too intensely.

"Seriously?" I moan.

"I'm kidding! Part of the process is that I have to let go. Just gotta let go," she says, beginning to fan her face.

"Um. Are you okay?" I ask.

"I'm fine. It's just . . . this will be the first break I've had from working in decades," she says, tears beginning to pool at the edges of her eyes. "I'm just overwhelmed with possibility. So much free time on my hands! What are you doing right now, Bea? Do you want to grab some lunch?"

"Uhhhh," I stammer, remembering Caleb's passport in my train case, suddenly feeling like it weighs a thousand pounds. "I think I need to go take a nap first. It's been a long week."

"You've only been here for one day," Sadie corrects.

"Exactly."

— ✈ —

I RUSH BACK to my room and flop onto the slightly less awful of the two awful beds, dumping Caleb's passport out of my train case. Before I open it up and read, I pause and take a second to hypothesize the ways that he died. Really, there are only two possibilities: it must've either been by doing something really heroic, like saving a child from a burning building, or something really stupid, like making a video of himself eating a packet of laundry detergent or an outrageous amount of cinnamon because his friends dared him to.

But isn't stealing and reading his passport equally as stupid? Why do I even care about how he died? It's probably because we're confined in a strange place together. It's like the summer before seventh grade, when my dad sent me away to Bible camp because it was cheap and convenient and "good for me," but I spent the whole time fixated on the only other kid my age there. Then, on the last day of camp, as I prepared to say goodbye to him, I realized he always smelled like Cheez-Its and had the face and personality of a foot and we would never make it in the outside world.

I realize I've been holding the passport for so long that my hands are making sweaty imprints on its vinyl cover, so I finally just open the thing up.

Name: Caleb Smith
Date of Birth: 1/3/2002
Date of Death: 12/12/2019
Time of Death: 9:20 p.m. EST
Location of Death: Intersection of Huntingdon Pike and Susquehanna Road, Northwood, Pennsylvania, United States
Cause of Death: Blunt-force trauma and internal bleeding caused by car accident

As I read the last two lines, I feel like I'm having déjà vu. This looks nearly identical to the report in my own passport. I pull mine out and compare the pages. The information on our deaths is nearly identical. This must be a printing error or some clerical mix-up. Like I'd ever trust the people who run this place not to make mistakes.

Yet even as I tell myself this, my chest begins to feel like it's being squashed by a cinder block.

Because why are our deaths recorded one minute apart?

I figured Caleb and I died on the same day because we

were on the same flight, but I didn't think we'd died in the *same exact place* in the *same exact spot*.

I thought he seemed familiar to me on the plane because he was wearing the most basic boy outfit of all time, but maybe he's actually familiar to me because he's the person who killed me.

7

"Stop right there!" a booming man's voice yelled, too mature sounding to be Dominic or even his friend. I froze where I was standing in the parking lot, wedged between two station wagons. Emmy was still staring back at me.

I turned around and saw Rick, our school security guard, or, as he preferred to be called, "school safety agent." Regardless, most kids called him Sergeant Rick behind his back because of his choice to pair his polo shirt that said SECURITY on the back with camouflage-print cargo pants. And also his militant attitude.

He clutched the walkie-talkie stuck to his belt like it was a gun, and I knew that he wished it was. Every time there was another mass shooting in the news, he would loudly complain to any student or teacher who would listen to him that the only way a tragedy could be prevented at our school would be if he, too, were armed.

"I saw what you did back there, young lady," he said. "You're coming with me to Principal Spoglio's office."

"Wait!" Emmy called, then walked back toward me. "She was just sticking up for me."

Then she added, "Sir."

Rick turned and stared incredulously at Emmy, but his face fell as he took in her neat ponytail and her pink puffer jacket and her calculus book—all signs that pointed to innocence.

"It's true," I said, stepping in front of her.

"Well then," he said, still staring at Emmy, "I guess you'll be joining her on her trip to the principal's office."

Emmy's eyes widened with sheer panic. She had never been to the principal's office before for anything other than to present him with a petition that she'd created to ban plastic straws in the lunchroom or to be congratulated on making it into the state's top percentile of standardized test takers.

"That doesn't make sense," I said, crossing my arms. "She didn't do anything! I mean, god, don't you have something better to do right now than patrol the parking lot?"

Rick grimaced at me.

"Young lady, it is my *duty* to patrol this area. I am dedicated to the safety of this school and that includes its parking lot. *Especially* its parking lot. In fact, I have taken an oath to make this parking lot a violence-free zone."

With that, he grabbed me by the elbow and dragged me up the hill.

"Don't touch me!" I yelped.

Rick opened his mouth to speak, but then Emmy interrupted him from behind us.

"Bea," she said. "For once in your life, you're just going to have to cooperate."

8

The first impulse I have after reading Caleb's passport is to burn it, but that would be too simple. Also, I don't know where to find any matches.

I need to play the long game. If he's the reason I'm here, then I need to make his life a living hell. Or however else you'd apply that metaphor to the afterlife.

I take a deep breath to calm down, and try to remind myself that I'm jumping to conclusions. There are other possibilities besides my theory that Caleb committed vehicular manslaughter resulting in my untimely death. Like, maybe he was just an innocent passenger in the car that crashed into mine and none of this is his fault. Or he was just a stupid, stupid pedestrian who walked into the middle of traffic at the worst possible moment. In fact, maybe we're both victims and have gone through a singularly unique experience that only each other can fully understand, bonding us together eternally! No. Before I conclude anything, I need to know the truth.

Remember: the long game.

First, I need to get it out of Caleb whether or not he was driving the night he died, but I have no idea when I'll see him again. I don't know his room number. I don't have a phone and he probably doesn't either. There's a chance I could run into him at breakfast tomorrow, but that feels too far away. I don't want to spend another second not knowing.

If I were someone who lost their passport in a gigantic airport, where would I be?

I stand up and walk over to look at a laminated map stuck to the back of my room door, but it's basically useless. The "You Are Here" sticker has been haphazardly placed in the area representing a plane landing strip, far away from wherever my actual room is situated. Among the tiny icons signifying bathrooms and elevators, I spot one that says L&F. I assume that stands for "Lost & Found."

If it really is a lost and found, maybe I can get someone there to page Caleb on the PA system because some Good Samaritan has so kindly returned his passport and he should come collect it immediately, and then I could just *happen* to be in the general vicinity when he arrives.

I know how to get to the waiting area, so I figure out a path from there to the tiny square signifying the lost and found on the map. When I get where I think I'm supposed to be, there's nothing, no office or door or counter or anyone else in sight. I'm about to give up when I notice a small window made of thick glass with a speaker in the middle, like a bank teller's station. No one is sitting in the chair behind the window, but there is a small phone attached to the adjacent wall with a sign above it that reads CALL FOR LOST AND FOUND. On the phone itself is a printed label that says PRESS 1 FOR LOST AND FOUND. Under *that* is a handwritten label that says, *Press 1 REALLY hard.*

I pick up the phone and put it to my ear. There's no dial

tone, which I immediately take as a bad sign. Still, I press 1. Silence. I press it harder. Nothing. I place the phone between my ear and shoulder to free a hand to simultaneously knock on the window while I keep pressing 1, in case someone is hiding back there.

"Hello!" I call, banging my fist. "Anyone in there?"

Frustrated, I slam the phone repeatedly into the receiver.

"Stupid piece of—"

"Hey!" a voice says behind me.

I turn around to see Caleb, his hands up in surrender.

"Hi," I say, taking a single gulp. I realize I'm wielding the phone like a weapon. Without thinking, I drop it, and it clatters past the counter and dangles toward the ground.

"Sorry, I didn't mean to interrupt," he says with a small smile. "You can keep, uh, doing whatever you were doing to the phone. In fact, I would very likely be doing the same thing if you weren't already."

"Oh?" is all I can manage to say. My stomach lurches.

Somehow I feel embarrassed looking at Caleb, like I'm coming face-to-face with a celebrity I've read R-rated fan fiction about, or maybe more accurately, like coming face-to-face with a serial killer I secretly found to be kind of hot in his mug shot.

"I've been here, like, ten times today. I lost my passport." He says, rolling his eyes at himself. "Two times out of ten, someone answered me, and even then, they totally blew me off. I thought I'd give it one more shot because, really, what else is there to do around here?"

"It's funny you say that," I say, standing up straighter and smiling just as Sadie taught me to. "Your name's Caleb, right?

Because I was coming here to return a passport. And, well . . . I think it's *your* passport."

I pull it out of my bag.

"No way!" he says, eyes widening. "How did you find it?"

"Well, actually someone else found it and then left it at the departures counter, where I was working today," I lie. "I looked inside and recognized your name, but I had no idea where to find you or what your room number was or anything, so . . ."

"Why didn't you just ask the front desk at the hotel?"

"I did!" I continue effortlessly. "They're not allowed to give out room numbers to strangers."

"Why didn't you just leave it at the front desk? I was checking there too."

"Wow! So many questions for me, a person who absolutely had no personal obligation to find the owner of this passport, but still did it out of the kindness of their heart!"

I pretend to place the passport back inside my bag.

"You're right," he says, shaking his head.

"But seriously," I say, pulling it back out. "I didn't leave it there because they told me to take it to the lost and found. And that . . . is the story of how I ended up here smashing the phone to pieces."

"I'm sorry. I shouldn't be so rude. It's just been a long day. I feel so stupid for even losing it."

"It must've fallen out of your shorts. I guess that's what happens when you die wearing shorts without real pockets."

"Whew, ice-cold!" he says, clutching his chest in mock offense. "But I guess you're right."

I step closer to him and hand him the passport.

"Thank you so, so much," he says, a smile spreading across his face. "Really."

"It's fine," I say. "So . . ."

"So . . ." he says.

"Blunt-force trauma and internal bleeding caused by car accident?"

Caleb's smile freezes.

"Excuse me?" he asks through his teeth.

"Your cause of death," I elaborate.

"Oh. Yeah," he says, blinking like this is something he either is just remembering or wants to forget. "I guess so."

"I peeked inside your passport. I mean, I had to figure out who it belonged to . . . Sorry," I say, trying to pull off a convincing embarrassed smile. "I'm not really sure yet what passes as socially acceptable small talk around here. Do we casually talk about how we died or is that, like, really weird, you know?"

I twist a piece of my hair around my finger, pretending like this social taboo is actually what's making me nervous, not something else entirely.

"It's not weird," Caleb says, relaxing slightly. "I guess it should be small talk. It's, like, the main thing everyone here has in common. Being dead."

"Exactly! That's what I was thinking."

For a moment he stares thoughtfully at the wall and puts his hands in his shorts pockets.

"I think I just have a hard time believing it's real, you know?" he asks, scrunching his shoulders up. "It's like, one minute I'm driving in my car and the next . . . I'm on an airplane?"

"You were the one driving?" I press, battling my face's muscles to keep my expression neutral.

"Thank god it was just me in the car," he says, shaking his head.

I clench my fists as the taste of bile climbs up my throat and hot rage thrums through my veins.

"Yeah," I say, nodding emphatically. "*Thank god* it was just you."

Permission to play the long game: granted.

9

—

"You know, Spoglio is a total softy. He'll still let you go to the dance tonight. He won't punish you. I mean, not that you even did anything," I said to my sister as we sat next to each other in the lobby of the school office, waiting for our fate to be delivered to us. Sergeant Rick was inside the principal's office, relaying the details of what happened in the parking lot.

"Yeah," she said vacantly, staring straight ahead at the bulletin board on the wall across from us that read TOGETHER WE CAN DREAM . . . BELIEVE . . . LEAD . . . ACHIEVE in giant paper letters.

"Really inspirational stuff, huh?" I said, nodding toward it.

"What?" she asked, like she'd just woken up. "Oh. Yeah."

"I didn't mean for this to happen, you know."

Finally Emmy turned her head and stared at me.

"What do you mean 'didn't mean'? You didn't mean to get caught?"

"Well, yeah. And for you to get involved. It just all kind of spiraled out of control."

"Okay. Thanks, I guess? What do you want me to say?"

"I didn't ask you to say anything. I was just explaining myself."

"Sometimes," Emmy started, then paused. "Sometimes I just think you're bad at picking your battles."

"What's that supposed to mean?"

"You didn't need to have an altercation in the parking lot over one stupid comment," she muttered.

"I was protecting you! You're my little sister. It's my job . . . it's . . . it's my *duty*. I took an oath," I said, smiling as I called back to Sergeant Rick's earlier ridiculous comments. Emmy didn't return the smile.

"Sometimes I don't need to be protected, okay?" she said. "Sure, I'd prefer to walk into school without being cat-called, but what can you do? I mean, maybe if I got to school earlier . . ."

"How would that change anything?"

"I don't know, like, if we actually got to school on time and parked at the top, where all the grody boys don't hang out, this wouldn't have been a problem and I would just be in class right now having a calm, normal morning thinking about the amazing time I would have tonight at Snow Ball with my boyfriend."

"So you're saying this is all my fault? That I asked for this?"

"No! That's not what I'm saying at all," she said, closing her eyes. "Sorry. I'm not making any sense."

"You're not going to get in trouble. And, hey, if you do, there will be other dances for you and Skyler to go to. You're only a sophomore, Emmy! You have so much time. Instead we can just have a chill night at home! We can watch *Real Housewives* and make pizza rolls and wear those gross slimy sheet masks you love."

"*Bea*," Emmy said, sitting up. "Do you not get it? I don't

want just a chill night at home. Tonight was supposed to be special."

"Beatrice Fox?" the principal's secretary called from behind her desk before I could say anything more. "Principal Spoglio will see you now."

10

In my room, I lie awake, attempting to plot my revenge against Caleb. I refuse to sleep knowing I'm sharing air space with the person who committed manslaughter against me.

The problem is there really isn't anything to plot with. Like me, and everyone else here, he has nothing important to his name. Nothing I can hold over his head and use to make him suffer. No money, no valuable possessions, no friends, no reputation, no embarrassing past social media presence that I could dig up and use to humiliate him. My earlier rant that we have nothing to show for ourselves except for our useless frozen bodies rings too true.

If all he has is his body, then could I physically hurt him? If I just punched him in the face, would it actually do anything? Is punching someone in the face one millions times over even close to the equivalent of them killing you?

I turn over and glance at the clock on my nightstand. It's 3:30 a.m. Before I can think too hard about what I'm doing, I'm putting my shoes on and heading up to the sixth floor.

"Good morning, Bea!" Sadie says, opening her door. She's wide-awake and panting, like she'd just been running sprints.

"Are you up?" I say, weary.

"Oh, I only need three . . . four hours sleep, max! I was just doing my morning aerobics routine. Want to join me?"

In the doorway, she high-steps in place.

"Uh, I'm good. I just had some . . . lingering questions that weren't really addressed in my orientation."

"Well, I'm sure I've got answers. Come in," she says, moving aside. "I can walk and talk."

When I step inside Sadie's room, I'm rendered speechless.

The furniture and the layout is identical to mine, but her room is full of *stuff*. Tons of it. Taped to the walls, the way girls line their bedrooms with printed-out pictures of them and their friends, are hundreds of bits of paper and napkins with notes scrawled on them.

Whereas my dresser is bare, hers is covered with cups of pens and markers, bottles of glue, piles of magazines, the jar of glitter she must have used to make my welcome sign, bottled toiletries with generic labels, and god knows what else. In someone's house, this would be considered "cluttered." Here, in an airport where most people arrive with no possessions and no one has money and there's virtually nothing to buy, I'd say this would be classified as "hoarding."

"You have quite the collection," I say at last.

Upon closer inspection, I realize the notes taped to wall all have messages that read like they belong in the back of a yearbook, things like, *Thanks, Sadie! LYLAS* and *I'll miss you! Never change!* and *BEVERLY + SADIE = BFF*.

"Oh yeah," she says, continuing to bounce up and down. "Those are all my notes from people who've moved on to Heaven. Some of them were people I helped. Some of them were coworkers."

"And this one?" I ask, pointing up at a napkin that says in calligraphy-like handwriting, *To Sadie, My Eternal Flame* . . .

"You said you had some 'lingering questions' for me?" she asks, squinting and gesturing for me to take a seat on her bed.

"Yeah," I say, crossing my arms and flopping down. "I was wondering . . . if our bodies are frozen in time, does that mean we can't feel pain?"

"No," Sadie says, doing a split on the floor and groaning as if to prove her answer. "Think about how you felt when you first arrived. You felt sick, right? All queasy and vomit-y."

"Ugh." I cringe. "Okay, but that was my body's own impulse, right? What about if something or *someone* were to hurt me? If I were to, like, jump out my hotel room window onto the tarmac right now or, say, I don't know . . . get punched in the face, would it damage my body?"

"No, but it would *hurt*. Your body is now indestructible, but it's not as if you're, like, totally superhuman, you know?"

"So I could get punched in the face a thousand times in a row and that wouldn't break my nose, but it would *feel* like I'd broken my nose?"

"Precisely!" Sadie smiles, but then her face immediately falls. "Why are you so obsessed with someone punching you in the face? Is someone threatening to punch you in the face?"

"No. It's just the first thing that came to mind."

"Well, no one would punch you in the face here. Anyone who would do that sort of thing was probably sent straight to Hell, but if someone here dared to try, they'd have to go in front of the Disciplinary Council for judgment."

"Disciplinary Council?"

"If anyone does something here that would've been considered a crime while they were alive, the Disciplinary Council decides if that person should be temporarily removed from the lottery or, if necessary, immediately removed from the airport and sent to Hell."

"That's a thing?"

"Yeah. They're, like, the closest the airport has got to a government," Sadie says, now turning onto her back to do crunches. "They live and work in the air traffic control tower, away from everyone."

"And no one mentioned this to me in orientation because . . . ?" I ask.

"The council doesn't like to publicize themselves. They don't want people to be on their best behavior just to avoid getting in trouble. They want people to be on their *normal* behavior, so they can weed out anyone who was placed here by mistake. Really though, they're barely needed. I've only heard of them swooping in a handful of times since I've been here. God is pretty reliable with sorting us out."

"Do you know what made them take action?" I ask, standing and pacing back and forth. The wheels in my head begin to turn. "Like, what crimes people committed that got their attention?"

"Phew," Sadie exhales, coming up from a crunch. "These are great questions, Bea! You're so perceptive. I would say—"

She's interrupted by a sudden knock at her door. Her body freezes. After a few seconds she turns and glances at the clock on her nightstand.

"He's early," she says under her breath.

"Who?" I ask, crossing my arms.

Sadie stares up at me as if she's just remembered I'm in the room.

"It's meeeee!" a man's voice booms from behind her door.

"Oh. Am I interrupting . . . your plans?" I ask, pretending to be polite, but actually super annoyed.

"I know the password, Sadie," the voice says, lower this time.

Suddenly she jumps up off the floor, sprints to the door, and opens it, revealing none other than Todd.

"It's Sadieisthemostbeau—" he starts, leaning into the doorframe.

"*Heyyy*, Todd!" she says, cutting him off. "You'll never guess who is here. Our new friend Beatrice."

"Who?" he asks, looking over her shoulder toward me.

"You know Beatrice, my *trainee*."

"Your . . . ? Oh!"

Todd blinks twice, then stands up straight and clears his throat.

"Hello, Beatrice!" he says, coming inside.

"Hi," I deadpan.

"Todd was just joining me for my morning aerobics routine, as he usually does."

"Yep," he says, putting his hands on his hips. "You don't get muscles like these just sitting around all day."

"Isn't aerobics cardio?" I press. "I thought strength training gave you muscles. Plus aren't our bodies frozen in time and impossible to change?"

"Well, I'll tell you what," Todd says, turning his head

toward Sadie. "These new arrivals are just getting smarter and smarter. I don't know what they're teaching them down there, but it is working."

"You guys don't have to do this whole song and dance for me. Whatever is going on or is . . . about to go on"—I pause to grimace—"is your business. Sadie, can you just please answer my question from before and I will get out of your way?"

She gives me a hard stare for a moment, but then breaks back into a smile.

"Sure thing!" she says, then turns to Todd. "Bea wanted to know what crimes people have committed here that have gotten the attention of the Disciplinary Council."

Todd blows air out of his mouth.

"Oh man. Where to begin . . . Well, there was that guy who kept flashing everyone. . . ."

"Oh my god, yes!" Sadie exclaims. "What ever happened to him?"

"I think they ruled that he couldn't be blamed because he didn't *choose* to die wearing just a trench coat and nothing else."

"Mmhm. Oh, do you remember that woman who ended up here with that guy she thought was her murderer?"

I perk up my ears.

"Yes!" Todd says, nearly jumping up and down. "But it turned out to be a guy who looked just like her actual murderer? And still she kept trying to stab him with a butter knife from the food court?"

"Poor thing," Sadie says, shaking her head condescendingly. "Like that would've accomplished anything. Still, the

Disciplinary Council really doesn't like it when people try to take justice into their own hands."

My stomach drops.

"Yeah, and they hate it when anyone tries to game the system," Todd says, sitting down on the edge of Sadie's bed.

"What do you mean?" I ask.

"Some people have it in their heads that they can get their number called without waiting," Sadie explains. "I blame it all on how they updated orientation for newcomers. They used to not tell you that once you get to Heaven, you'll be able to watch over your loved ones and see how they're doing."

"You can?" I ask, estimating in my head how old Emmy will be when I finally get out of here. With my luck, she'll probably be in a retirement home by the time I can check in on her.

"Yeah," she says. "It's supposed to be an incentive to get people to cooperate with our team. Now that everyone knows, they're just chomping at the bit to move on, as if they weren't already. As if the reward of Heaven weren't enough for them."

"It's true. People are getting more entitled than ever," Todd says, taking off his shoes. "I don't know what's happening on Earth, but these new arrivals do not seem to understand we are not a commercial airline company that they can just . . . *fax* . . . or *tweet* . . . whatever that is . . . their complaints to and get what they want. This isn't a business. They can't just harass us into getting their numbers called."

The stench of Todd's feet fills the room and I cover my nose.

"Or worse," Sadie says. "They think they can sweet-talk you into doing them a favor."

"Yes!" I blurt out. "That exact thing happened to me this morning when . . . a person saw I was wearing a Memory Experience uniform."

"Already? Typical," Todd spits. "These people will just prey on any fresh meat they can find."

I wince at his description of me.

"So what happens?" I ask, looking between the two of them. "Theoretically, if that same person were to keep bothering me?"

"Well, yeah, that would be considered harassment and you'd need to file a complaint with the Disciplinary Council office, which I've never actually seen open during the day, so you'd have to leave it in their mailbox," Todd says.

"And then," Sadie adds, "they're required to go through surveillance camera footage to find proof of the claim and then review that footage before they can even schedule a hearing and call on witnesses and—"

"Surveillance camera footage?" I ask, leaning forward. "We're being watched?"

"Eh," Todd grunts. "We're not so much being *watched* as we're being *recorded*. The footage is there if it's needed."

I look up at the corners of the room, searching frantically for a camera.

"Bea, I don't meant to be, like . . . rude," Sadie says, continuing her exercise routine by moving into plank position with her toes pointing down and her forearms flat on the floor. "But has it really not occurred to you that your entire life was surveilled and that's why you're here now?"

I stare at her with a gaping mouth.

No. It hadn't.

"Don't worry, though," she says, looking up at me. "Our rooms don't have cameras in them. They're the only places that don't. Well, and in the memories."

"What do you mean?"

"The memory sessions can't be recorded since they only happen inside people's brains. The Memstractors are only capable of taking transcripts of people's neural patterns to prove they are ready to move on."

"Oh, well, of course," I mumble.

"Speaking of," Sadie says, collapsing onto the carpet at last. "Are you nervous for tomorrow?"

"What's tomorrow?"

"Your first session without me, silly!"

I had, to be honest, completely forgotten about my job and the whole memory thing over the course of the night. It had been completely absorbed by my desire to ruin Caleb, which, I now realize, could very well be possible.

"Oh, *that*?" I say, smiling and waving my hand. "I'm not nervous about it at all."

11

My first solo soul is Charlie Blunt, a fifty-seven-year-old man who died of a heart attack.

I ask him to tell me a little bit about himself and the first thing he says is he worked as something called a "chief risk officer" at a bank that I've only heard of because they have a drive-through ATM at the shopping center near my house.

"So you were, like, the security guard at a bank?" I ask.

"No, I worked on *Wall Street*," he scoffs.

I take a deep breath and plaster on a smile.

At the beginning of our session, he shows me vivid memories of himself sitting at the head of long, important conference tables and staring at screens with rapidly moving numbers and laughing with other businessmen in dimly lit restaurants while they eat giant cuts of steak.

Yet when I press him about his personal life, the memories get fuzzier. He can't seem to remember what color his wife's hair is or if his son plays soccer or football. When he recalls their last vacation together, he can only think of himself searching for cell reception on a cruise ship so that he can take an important work call.

It doesn't take me long to zero in on the regret that's holding him here.

"Okay, yes, you're exactly right," he exclaims an hour into our session, blubbering like a baby. "I overworked myself to death! I didn't make time for my family when I should have!"

The green light on his helmet lights up, signaling that a neural pathway of self-realization, or whatever, has been formed. Still, he continues to weep and weep and weep, even when we return to the airport to file his departure paperwork.

"There you are. Finally," Sadie says, clutching her chest with relief when she sees me, even though I managed to finish up a half hour before our four-hour window was over. She must have been waiting at the departures counter since the early morning. "So, how'd it go?"

"Fine." I shrug.

"Define 'fine,'" she says, squinting. "Do you need some more time for his case? Did you—"

"No. He came to a conclusion. He'll be on the next flight out."

"That's amazing, Bea! Your first solo soul and you got him moving in a day. That means you only need to move one more person along and then it's my time to go." She smiles, but falters as she looks at me. "Why aren't you more excited? You should be so proud of yourself!"

"Honestly? It was a huge bummer."

I didn't feel amused or invigorated the way I did when our first soul, Wendy, revealed to us that she ran a guy over with her car. I felt weird and sad, like I just witnessed a classmate I barely know's dad have a breakdown in front of me.

Sadie pulls me aside so we're out of earshot of anyone else. The waiting room is emptier this morning, which I assume means most of the people whose numbers weren't called have retreated to the hotel until tomorrow.

"What do you mean?" she presses.

"I mean, look at him," I say, glancing at Charlie. He's sitting on a bench a few feet behind us, absolutely bawling like a newborn in a business suit.

"Yeah, but you got him to realize what was holding him back! He had been living in denial for so long and you're the first person he admitted it to. That's what's important."

"He doesn't seem at peace about it, though."

"Well, he's grieving now, but he's got it off his chest. Peace will come to him in due time."

"If you say so," I mumble.

"It can be hard at first. Believe me, I know," Sadie says, placing a hand on my shoulder. "But soon you'll have gone through so many people's memories, nothing will faze you. Look, let me use the analogy the person who trained me used: It's like being an ER doctor. The first time you have to pump someone's stomach will be disturbing, but after a while, your job just becomes one big blur of bodily fluids all the time. You won't even give it a second thought."

Great.

Two souls down.

Only 4,998 souls to go.

—✈—

WITH THE WORKDAY over, my mind returns to the Caleb Problem. If I knew that harassing an agent was a punishable offense from the beginning, I wouldn't have freaked out at him that first day. I would have strung him along until the last second, when I would've reported him for bribery to the Disciplinary Council, just for being an entitled prick, regardless of whether he hit me with his car or not. They could've had him in their grips and punished him.

But would they have? Sadie said they don't like when people take justice into their own hands here.

My stomach grumbles and I'm too exhausted from a morning of solving a businessman's deepest emotional regrets to figure out the answers. First, I need to eat lunch. Then I need to take a nap.

Instead of sitting down to eat, and potentially running into Caleb before I'm ready, I stop at the hot dog cart I spotted on my first day. Although, maybe it's a completely different cart. The main hall loops around the center of the airport, so that when you walk through it, it feels like the repetitive backdrop of a video game level you can't seem to beat.

Hot dog cart. Newsstand. Food court. Bar. Hot dog cart. Newsstand.

I know I shouldn't be surprised when I'm handed a hot dog submerged in red Jell-O inside a bun covered in yellow Jell-O, but it still makes me gag.

I return to my hotel room, and as I kick off my shoes and sit down on the edge of my bed, I feel the creeping sensation that something isn't right. I look over at the other bed to my left and jump up, accidentally dropping my fake hot dog mustard-side down onto the carpet. A pair of beady eyes is peering into my soul. A pair of beady eyes that belongs to a pink stuffed poodle, but still.

I carefully pick up the toy dog and flip it over, convinced it must be bugged, or worse, contain some kind of explosive device. But before I can inspect it further, I hear the toilet flush in the bathroom and the sound of the sink turning on and off. The door opens. I drop the poodle onto the bed and instinctively put my hands up.

In the doorway stands a petite white girl with a super-cropped red pixie cut, wearing a baby-pink velour sweat suit that's a size too big for her frail-looking frame.

"Oh, hi!" she says, walking over to me. "I'm Jenna! You must be my roommate!"

12

——

"**So, let me** get this straight, you assaulted Dominic Reed with a Hot Pocket?" Principal Spoglio asked me, eyes closed, pinching the bridge of his nose with his fingers.

"More or less." I shrugged.

He opened his eyes and stared at me, incredulous.

"It was in self-defense!" I exclaimed.

This was not my first visit to Mr. Spoglio's office, which itself was way less intimidating looking than you'd think a principal's office would be. Or, at least, it wasn't even trying to be intimidating the way most principal's offices tried to be on TV, with their heavy wooden desks and fancy trophies that said useless things like AWARD OF DISTINCTION FOR EXCELLENCE IN EDUCATION.

His office had only one small window, cinder-block walls, a ceramic football-shaped pencil holder, and an abundance of dusty Penn State football merch. Like many teachers at my school, Mr. Spoglio thought being obsessed with his college football team was a replacement for a personality.

"Beatrice, look: I know being a young woman in this day and age is not easy. As the father of two girls of my own, I get it."

He gestured to a framed professional portrait of him and his wife holding hands with two toddlers on the beach, the whole family wearing matching white shirts and khaki shorts. This was approximately the third time this year he'd said something to that effect to me, then pointed to the picture as proof of his undying understanding of my womanly struggle.

"And between you and me, I know Dominic Reed doesn't have the, uh, most outstanding character."

"You don't say."

He gave me an exhausted look.

"But, Beatrice, you need to exhibit some impulse control!"

I slouched down, letting all my hair fall behind the back of the uncomfortable chair I was sitting in.

"Listen to me, I know you're not stupid," he said.

"Oh, thank you so much!"

"In fact," he said, ignoring me, "I think if you didn't get so distracted by all these petty squabbles all the time, you could be one of our brightest students. Just like that little sister of yours!"

"I don't know," I said, staring up at the dropped ceiling and counting the number of dots on the tiles. "Emmy spends all of her free time on homework and extracurricular stuff. She lives for it. My free time is for me. There're just so many stupid Instagram videos of people doing their eye shadow and making slime out there and so little time to watch them, you know? Plus, have you ever considered that my quote unquote 'petty squabbles' aren't distractions? Maybe I'm doing every-one a favor by putting someone like Dominic Reed in his place."

"Beatrice. Seriously. Cut the crap."

"Wow, the *C*-word, Mr. S? In the presence of a young lady such as myself?"

At this, Mr. Spoglio placed his head in his hands and began intensely rubbing his face. This was how our interactions usually went. He would try to guilt me into becoming a better person or whatever. I would try to wear him down with increasingly irritating comments. Finally he would just get so tired, he would let me off the hook.

"Here's what I'm going to do," he said at last. "I'm not going to suspend you for this morning's incident, but—"

"And Dominic?" I asked, sitting up straight. "Will he be suspended for what he said to my sister?"

"No. He will not. I think he has endured more than enough punishment today."

"Oh, so you condone him telling my sister that she has, and I quote, a 'tight as—'"

"Enough!" he said, squirming and gripping the arms of his chair. "No! I do not condone whatever he said, just like I don't condone whatever the heck it is that you did to him. But . . . next time I will suspend you. And there will be no next time. Is that clear?"

"Hmm," I said, tapping my hand to my mouth. "How about this: there will be no next time *only* under the condition that my sister is free to attend the dance tonight even though she was late to school."

"That's not how this works, Beatrice. This isn't a negotiation. I am the authority here."

"Please, Mr. Spoglio," I begged. "This isn't about me. You know *I* couldn't care less about the dance. The last thing I want to do is come to school in my free time to drink room-temperature punch and watch my classmates grind on one another, but it's really, really important to Emmy."

Mr. Spoglio stared at me, nodding very, very slowly.

"Okay," he said with purpose, like he had just made a powerful breakthrough. "Your sister is free to attend the dance."

"Great!" I yelped, bolting out of my seat.

"On one condition," Mr. Spoglio added, lifting his hand for me to pause.

"And that is?"

"You must also attend the dance," he said, a maniacal smile spreading across his face.

I stared at him stoically, hoping the intensity of my eyes would make him back down. It didn't.

"Fine," I said at last.

"Well then, we're all done here," he said, writing me a pass to my second-period class. "Here you go."

"Gotta hand it to you, Mr. S," I said, pulling the pass from his grasp. "That was a savage move you pulled on me."

He smiled to himself and stood to open the door to his office.

"Emily Fox," he called out into the waiting room. "You're free to go. See you *girls* tonight."

Emmy breathed a sigh of relief.

"See?" I whispered to her as I collected my backpack. "You're fine. I told you everything would be fine. I'll see you at lunch, kay?"

She gave me the tiniest smile that I knew meant she'd forgiven me.

13

"**Uhhhh,**" **I say,** eyes wide, reluctantly reaching out my hand. "I'm Bea."

The girl, Jenna, ignores my hand. Instead she comes in for a hug. My whole body freezes. Awkwardly, I pat her back and when I do, I feel small hard bumps on the back of her sweat suit. Rhinestones.

"I see you've already met Sprinkles!" she says. "He and I have been through soooo much together, but I'm relieved to see we've both come out on the other side. Aren't we so relieved, Sprinkles?"

She looks at the toy and blows it a kiss. It occurs to me that the only way she could've brought it with her here would be if she died clutching it in her arms.

"I'm sorry, did you say 'roommate'?" I ask, pulling out of her hug. "Are you sure you're in the right place?"

"Yeah!" she says, pulling a key inscribed with the same number as mine out of her hoodie pocket. "This *really nice* lady at the front desk told me she was giving me this room as a special treat."

"Did she happen to have a bunch of lipstick smeared on her teeth?" I ask.

"Yes! Exactly!"

Damn Belinda.

"I'm so glad they paired me with another girl my age," Jenna continues. "My plane was full of old guys. I mean, it sucks that you and I passed away so young, but at least now we have each other. It'll be super fun! Just like bunking at sleepaway camp!"

"Wait, sorry again, but just to clarify . . . you're also seventeen?"

"Yeah. I know," she says. "I look really young. I haven't spent that much time outside these past few years because of the cancer."

She frowns and stares at the floor for a second, but looks back up at me with a smile before I can even ask if she's all right.

"So what do you do for fun around here?"

"Fun?" I say, bending over to pick up the sad excuse for a hot dog I dropped on the ground. "I don't know if 'fun' is physically, or even mentally, possible here."

"Oh no, was that your lunch?" she asks, a look of pity on her face. "You must be hungry. C'mon, we should go eat and catch up and get to know each other! There was an ad for this uh-mazing-looking pizza place on the TV."

She reaches to pick up the remote, which would inevitably turn on the TV and play the song of my nightmares.

"No!" I say. "I mean, um . . . I dunno . . . I should probably not . . . There's this . . ." I gesture vaguely with my fingers around the room toward nothing.

"What?" she says, raising her eyebrows. "Do you have something better to do?"

She doesn't say it like she's offended. She says it like she's hopeful, as if there's some secret nightclub for the prematurely dead that I can get us into.

I shake my head. As painful as it is for me to admit, I truly do not have something better to do.

"THERE'S JUST SO much to choose from!" Jenna exclaims when we get to the food court.

Really, there isn't. There's a burger place, a pizza place, a salad place, and something just called Home Cooking, which strikes me as particularly depressing given that no one here is going home ever again. Behind all of the counters are plastic menu boards printed with faded stock photos of food lit up by fluorescent lights, but there's no need to order. Like the continental breakfast in the hotel lobby, the food is serve yourself and protected by plastic sneeze guards.

"So how'd you end up getting a job at the airport?" Jenna asks, loading up her tray with a clump of fries from the burger counter. "Seems fun!"

"It's sort of interesting," I say, dropping a goopy cheeseburger onto mine. "But it's definitely not 'fun.' My job is my punishment for being a huge bitch on Earth. Or something like that."

"You don't seem like a . . . bitch. . . ." Jenna says, whispering the word. "Not to me."

She wanders over to a tray of "spaghetti and meatballs" at the Home Cooking counter.

"Yeah, well, you don't know me," I say, walking behind her.

"No, I can tell," she says. "I'm good at seeing the best in people. My mom calls it my 'gift.'"

"Wow," I mumble. "How convenient for me."

As Jenna and I turn to take a seat, I stop in my tracks. There at the other end of the food court, I spot Caleb. He doesn't see me, but he's moving quickly in our direction. Far too quickly, because he's . . . jogging? What a show-off. What is with everyone exercising? There's no point in doing it after you've already died and your body is suspended in limbo. Possibly the only nice thing about being here is that the whole concept of "health" no longer exists.

I pull Jenna by the elbow. She squeals.

As Caleb gets closer, I panic and I flip my tray toward myself to cover my face, dropping the burger onto my toes.

"Oh, Bea!" Jenna exclaims, bending down to pick it up with her napkin. "You're so silly. Always dropping food on the ground. What's going on with you today?"

"I'll explain later."

"But, Bea, tell me, Bea! Please!" she whines, wiping off my shoes.

I dart my eyes over the edge of my tray to make sure Caleb didn't hear my name.

"Shh!" I whisper.

"Who's that?" she says, following my gaze toward him as he closes his eyes and pulls the lower part of his shirt up to wipe sweat off his face, exposing a pair of abs that are defined enough to be impressive but not enough to suggest he spends a completely personality-crushing amount of time at the gym. I hate myself for even making this analysis.

"Just be quiet and I'll tell you in a minute," I say through gritted teeth.

Finally Caleb jogs away, looping around the other end of the food court, completely unaware of my presence. I wait a few seconds after he passes, and finally exhale.

"So?" Jenna says, standing up with the gut-like remains of my burger in her left hand, her tray of food in the other.

"He's no one," I say conclusively.

She raises a single eyebrow.

"Oh, c'mon! You have to give me more than that!"

I purse my lips together.

"We have history together, you could say."

"Oooooh!" she exclaims.

"Ew, no, not like *that*," I say, remembering the nausea-inducing sound of his car colliding with mine.

"So you wouldn't mind if I went for him then?" she asks, biting her lip and smirking, her eyes going wild.

"*Yes*," I say a little too loudly. "I mean, no. I don't know. I don't care."

Jenna observes my face for a few thoughtful seconds.

"Well, I guess there are plenty of other fish in the sea. I mean, I think. Statistically speaking, how many teenage boys die? Probably more than girls . . . Boys are always getting into dangerous antics. . . ."

I look her squarely in the face.

"Jenna, do you understand where we are? This isn't sleep-away camp. This isn't high school. This isn't some prom with an ironic theme of 'crappy airport.' Now is not the time for meeting boys and having fun. This is some serious existential stuff, okay? We're *dead*."

"Yeah, I know . . ." she says, continuing to smile.

"We are in purgatory," I say. "PUR-GA-TO-RY!"

Several people in line at the salad counter turn and stare at me with gaping mouths, including a man wearing a race car driver's outfit.

"What? Is no one gonna just come out and say it?" I ask, making eye contact with him.

"I mean . . ." Jenna says, her smile faltering slightly. "I just thought this could still be a *little bit* fun. I've always associated airports with the excitement of going on vacation. . . ."

"It's not fun! I'm *doomed* to be here for a long, long time. So now, if you don't mind, I need to leave and go to bed so I am well rested for yet another day of selflessly helping others."

Before she can say anything, I throw my tray onto the top of a trash can and storm off.

"Bea, wait!" Jenna calls after me. "Bed? It's only the afternoon. You really should eat lunch."

I turn around and there she is, dumping the remains of my burger into the trash and then skipping to catch up to me like some kind of pink velour puppy.

Jenna may be a pain in my butt, but I can already tell: she's loyal. Trusting. Possibly too trusting. If I were her mother, I'd be in a constant state of panic that she'd get into a white van with an old guy who offered her candy, or, maybe more realistically, that she'd be catfished by an old guy posing as a male model online.

14

"Anything!" Jenna exclaims, fists clenched with excitement and eyes bright. "I'll help you with anything."

I stop and look around the food court dramatically like I'm about to drop some classified information.

"So that guy you noticed a few minutes ago?" I say quietly.

"Yeah," she says, smiling.

"He tried to bribe me into getting his lottery number called."

"No way!" She gasps. "How?"

"Flirting," I say. "How else do guys like him get what they want? They think they can charm their way into anything."

"So annoying," she says emphatically.

"It's not just annoying, Jenna. Here, it's a punishable offense."

"Oh. Wow!"

"So here's what I need you to do," I say, putting my arm around her shoulders and whispering into her ear. "When he loops back around on that little jog of his, I'm going to invite him to eat with us. You'll be there to witness the conversation. Because I have a feeling he's going to pull something on me again, and I want you there to back up my claim that he's trying to game the system."

"Oh my god," Jenna breathes. "A witness! So official."

"I want you to ask me if I know of any hacks to get *a* number drawn. Not *your* number, of course. I don't want you getting in trouble. Just mention it . . . in a theoretical way. Let's make him feel like it's a safe space to bring up rigging the lottery. Does that make sense?"

"Wait, you want him to try to bribe you again?" Jenna asks, squinting. "Even though it's against the rules?"

"Well, no, of course not. As someone who obeys and respects the rules, obviously, I don't *want* that to happen. I just . . . Look, Jenna, I just need you to do as I say. So will you be my official witness or not?"

She swallows and nods furiously.

"I knew I could count on you," I say, patting her on the back.

Across the sea of tables, I spot Caleb coming around for another lap, this time at a slower pace. He eventually pauses at the salad counter and looks over its offerings like they're actually appetizing.

Of course he does.

"Okay," I mumble to Jenna. "It's go time."

"Hey! Caleb!" I call. He looks around at the gaggles of lunch eaters, then his eyes settle on me.

"Bea," he says, smiling and walking over.

"Have you scoped out which one's the cool table yet?" I ask.

"Yeah." He looks toward a group of three white-haired men in leather biker outfits. "But they rejected me."

I plan to put on my fakest friendly smile, but somehow it comes without even trying.

"That's too bad," I say. "My new roommate, Jenna, and I were about to eat. Maybe you could join us and we can be the second-coolest table?

"Oh, hi," he says, noticing Jenna next to me. "I'm Caleb."

"I know," she says, scowling.

I turn my face so only she can see it and widen my eyes at her.

"I mean," she says, with an unconvincing half smile, "hi."

"Why don't you find us a place to sit, Jenna?" I ask. "While we go grab some food."

"Sure. I'll do that," she answers, walking backward with her tray, continuing to watch Caleb with eyes like a hawk, and bumping into a chair. "Ow!"

Caleb twists his head toward her with concern.

"Is she okay?" he asks me.

"I'm fine," Jenna blurts, continuing to walk backward.

"She's fine," I repeat with a wave of my hand. "So, Caleb, it's my first time dining around these parts. I've only had a chance to experience the stunning breakfast buffet. What's good here?"

He gives me a skeptical glance. *Around these parts?* Who even am I?

"Okay, let me be more specific," I elaborate. "What can I eat here that *won't* make me want to sever off my own tongue with a knife so I never have to experience flavors again?"

"Well, when you put it that way," Caleb says with a grin. "Honestly? I got a salad last night and it was . . . edible."

"What? No! How?"

"My theory is that because Jell-O salad was a real thing on Earth, my brain can actually process what I'm eating, as opposed to like . . ."

He looks around and his eyes settle on a woman struggling to pick up a Jell-O–encrusted sub sandwich without it sliding from her fingers.

". . . that."

"You make a good point," I say.

Even though I think Caleb's logic is totally unreasonable and there is no way Jell-O salad makes sense as a concept, I follow him to the counter and plop a yellow dome filled with slices of tomato and cucumbers and carrots and topped with a tiny jiggly dot of ranch dressing onto my tray.

I'm about to turn away when I notice a familiar-looking man with bleached-blond spiky hair mopping the floor behind the counter. Barf bag guy from the plane! Instead of a Hawaiian shirt, he's now decked out in orange coveralls.

"Not so fun cleaning up someone else's mess, is it?" I ask, calling over the counter. The man pauses and stares at me for a moment, then turns back, mopping even harder. I take this as a good omen. Karma is real. Consequences exist. My plan to get Caleb in trouble *will* go well.

When Caleb and I get to the table where Jenna sits, her steely resolve has disappeared. Her eyes are closed, one hand hovers over her mouth, and the other holds a fork in midair.

"Jenna?" I ask, placing my tray down next to her. "Are you okay?"

She shakes her head once but doesn't open her eyes.

"Jenna!" I repeat louder, tapping her shoulder.

"Sorry," she says, opening her eyes as if she's waking up from a coma. "I got overwhelmed because . . . it's just . . ."

She takes a ragged breath and moans. Caleb gives me a panicked look.

"The food!" she exclaims at last. "It's . . . so . . . GOOD!"

"What?" Caleb and I both blurt.

Jenna forks a meatball and eats it in one bite.

"Chemo," she says through a full mouth. "I had to get chemo for the last few years. It stopped me from having a real appetite. But now my appetite is back! This rules!"

Caleb relaxes in his chair and gives her a sad smile.

"That's great," he says. "Hey, if you think this food is good, just imagine what it will be like when we get to Heaven."

"Speaking of—" I say.

"Do you think they'll have breadsticks in Heaven?" Jenna asks him, interrupting me with an urgent look in her eyes. "That's my favorite food. The endless breadsticks from Olive Garden."

"Um. Sure," he reassures her. "There will probably be endless everything."

"Even Cinnabon?" she presses, sucking up a clump of noodles.

"I'm guessing yes," Caleb answers.

"Subway?" she asks through a full mouth, so it sounds more like "Shoveway."

"Hmm. Probably not, if I'm being honest. God would probably consider their sandwiches an abomination."

Jenna frowns at this and swallows hard.

"But you know," he pipes up, noticing her face, "some

people believe that Heaven will just be a manifestation of all your individual desires, so if that means Subway for you . . . then yes."

"Wow," Jenna says, staring off dreamily. "I love that!"

No wonder Jenna seems so happy to be here; her idea of Heaven is a fully loaded mall food court.

I clear my throat and stare her down.

"What food are you hoping to find in Heaven, Bea?" Caleb asks me with amused eyes.

"I don't know. I haven't really given it much thought," I say without breaking eye contact with Jenna. "I've been too busy *working* since I got here."

"Oh!" Jenna exclaims, scraping the remains of her meal off the plate and practically licking it clean. "I feel like there was something I was going to ask you about that, Bea. Your job . . . memories . . . lottery? Yes! That was it. So, what's the deal with the lottery?"

She tries to wink at me, but just ends up blinking both eyes.

"What about it?" I ask her in a strained voice.

"Like, why do I have to wait around for my number to be called randomly? They should be called in order of who arrives first! Don't you agree, Caleb?"

"Sure." He shrugs. "But if it worked like that, we might be stuck here even longer."

"True," she says. "I just *wish* there was something I could do to get my number moved to the top. Don't you?"

Jenna looks at him, then me, as if I'm supposed to hand her a treat for asking this question.

"Yeah, but there's nothing you, or any of us, can do," he says, glancing at me and smiling crookedly. "I was frustrated about that too. But then I realized the nice thing about a lottery is that it lets everyone wake up with the hope that today's the day they move on and, if not, maybe tomorrow. Sometimes that little bit of hope, even if it's false, is all you need to get through the day."

Not only did Caleb listen to and absorb what I said yesterday, but now he's trying to put his own inspirational spin on it? What kind of psychopath just does that?

"Hm," Jenna says. "You know, that's a really positive way to look at things, Caleb. I really respect that, as a positive person myself."

I throw my fork down on my tray in defeat. Both of them stare at me.

"Well, I think it's time for me to have dessert," Jenna continues, pushing her chair back. "You guys want anything?"

Caleb stares down at the sculpture of a salad he's barely touched.

"No, thanks. I think I'm gonna go check out one of those newsstands. Have you guys been? I'm hoping they have some books. There's probably only, like, James Patterson paperbacks, but it could be worth a shot."

"Oh, I love James Patterson!" Jenna says. "My mom and I are obsessed with his Women's Murder Club series. Or . . . were, I guess."

Her face falls and tears begin to pool at the corners of her eyes.

Caleb makes panicked eye contact with me.

"Sorry, Jenna," he says. "I didn't mean to—"

"No, no. It's okay," she says, sniffling. "How would you have known James Patterson would be such an emotional trigger for me? I didn't even realize until now."

She hugs herself and looks self-consciously around the cafeteria.

"Hey, if it makes you feel any better," Caleb says, leaning forward, "I miss my mom too."

Jenna tries to give him a grateful smile, but instead she lets out a ragged sob. She sits back and closes her eyes, her chest still heaving.

Welcome to the No Moms Club, I want to scream out to them. I've been a member since 2004; every Disney character has been since forever.

"It's probably a good time for you to go check out that newsstand," I say quietly to Caleb.

"Yeah." He nods gravely, picking up his tray.

He waves goodbye and walks away.

"Bea, I just have to say," Jenna says after a few minutes, her breath becoming steadier. "Caleb seems like a *very* nice young man. I don't know how you got such a bad first impression of him."

"He was probably just on his best behavior because you were here."

"No. I told you," she says, sitting up and wiping her face with a napkin, "I have a gift for seeing the best in people."

"Well, I have the gift of an amazing bullshit detector and I think both of you are full of it."

15

"Look what the cat dragged in," Taylor Fields stage-whispered as I arrived late to second-period American history class.

"Is that something people actually say in real life?" I asked, handing my pass to Ms. Walsh. "I thought only stereotypical mean girls without personalities said that in movies, but I mean, if the shoe fits . . ."

"Beatrice," Ms. Walsh intervened. "Please take a seat."

Taylor Fields had always annoyed me. Every day, with the exception of mornings she'd walk in fifteen minutes late to school with Starbucks in hand, she would sit down in front of me, and her jeans would gape in the back, exposing an infinity symbol that had the words *LIVE. LAUGH. LOVE.* interwoven through it. It made me want to never do those three things again. But Taylor went from annoying to just plain enemy status a few weeks before this particular day.

I was also *blessed* enough to be in the same health class as she was. "Health class" being a generous descriptor of the one period a week our gym teacher would play us VHS tapes made before we were born that outlined information we probably should've been taught as soon as we'd hit puberty, not during our junior year of high school.

"Any questions or concerns?" Mr. Scruggs, a shy guy in his mid-twenties who clearly possessed way more knowledge of kickball etiquette than he did of the female reproductive system, had uncomfortably asked us after our viewing of *Birth Control: The Final Frontier*.

"Yeah, um," Taylor said, raising her hand and speaking without being called on. "I just want to say that I think anyone who takes birth control is a hypocrite. It's just unnatural."

Those were the words that came out of her mouth when I decided her life was definitely too easy and I should do something to make it harder. It was my moral imperative.

"It's not unnatural, Taylor!" I blurted out without raising my hand. "It's modern medicine. It changes and saves people's lives."

"It doesn't save lives," she said, turning toward me. "It kills them. Birth control kills babies, Beatrice."

She said my name with an exaggerated *uh* sound in the middle (Be-uh-trice) and flipped her long blond hair that had been curling-ironed meticulously to look like effortless beachy waves.

I rolled my eyes.

"Did you not absorb any of the thrilling information provided in that high-quality short film we just endured?" I said. "The hormones in the pill stop ovulation. No ovulation means there's no egg hanging around for sperm to fertilize. No egg equals no pregnancy. Pay attention, please."

"Ladies," Mr. Scruggs piped up, his voice breaking. "Please. While I'm, uh, ninety percent sure what you just described is true, Beatrice, I do want to remind everyone here that North-wood School District officially endorses *abstinence*. Uhhh . . ."

He frantically reached for a pamphlet on his desk.

"That's so irresponsible," I cried. "This is how girls my age end up having kids when they're not prepared for them."

"Oh, you mean like *your mom*?" Taylor asked.

A chorus of "Oooooh!" came from a row of boys in the back of the classroom.

"You know what? Yeah, I do mean my mom," I said, leaning over Taylor's shoulder. "If someone taught my parents how to correctly use birth control when they were our age, then I wouldn't be stuck here in this room with you and your signature scent that smells like fried hair and desperation."

"Beatrice," Mr. Scruggs said. "C'mon. Keep it *civilized*."

"I'm not going to keep it civilized if she's just going to keep saying this nonsense. She clearly needs to go home and google some basic facts about the human body, because you're obviously not going to teach them!"

Mr. Scruggs nervously eyed the rest of the room, practically begging for someone who was not me or Taylor to participate in the discussion. Or maybe he was just silently praying for the ceiling to cave in on us all.

Mercifully, the bell rang before it could go any further, but I knew I wasn't going to leave the argument in the classroom.

The plan was simple: I'd find Taylor Fields's most morally reprehensible posts on social media and send them to the manager of our local Chili's, where she was employed part-time as a hostess.

It sounds stupid, and it was, but Taylor wielded the little power she did have to act like she was the queen of our local Tex-Mex establishment. When people she didn't like, or the parents of people she didn't like, came in to eat, she'd purposely seat them right near the bathrooms. She'd get all of her friends free, illegal tequila shots by flirting with the middle-aged bartender. Also, most disturbingly of all, she was obsessed with bringing her Chili's leftovers in for lunch, flaunting her to-go bag of cold Southwestern egg rolls like we should all be jealous.

But when I went home and scrolled back several years through her Twitter, Facebook, and Instagram, I was surprised by the lack of offensive content. Based on her track record of comments, I expected to at least find some misguided screeds about how "all lives matter." I knew I should have been relieved that there was one less person spewing harmful crap on the Internet, but part of me wanted something to physically point to in order to prove she was bad. Maybe she kept it all in private accounts, but I doubted she was that savvy. Then I realized, though, there were some pretty stupid thoughts she found worthy of documenting for the world to see:

HMU if u wanna get SCHWASTED tonight at chili's y'all!!!

Ugh no one order the awesome blossom, p sure the secret dipping sauce is made of the cook's u kno what 😬

Ugh my boss is always up my ass and i'm like welcome to Chili's bitch!!! Crawl inside.

On a Thursday night, I emailed the screenshots of this thrilling content to the manager using a burner email account I made especially for the occasion (lavacakeluvr42069@gmail. com, in honor of Chili's molten chocolate cake, the only good item on their menu).

By Monday morning, the big news around school was that Taylor Fields was fired from Chili's and had to be escorted off the premises by the police after she allegedly whacked her manager in the head with a sizzling hot fajita skillet. And that was that. My revenge plot worked to an extent, but sadly it couldn't get Taylor fired from school. I was still stuck with her in my classes, still stuck with her ridiculous opinions.

Like the one she had on the day of the accident. The only upside to that day was that it was the last time I ever had to hear Taylor speak.

When I entered the class late, Ms. Walsh was in the middle of presenting a PowerPoint on the history of *Roe v. Wade*, the Supreme Court decision that made abortion legal in the United States. When she was done, she opened it up to a class discussion on the topic.

"I just think more people need to take responsibility for their actions," Taylor said, raising her hand, but already speaking before she was called. "If you have sex and get pregnant, you need to learn your lesson and not be so sloppy next time. It's not right that the government is letting people off easy by allowing them to kill babies."

It was like déjà vu. I'd braced myself to hear her views on other divisive topics, like gun control or Confederate statues, but I'd thought we'd left this particular argument in health class.

"So you think in order to learn a lesson, people should be forced to take care of a child they're not prepared to have?" I piped up as I settled into my seat behind her, taking a pencil out of my backpack.

"Yeah," Taylor said, turning around and shrugging at me like it was obvious. "Or they can give it up for adoption. I'm sure there are lots of families who can't have babies themselves who would love to adopt. There are other options.

"In fact," she said, flipping her hair again and turning back to Ms. Walsh, "I do a lot of volunteer work related to this issue. I go with a group from my church and hand out flyers outside of Planned Parenthood encouraging women to rethink their decision."

"So you harass these women?" I press.

"No, Beatrice. We don't threaten them or block them from going inside. We're there to be compassionate listeners and make sure they are aware of every option available."

Ms. Walsh nodded vaguely. For an American history teacher, she was almost disturbingly good at never revealing her own opinions. Somehow, this made her almost as evil as Taylor to me.

"So if you got pregnant tomorrow, you would go through with giving birth? Even though you're only seventeen and clearly have no way to support a child? I mean," I say, leaning forward, "you're seventeen. You can't even hold down a part-time job at Chili's. How would you expect to pay for diapers?"

Taylor turned around and looked at me with a pained expression like I'd just thrown a dart into her chest.

"I wouldn't get pregnant tomorrow!" she sputtered. "I'm not stupid . . . *like some people you know.*"

"We're veering off topic," Ms. Walsh said. "Anyone else?"

Even as the discussion moved on, Taylor kept her eyes on me for a minute, trying to impress some kind of meaningful look.

"Can you stop being so obsessed with the fact that I was born to a teen mom?" I mumbled through my teeth. "It's getting kind of creepy. If you're interested in the topic, there are entire exploitative TV shows that you're welcome to watch."

"I wasn't talking about your mom," Taylor whispered back. "All I'm saying is . . . it's clear the apple doesn't fall far from the tree."

Did she even know what that expression meant? What was she trying to get at? That I was like my mom and having unprotected sex? Something that was impossible given that I had never even kissed a boy, not that I would ever reveal this to anyone besides Emmy. Deep down inside, I hoped that everyone just assumed I had some cooler, older boyfriend who went to another school and took me on rides on his motorcycle.

I gripped the pencil in my hands and prepared to throw it at her, like an actual dart to her chest, but then I remembered what Emmy had said to me earlier that morning. I shouldn't get into an altercation over one stupid comment. I should pick my battles. Plus, I couldn't stand another trip to Mr. Spoglio's office. I had to at least appear as if I'd learned some kind of lesson.

"Tell your sister," Taylor muttered to me under her breath, "that she shouldn't have ignored me on her way in. She'll know what that means."

16

The next morning I awaken with a start to find that my bed is shaking.

"Wakey, wakey!" Jenna says, jumping up and down at the edge of my mattress. The bed frame makes a squeaking sound that reminds me of when people have sex in romantic comedies. Except this situation could not be further from romantic. Maybe it's a comedy, objectively, but not to me.

"What time is it?" I grumble.

"Five of eight!" she says, letting her body collapse next to me on the bed.

"Seriously?" I say, bolting upright. "I'm late."

I'm supposed to be ready to take today's lottery number winner over to the hangar by eight. I don't know what happens if I'm late to work, but I don't want to test it in case it means piling on more souls to my sentence.

Frantically, I pull off my pajamas and slip into my uniform, pulling up the back zipper as I head out the door. I skip past the elevator and make a beeline for the stairs, taking them three at a time, nearly falling forward over something gray and lumpy lying along the steps between the third and second floors. I catch myself against the metal railing with a yelp.

It's a human.

The witchy-looking old lady who wouldn't stop moaning in the bathroom on my first day. What did Sadie say her name was? Gladys?

She stirs from her slumber, widens her eyes at me, then barks. Literally barks like a dog.

"Well, good morning to you, too," I mumble, continuing on.

I make it through the hotel lobby, then run down one of the moving walkways, completely unnecessary here given that no one has any physical baggage.

I'm almost at departures when I run headfirst into another person. My head bangs into their hard chest and I'm knocked off my feet, onto the floor.

I sit up when I see the shoes. A pair of black Nike slides with white ankle socks. Caleb. He must be jogging for at least the second time in twenty-four hours.

"God, why can't you just stay in your lane?" I yell, not realizing the double meaning behind my words until I've already said them.

"Sorry," he says with a laugh. "You all right?"

I stare up at him blankly and wonder if ending my life wasn't enough for him. He just *has* to make my afterlife harder too.

"Seriously, Bea, are you okay?" he asks again, his face falling and his eyebrows knitting together with a look of genuine concern. He reaches out a hand to help me up.

"I'm fine," I say, ignoring his hand and pushing myself up. "I'm not some damsel-in-distress type, okay?"

"Oh, believe me," he says, smiling again, "I don't think you are. Hey, is Jenna okay? I noticed you guys weren't at breakfast. I still feel really bad that I brought up James Patterson and made her cry."

"Oh, Jenna? She told me she hates you," I deadpan.

Caleb's eyes go wide.

"I'm kidding," I say. "She's fine."

Suddenly a voice comes over the loudspeakers.

"Number 07259, please report to departures. Again, that's number 07259, 07259, please report to departures."

"Shoot," I say, dusting myself off. "They're already drawing lottery numbers." I wobble slightly, more dazed from my fall than I'd ever admit.

"Here, let me take you over," Caleb says.

"It's, like, a thirty-second walk," I say, starting toward the departures counter. "But okay. You know, I wouldn't have fallen over just now if it weren't for your pointless act of athleticism."

"What's that supposed to mean?"

"The jogging," I say. "How are you even doing that without your sandals sliding off your feet?"

"For your information, Beatrice Fox," he says. The sound of my full name coming out of his mouth makes me feel simultaneously nauseous and like my whole body is on fire. "Some of us don't have very important jobs to do during the day. We get tired of sitting around and doing nothing. Jogging gives us *something* to do. And as for the sandals, I have very adept feet."

I just nod, unable to speak due to my body's conflicting sensations.

"Anyway," he continues. "You were missed at breakfast.

Not by me necessarily though; it's just, you know, everyone in general misses you and your repeated footwear insults."

"Sounds like you're having trouble making friends."

"Oh, but I thought *we* were friends. By my count, we've partaken in *1.5 terrible meals together* at this point," he says.

"Maybe I'll make another appearance one of these mornings," I say, like an idiot.

We get to the departures counter and the omniscient voice is still blaring from the loudspeaker, crying out the same lottery number.

"Where the hell is 07259?" I ask Todd before he can make any mention of my late arrival. I'm the only one in a uniform left—07259 must be mine.

"Apparently his plane is landing right now," he says without looking up from some paperwork.

"Wait. It hasn't even *landed*?" I turn and complain to Caleb, like this is his fault. "So you're telling me his lottery number is being called before he even *lands*? While all these people just wait around for days, even months, just to get through? And of course it's a *he*. Let's just let a *man* bypass the line, huh? It's not like he hasn't gotten enough privileges on Earth; let's give them to him in the afterlife too!"

I realize as I'm talking that I've also been pacing closer and closer toward Caleb. Now our faces are only an inch or two apart.

"Hey, it's some stranger you're talking about, okay?" he says, backing away from me slowly. "Not me, remember?"

"Oh yeah sure, '*not all men*,' right?" I say, making air quotes.

He snickers.

"Didn't you say you had something you have to go do? Sit around and do nothing?" I say.

"Oh yeah. That. It's okay. I can reschedule that. I've decided it's a lot more fun to watch you rail against the patriarchy."

"Is it? Because I'm just getting started!"

Just then, I notice an elderly man with a full head of white hair shuffling up the aisle at .01 miles per hour in a flannel robe and pajamas. He waves his passport up in the air.

"07259," he says, squinting at his passport and reading off of it. "That's me!"

I go over to him and snatch the passport out of his hand.

"You'll be coming with me, sir."

"Say, hon, do I have time for a cup of coffee first?" he asks.

Caleb covers his mouth with his hand in an attempt to suppress his laughter. I narrow my eyes and take a deep breath, remembering the more this old man trusts me, the faster he will move on to Heaven and the sooner I can too.

"No, sir, you do not have time," I say, plastering on a smile. "But I promise you after this, you'll have an *eternity* for a cup of coffee."

I pull the old man by the arm toward the exit onto the tarmac.

"Have a great time out there!" Caleb calls after us.

I turn and stare at him. If looks could kill, he'd be dead right now. That is, if he wasn't already.

17

I spend my whole walk back to the hotel from the hangar internally praying that Jenna won't be in our room. After spending the whole day listening to that old man blabber on, only to reveal that his greatest regret in life—the thing that weighed on him so hard that it held him back from Heaven— was losing his childhood dog, I just want to lie down in silence.

Of course, when I open the door, she's sitting up in bed, catatonically watching the weather report on the TV like a grandma absorbed in her daily soap opera.

I sit down on the edge of my bed without saying hello and take off my shoes. After a minute she peels her eyes from the TV and stares at me.

"Hey," Jenna says after a moment.

She shuts the TV off and sits on the edge of her bed, facing the nightstand we share.

"Hey," I say.

"Are we . . . okay?" she asks.

The question takes me aback given that I don't know if I would go as far as to describe us as a "we" just yet.

"Uh, sure," I say.

"Really?" she presses.

"Yeah."

"Because I was thinking it over and I realized what you said to me yesterday about this not being a place like summer camp or prom and that I needed a BS detector . . . I sorta kinda realized all of that was a little bit, um, harsh of you?"

"I don't know about that," I say defensively. "I mean, you were supposed to help me catch Caleb in the act of bribery, but then you botched the plan and ended up acting like he was the greatest person you've ever met."

"Well, he didn't *do* anything in front of me, so what am I supposed to say? Want me to lie on your behalf?"

Yes! I want to scream, but I don't.

"I know I disappointed you," she says. "But I don't want there to be any hostility between us. No bad vibes. As room-mates, communication is key."

I'd swear Jenna just googled "fight with roommate" and is now reciting what she learned from a wikiHow article, but I know that's impossible since we have no Internet access here.

"We can understand each other a little better if we're just open with one another," she continues. "I think our first step should be sharing how we both ended up here at the airport."

"Jenna, it's fine. You don't have to—"

She places a hand on my shoulder.

"Look, I know you said this isn't a slumber party or whatever and I get that. But I still think we should have a slumber-party-style heart-to-heart, okay?"

"I don't think those are initiated by someone saying 'I think we should have a heart-to-heart,'" I mumble. "But what-ever. Fine. Tell me how you got here."

At best, this will provide me with some entertainment.

Jenna moves over onto my bed and crisscrosses her legs into a pretzel, then closes her eyes and takes a deep breath.

Here we go.

"So I was diagnosed with leukemia when I was thirteen," she declares, the words spilling out of her mouth like she's been rehearsing this all day. "I kept getting all of these mysterious bruises and then one day, in the middle of my hip-hop dance class, I just blacked out all of a sudden and face-planted in the middle of the floor while 'Uptown Funk' was playing.

"After that, I was in and out of the hospital all the time. I had to be homeschooled instead of going to actual high school. I never went to dances or walked around the mall with my friends. I never had a boyfriend or even just a crush on someone who wasn't a celebrity. I never got to do anything fun, unless you count sitting in on my mom's erotic book club that she started to blow off some steam with the other cancer-ward moms."

I wince at the thought of Jenna sitting there with a bunch of moms discussing *Fifty Shades* and drinking white wine.

"It just felt like the world was happening without me. But, I dunno. I really try not to think about it too hard. I'm one of five kids—the oldest girl. My mom had to quit her nursing job to take care of me full-time. It was already stressful enough on my family, me being sick. I figured it was just a lot easier to have a positive, cheery attitude around everyone so they'd be stressed-out just a little bit less. I mean, why should my tragedy be theirs too? So I guess you could say that's why I'm such an upbeat person. Though these last few months, things got worse than ever before. My doctors decided the chemo was causing more harm than it was helping. So finally I decided, 'What the heck? I'll do Make-A-Wish.' I asked for a trip to Disney World for my whole family. And this might surprise you, but I don't even like Disney stuff that much!"

I raise my eyebrows a sliver. This does indeed surprise me. Jenna strikes me as the type of girl whose ultimate life goal is to get engaged in front of Cinderella Castle. The type of girl who has taken several different "Which Disney Princess Are You?" BuzzFeed quizzes and cross-examined the results for accuracy.

"But my siblings go wild for that stuff, so I figured I should take advantage of it. I mean, do you know how much a vacation to Disney for seven people costs? I don't mean to sound ungrateful or anything. The trip was really, really nice. We got to skip the lines to the rides and everything and they gave us all these waffles shaped like Mickey Mouse's head, but my real dying wish was to go see the Grand Canyon. You know, ideally I would've taken a road trip, camped out with my friends who don't exist, made s'mores, and watched the sun rise."

She stares off for a second, her eyes going glassy.

"It's stupid. I know."

"That's not *that* stupid," I admit. "It's okay to ask for what you want."

She smiles at me.

"Sure, sometimes I wish I'd lived a little bit more for myself than everyone else, but what can you do, you know? At the end of the day, family is what's most important."

"I'm sure your siblings would've survived without getting Mickey Mouse's autograph," I say. "Just because you're related to people doesn't mean you need to sacrifice your own happiness for them."

The words come out of my mouth, but I don't even know if they're true. My mind goes to Emmy—the only person I truly consider family. Not just the Emmy who sends me texts throughout the day to remind me to drink water because she knows my body is 75 percent coffee and Diet Coke. Not just the Emmy who reassures me that I'm cute even when I get spooked out by accidentally opening the front-facing camera on my phone while lying down on my bed. Not just the Emmy who I fiercely protected when we were around everyone else, but who was the only person I could trust being vulnerable with when we were alone.

Instead I think of the Emmy who exists somewhere else right now. The Emmy whose life I've ruined, hopefully just temporarily. The Emmy who probably hates my stupid guts, even if they are currently sitting in a grave, all thanks to Caleb and his shiny SUV.

"Anyway," Jenna says, smiling sadly and rubbing her head. "My hair started to grow back before I died, so at least I'm stuck with a semi-cute pixie cut. Enough about me, though. How about you, Bea? What's your story?"

I hug my arms to my chest, protecting myself against the chill of the blasting hotel air-conditioning. Or maybe it's just the thought that this is it; my story has truly ended and I have nothing to show for it except the permanent flecks of mascara running down my cheeks.

"I don't really have a story," I answer. "I died alone in a car accident and now I'm here."

"I'm sure that's not true, but I won't push it any further for today. You know . . . you're a tough nut to crack, Beatrice," Jenna chides. "But you're a nut I'm gonna crack one day!"

I grab a pillow and unsuccessfully try to smother my face with it.

THE DOOR TO the staff room is locked, which by now I realize isn't so much a precautionary measure as it is a ploy to stroke Todd's extremely inflated ego.

"What's the password?" he calls as I knock at the door.

"I refuse to say it."

"Beatrice?"

"Yeah?"

"What's the password?"

"You just acknowledged that you know it's me."

"It's protocol."

"It's 'Toddcanshoveastickuphisass.'"

"Beatrice."

I sigh. Deeply.

"It's 'Todd can flip an omelet without it breaking.'"

The door opens.

"You know, that's not that impressive of a skill," I say.

"I don't even have to use a spatula. I just," he says, miming flipping a pan, "flick of the wrist."

"Ugh."

Inside, Sadie sits at the front of the room and waves me over to the seat next to her.

"Good morning, everyone!" Todd yells from the front of

the room. "It is with a heavy heart that I must announce our beloved team member Sadie will be leaving us today. After selflessly helping thousands of people move on to Heaven, she has officially fulfilled her quota.

"Sadie," he says, looking into her eyes, "I just want to personally thank you from the bottom of my heart for your commitment to the work that we do here."

It feels like Todd is giving a wedding toast. I half expect him to pull out flutes of champagne for all of us.

"Let's all give her a round of applause," he concludes.

"Thank you, thank you so much," Sadie says, before anyone has barely put their hands together. "Todd, if you don't mind . . ."

She stands up and gestures for him to move aside.

"I just wanted to really quickly say to all of you that I know you're jealous of me and that's okay. I will be looking down upon all of you from my beautiful Jacuzzi-filled mansion in the sky and laughing for the rest of eternity. Ciao, losers!"

With that, she takes off her white gloves, throws them onto the floor, and walks out of the room for the very last time.

For the first time in my whole existence, I spontaneously applaud.

"NUMBER 03675, NUMBER 03675," blares over the intercom.

I'm waiting at the departures counter for my assignment when I see Caleb ambling up the aisle toward the counter. He's probably back to witness the big show of me freaking out at someone for some reason or another. But as he gets closer, his face looks like he's just seen a ghost. I mean, in the earthly sense given that everyone here is technically a ghost.

He walks up to me and stands uncomfortably, shifting his weight back and forth on his slides.

"Bea," he says.

"What do you want *now*?" I say, inspecting my eternally chipped nails.

"I have something really important to tell you," he says with a sober look.

I stand up straight, suddenly alert.

"What is it?" I ask.

"It's just that," he breathes. "I . . . am . . . number 03675."

18

Caleb slides his passport over to me, breaking out into a smile. I look at the random number printed on the inside, what I thought would be the least relevant bit of information the passport contains. It really is his lottery number.

"And I swear to you, I did not bribe anyone else to get called this soon," he says as I continue to stare down at the passport.

It's not fair that he gets to move along to Heaven this soon. I can't let him get away from me that easy. He *deserves* to suffer.

"Todd," I call behind me, my voice shaking with anger. I cough once to hide it. "His number was called."

"All right, line up in the sectioned-off area over there," Todd says to Caleb. "Actually, you know what? Why don't you just take him out to the hangar, Bea? He can be your assignment."

"What? No!" I blurt out.

Both Caleb and Todd turn to stare at me.

"Is there a problem with that, Beatrice?" Todd asks.

My body freezes and my heart pounds. I'm not prepared for this. I still haven't gotten back at him. My plan to frame him was a failure. I haven't had time to figure out my next big move in seeking vengeance on my unsuspecting murderer. I'm back to square one. How am I going to get even with him if I'm always being watched?

I look at Caleb.

His face is open, innocent.

Maybe this *could* work. Sadie said that inside memories is one of the few places that aren't under constant surveillance. I could do whatever I want with him. I can drag him through his most embarrassing, most painful memories so he's forced to revisit them and feel the discomfort all over again.

I can make the process as long and excruciating for him as possible.

Sadie even said that if I can't move someone along after thirty sessions, they get pushed backed into the lottery, forced to wait to be called again. I could make his life hell for a month, then get him pushed backed into the lottery so he's stuck here indefinitely.

I still have a few thousand souls to go. What's wasting a little extra time on one of them going to matter to me in the long run?

"No," I say at last. "It's no problem at all. As long as . . . Sorry, what's your name again?"

"*Caleb*," he answers incredulously.

"Right," I say, not looking at him and turning toward Todd. "As long as Caleb here is fine with that."

"Um. Sure," he says.

"Okay then," Todd says, looking back down at his paper-work. "Get to work. You're already five minutes into the first session. Ticktock!"

I wave for Caleb to follow me.

"I hope you're ready to spend *a lot* of quality time toge-ther," I say once we're almost out the door.

"Oh, believe me, I was born ready," he says.

But out of the corner of my eye, as I turn to lead him off toward the tarmac, I see Caleb take one big nervous gulp and his face goes pale.

WHEN I DIRECT Caleb to hop on the passenger seat of the golf cart, I expect him to crack a "You got a license for this thing?" joke or something, but he just stares solemnly off at the sky and gets in.

"Do you ever . . . get freaked out by the concept of infin-ity?" he asks instead.

"No," I say, giving him a sidelong glance.

"Really?"

I think it over for a minute.

"Well, there was this girl who sat in front of me at school and got an infinity symbol tattooed on her lower back," I admit. "It kind of ruined the whole concept for me."

"Okay, maybe *infinity* is the wrong word," Caleb says with a half smile. "I guess I meant *eternity*? Like, don't get me wrong, I'm relieved that there's clearly something after death. And that I'm here and not Hell. But doesn't *forever* seem, I don't know, kind of excessive? Like, why can't we just appreciate the time we have on Earth? Why do we think we deserve forever? And say you've been existing for, like, even just ten thousand years out of forever. Won't you start to forget old memories just because there're too many of them to keep track of? It all just makes me feel more sad than hopeful."

I stare straight ahead and say nothing. The truth is, I know exactly what he means. That in some ways the idea of going to Hell makes more sense to me because at least we as a society agreed upon what it looks like: fiery and horrible. But Heaven seemed just way too rife with possibility. It was overwhelming to think about in its own way. But how am I supposed to just nod along and agree with him when it's his fault that my own time on Earth was cut short before I could really even appreciate it?

I pull up next to the hangar and park.

"Sorry," Caleb says. "I'm not really making sense. You're probably just gonna say that moving on to Heaven is yet another privilege I have that I'm taking for granted."

"Well, yeah," I say, looking down at the tiny steering wheel. "But Heaven seems kind of boring, if all of the earthly depictions of it are true. I picture myself stuck in some medieval-looking garden wearing a robe like the one Mary wears in that Christmas farm scene for, like, all of eternity."

"You mean the manger scene?" Caleb asks, his face lighting up.

"Yeah. You know what I meant."

"I did, because, as you can probably tell by this conversation, Catholic school really messed me up."

"I get that. As *you* can probably tell, that one week of Bible camp I went to really shook me to my core."

Caleb just shakes his head at me.

"Anyway," I say, pointing to the hangar door. "Time for us to get to work."

I step out of the cart and walk ahead of him to unlock the door. I close my eyes and take a deep breath, hoping to erase the last five minutes of conversation. Now is not the time for us to relate to each other.

"Take a seat," I say, trying to sound as nonchalant as possible while Caleb follows me inside.

He stops in his tracks and stares at the Memstractor 3000.

"This thing won't kill me, right?" he asks.

"You're already dead, genius," I say, leading him over to the chair. "I'll need to see your passport again."

"Oh, you mean you haven't memorized it by now?" he jokes, taking it out of his pocket.

"No," I say a little too seriously. I grab it and turn away, inspecting it like I really haven't seen it before, and take a deep breath.

Caleb is not my friend.

Caleb is the reason I died at that intersection.

Caleb is not interesting.

Caleb is not cute.

Definitely not cute.

"Anything interesting?" Caleb asks as I stand and stare at his passport.

Not YOU! That's for sure! I scream internally.

"Mmm," I mumble.

I flip the passport shut and hand it back to him, as if it not only has a transcription of his death, but of my very thoughts, and I can't stand to look at them any longer.

Obviously, I don't want him to know that when and where he died has any significance to me. If the crash and, subsequently, my death, are the things that are holding him back, I have to make sure he doesn't conjure memories of it for as long as I can. Or else he might realize the truth and move on to Heaven too soon. And that would just be so unfair.

I walk back over to him and lower the helmet from the chair onto his head with a harsh thud.

"Comfortable?" I ask.

"Never been better," he says sarcastically.

I take my own seat and explain how the Memstractor 3000 works.

"That doesn't sound real," he protests when I'm finished.

"Do you think I would mess with your head like that?"

"Absolutely."

"Fine," I say, lowering my own helmet. "What did you eat for breakfast this morning?"

"What?"

I flick the switch and turn the machine on.

Suddenly we're inside the hotel lobby. Caleb gasps as he realizes we're standing before a past version of him, shoveling a plate of jiggly scrambled eggs into his mouth.

"Jeez," he says. "Is that what I really look like?"

A blurry figure carrying a tray of food walks right through our invisible bodies. Caleb jumps.

"Do you believe me now?" I ask.

He nods and looks back at himself eating.

"This is so embarrassing," he says, cringing. "It's like hearing the way your voice sounds on a recording, but a million times worse."

"Don't be embarrassed," I say, even though my true goal is for him to feel constantly, deeply embarrassed. "The more honest you are with your memories, the sooner we can get to the bottom of why you're here. Just be open. I won't tell anyone about what you show me. Everything that happens while you're connected to the machine stays in the machine."

At that last sentence, he suddenly stares into my eyes for a long second.

"What?" I say, arching my brow.

"Nothing," he says quickly, turning his eyes to the ground.

"Okay," I say. "Let's get started, for real this time."

Although, I'm not sure where to begin. His most traumatic memory? The time he felt most embarrassed in his whole life? The last time he had the flu? His first wet dream? Ugh. No. I need to ease into this.

"Think back to when you were a kid," I say. "What's your earliest memory?"

"Umm," he ponders, closing his eyes.

Suddenly we're in a small combination living and dining room with bunches of balloons tied to the furniture and streamers taped to the walls.

The room is full of people, but most of them are blurry and unidentifiable. Except for three: a toddler who looks like a miniature version of Caleb; a woman in her late twenties with tan skin, wide-set eyes, and a long dark-brown ponytail; and an older woman who looks a lot like her but with short graying hair and glasses.

The younger woman is clapping her hands and laughing. Caleb gasps again, this time in amazement rather than shock.

"My mom and my abuela," he explains.

Just then, toddler Caleb smears what appears to be blue cake frosting onto her nose.

"It was my third birthday party. I had two cakes. A Cookie Monster cake and my abuela's famous—well, at least famous in our family—tres leches cake. I probably only remember this so well because she kept a photo of me eating both cakes at once on her fridge for years."

"I thought the whole eating cake with your hands thing happened at first birthday parties. Aren't you supposed to know how to use a fork by age three?"

"Yeah," he says, too mesmerized by the vision of his family to even register offense at my remark. His eyes well up as he watches his mom laugh and wipe the frosting from her face with a napkin.

I guess I'd always assumed everyone else's early memories were sad and embarrassing, not happy and sweet and literally filled with more cakes than one child can handle. Personally, my first memory is finding out my mom had died and immediately peeing my pants. I need to steer Caleb away from this before he gets too emotional.

"Did you have a lot of friends as a kid?" I press.

"Yeah," he says absently, but his memory doesn't switch. He keeps gazing at his mother and walks closer to her, then reaches out to touch her shoulder, but his hand begins to pixelate.

"It's just a memory. You can't touch her," I remind him. "Uh, you said you went to Catholic school. What was that like?"

Finally he turns and looks at me.

"It was, you know . . ." he says, his memory suddenly

transporting us to a classroom where an elderly nun in a blue habit vaguely gestures to a diagram of the male body with a pointer stick.

"And that is why you must resist your urges!" she yells to the classroom of boys who look to be no older than twelve. "Sexual intercourse outside of marriage is a *sin*! Fornicators will be sent to *Hell*!"

"Catholic school." He shrugs, finishing his thought.

"Wow, guess you weren't a 'fornicator' then?"

"What?" he says, eyes going wide.

"Because you weren't sent to Hell," I elaborate.

"No!" he protests, blushing. "I mean, yes. I mean, no, that's not what I mean. Whatever."

"I'm just kidding."

"Anyway," he says a little too loudly, our setting quickly changing so that we're now standing outside the entrance of a big brick-and-glass building that looks like a fancy high school. "I switched to public school when I was in seventh grade because my dad decided Catholic school wasn't academically rigorous enough."

"Okay," I say, a hint of excitement in my voice because I think I'm finally onto something. "Do you remember your very first day of public school?"

"I . . . do," he stammers. "But I wish I didn't."

The memory shifts again. Now we're sitting on the bleachers of a school gym full of students sprawled out, waiting for the school day to begin. A banner hanging on the wall says BRENTWOOD SCHOOL DISTRICT: CELEBRATING 100 YEARS OF EXCELLENCE!

Of course Caleb goes to Brentwood. They're a town

rumored to be so rich, they built a Starbucks inside the high school with leftover tax dollars.

"Yo, what is this kid wearing?" someone at the bottom of the bleachers yells. "He looks like a motherfucking Minion!"

Several students turn their heads to stare. What feels like the entire gymnasium erupts into laughter. There's a clarity to this memory. It's not fuzzy at all, unlike the ones belonging to my other assignments. Each glaring student's face is perfectly etched into his subconscious.

We turn our heads and look to where Past Caleb stands. He looks about half a foot shorter, with a slightly paunchy belly and acne covering his cheeks. He's wearing a neon-yellow T-shirt underneath a pair of denim overalls. He does indeed look like a Minion.

Caleb, of right now, puts his head in his hand, half obscuring his eyes so he can't see the memory. He's absolutely mortified.

I'm thrilled.

"Why . . . did you . . ." is all I can get out between my gut-busting laughs.

"I don't know!" Caleb says, his cheeks resembling two vine-ripened tomatoes. "I mean, I do know. My mom bought me the overalls. She told me they were cool and . . . hip."

"When was your mom last in seventh grade? 1993?"

"Uh. Approximately. She has really good taste though! I just, I hadn't really thought about clothes my whole life. I wore a uniform to school up until then."

"And you paired the overalls with a yellow shirt because . . ."

"I honestly don't know," he says. "It was my favorite T-shirt, but not after that. It took a little while for me to live that down. By a little while, I mean . . ."

The memory changes again. Now Caleb is older. He looks like he does now, except, I have to admit, his outfit doesn't suck. He's wearing nice black jeans and a blue chambray button-down shirt, the short sleeves rolled up just slightly. It's a better outfit than what 99 percent of boys wear to school, which still isn't saying much.

"Bello!" one jock-looking boy yells to him in the hall. "What's for lunch, Caleb? Bah-na-na?"

"Hilarious," Past Caleb mumbles, trying to put on a good-natured smile.

"Well, hey, at least you grew out of the overalls. That's something," I say to Present Caleb next to me. "I mean, you even started dressing *too* normal."

I gesture to his now permanent basketball shorts outfit.

"I know you're so obsessed with my stupid shorts and sandals, but I swear to you, this is not how I usually dress, okay? It was just that the night that I, you know"—he swallows—"*died,* my judgment was just so . . . so . . . poor. . . ."

Our setting changes again, way too soon. I can't let him think about that night just yet. This is only the first of thirty sessions that I need to drag out.

Now we're in a dining room again, except this one is huge, with a table that could fit a dozen people and upholstered white chairs that look like they're begging to have food spilled on them. A past version of Caleb that looks identical to Present Caleb is unlocking a liquor cabinet in the corner of the room and reaching for a bottle inside. He pulls out some kind of fancy-looking whiskey and stares at it in his hands.

Before I can even open my mouth, his memory flashes instantly. Now we're outside, standing in the driveway, and he's opening the door to a silver Range Rover.

Wait.

Does this mean he was drunk the night he crashed into me?

"*Stop!*" I yell.

His memory flashes to darkness and we're floating in nothing.

"What?" Caleb asks. "Everything okay, Bea?"

"Yeah. It's just, um," I say, closing my eyes and swallowing. "I think you're getting ahead of yourself. We kind of skipped over the Catholic school portion of things. Let's take it back there for a second. Cool?"

"All right," he says.

I can't decide if dragging this out over the next month will be the easiest thing I've ever done or the hardest.

19

"**Do you want** to grab some lunch?" Caleb asks me when our session ends and we're driving back toward the airport. "Or we could . . . Well, I guess there's really nothing to do around here except eat lunch."

"Ummm," I say. "I'm not really hungry yet."

My stomach audibly grumbles. A look of realization passes over Caleb's face.

"Oh," he says, cheeks reddening. "You just don't want to eat . . . with me. I get it. That's totally cool. Honestly, no pressure. I wouldn't want to eat with me either after seeing what I was like for the past four hours."

He gives a self-effacing laugh and smiles, but it doesn't reach his eyes.

"No. It's not that," I say, hitting the brakes on the golf cart and pulling the keys out of the ignition. "It's just . . . we can't hang out while I'm working on your case."

"Oh," Caleb says, following me out. "Is that a rule?"

There are Sadie's warnings that I not get too close to any-one. And of course, there's my self-imposed rule, which is: Do Not Become Friends with Your Murderer, Especially While You're Trying to Emotionally Torment Him.

"Well, not officially," I say, walking across the tarmac to the airport entrance. Caleb catches up to me.

"If you don't want to eat lunch with me, you can tell me."

"No," I say immediately, surprising myself. "That's not it."

"What is it then?" he asks with an incredulous smile. "Because I kind of thought that we were becoming, I dunno . . ."

"Friends? Not this again," I say. "It's nothing. I'm just being paranoid because . . . I haven't spent time outside of the hangar with any of the other souls I've guided."

"Yeah, well, I guess none of them were as youthful and charming as me," Caleb says, opening the door for me.

"What's with all of this?" I ask, curiosity getting the best of me.

"What do you mean 'this'?"

"Here," I say as we walk back inside the airport, "and please don't take this as a compliment, you seem kind of confident and forward about stuff, too forward I would say, but in your memories . . ."

"Hey," he says, raising a hand. "You said you wouldn't talk about my memories outside of the hangar."

"You're right," I say. "Never mind."

"But I'm curious. What did I seem like? A total loser?"

"Yeah," I admit.

"Well, who isn't a loser in middle school? I'm sure if we looked at your memories, for instance . . ."

"Actually, I was very cool in middle school. Thank you very much."

"And things just went downhill from there?" he asks, giving me a sidelong glance.

He's right. My actual nickname was Queen Bea until the eighth grade, when I refused to have sex with my boyfriend of two weeks, who I hadn't even kissed yet, so then he started a rumor that my parents didn't believe in vaccines and I was single-handedly responsible for a county-wide measles outbreak.

"You know, you should be nice to me, Caleb," I say, the corners of my mouth turning up. "I'm the only one who can help you here."

"But when I say nice things to you, you freak out."

"So maybe then you should just be quiet," I say, approaching the departures counter to hand in my keys and sign out for the day. "Everyone appreciates a boy who can keep his mouth shut."

"Unbelievable," Caleb says, shaking his head.

"Stay here for a second," I say, pointing behind the stanchion and rope in front of the counter.

Behind the counter, Todd is slumped over with his head in his hands.

"Hey there," I say. "How are you holding up without your, um, coworker?"

"Who?" he says, without lifting his head.

"Sadie."

"Oh, her? I'm fine without her. Fine. Totally happy for her that she's moved on forever. She totally deserves it. Totally."

He makes a sound through his nose that's half sniffle, half snort.

"How was it with that one?" he says, glancing over at Caleb. "I assume he's moving along today, given your impressive track record so far."

"Actually, no," I say so only Todd can hear. "I think I've got a complicated case on my hands. He might take a little while."

"Happens to the best of us." He shrugs, lifting his beefy shoulders in the orange vest that's too small for his frame.

He collects my keys and signs me out for the day. I head back toward Caleb.

"You're free to go," I say, and start walking, but he keeps pace with me.

"I was thinking," he starts. "Wouldn't this whole process actually be much more efficient if I got to know you? Like, if we were comfortable around each other, wouldn't my memories surface more easily? And then I could move along faster?"

"You know enough about me," I scoff.

"No, I don't! You're kind of an enigma, honestly."

"I'm an enigma? That's so cool," I say. "I've always wanted to be an enigma."

"C'mon, Bea!"

"I'm supposed to be mysterious," I say seriously, stopping to look him in the eye. "It's like if I were your doctor or your teacher or your therapist."

"I get that," Caleb says, scratching the back of his neck. "It's just I've never had a doctor or a teacher who was a sixteen-year-old girl."

"How do you know I'm sixteen? Maybe I'm sixty-one. That's a real possibility here. Todd over there is probably, like, eighty."

"I'm just guessing that you're sixteen. But I know you're definitely not sixty-one, because we arrived on the same plane, Bea."

"Did we really?" I say, walking again. "Or was that your

mind playing tricks on you? As we learned today, memories can be quite fickle things."

He gives me an exhausted look.

"I'm actually seventeen," I admit. "But thank you for thinking I'm sixteen. Good to know all those antiaging creams weren't a waste of money."

"Okay, since you know my earliest memories, what are yours, huh? How was your first day of middle school? Where *was* your middle school even?"

"Nope. I'm not telling you that. That's not how this works," I say. "You're not the one helping *me* move on, okay? I have no obligation to share that stuff with you. I will answer superficial questions only."

"Fine then," he says. "What's your favorite color?"

"Holographic lavender," I answer immediately.

"So . . . purple?"

"No, *holographic lavender*."

"That's not a color! Bea, look, I'm just trying to get to know you. Stop trying to mess with my head by making up some fake color."

"I'm not trying to mess with your head! I decide to let my guard down and be honest with you for one minute and all you can do is deny the existence of my favorite color. Typical. If you're such an expert on what constitutes a real color, then what's your favorite, Caleb?"

"Red," he says.

"Red?"

"Yeah. So?"

"No one's favorite color is actually red past, like, the age of five," I say.

"This is ridiculous. Fine. Next *superficial* question, Bea. What's your favorite food?"

I purse my lips for a moment.

"Salt-and-vinegar potato chips," I admit.

"No way. That's such an old person food. That's like saying your favorite food is butterscotch. Maybe you are sixty-one. Salt-and-vinegar chips are one of those foods you see in articles like, 'Millennials Are Killing the Salt-and-Vinegar Potato Chip Industry.'"

"Yeah, well, I guess I'm single-handedly keeping the industry afloat. Or was."

Caleb's face falls.

"Anyway," I say, looking up and realizing we've walked all the way from the waiting area to the food court. "That's enough questions for me."

"Wait," Caleb protests. "I'm sorry, Bea. I didn't mean to insult your favorite color. Or your disgusting favorite chips. C'mon! The day is young. We should do something. Besides lunch."

"What kind of something?" I ask, crossing my arms.

"I don't know exactly. Let's go on an adventure."

"Here?" I ask, gesturing to all the busted neon food displays and artificial plants that somehow look dead even though they're made of plastic.

"Yeah! I bet we can figure something out."

"Why?"

"Honestly? I think I'm starting to lose my mind. I need to stay occupied. I went to the newsstand last night and all of the books had blank pages. All of them. And the newspapers? The only thing printed in them was daily reports of how many people had moved on to Heaven. And if I have to spend another night in my room watching stock footage of sunsets and breakfast and airplanes, I will start clawing at the walls."

"Fine," I say, surprising myself again. "An adventure."

This is so breaking my self-imposed rule of Do Not Befriend Your Murderer.

CALEB AND I find ourselves walking aimlessly around the airport in circles like we're just two bored kids wandering around a mall. Which is all to say, our "adventure" is kind of a bust, but I don't even know why I'd want it to be a success anyway. Maybe because I feel like I'm starting to lose my mind as well and would do anything to break up the constant sameness of the airport.

"Do you think it's weird that everything is written in English here?" he asks as we walk past the bar sign that reads IT'S FIVE O'CLOCK ANYWHERE! "Most airports have signs in multiple languages."

He looks ahead of us like he's staring at an equation he can't figure out.

"And why does everyone *speak* English here? I wonder if this means that there are a bunch of these airports. Maybe only people who live in English-speaking countries get flown to this one? But that wouldn't make sense because plenty of people don't speak English but live in countries where English is the dominant language—wait."

Caleb stops in his tracks. I walk ahead of him for a step, then turn around and pause.

"What?"

"Do you know any Spanish?" he asks with an intense stare.

"Um," I say. If by "any" he means enough to consistently get straight Cs in Spanish class for the last five years. "A little. Why?"

"I'm not fluent," he says, sticking his hands out. "But I'm pretty good. My mom's Mexican and she would speak it around the house. Plus, I was in AP Spanish."

"That's cool," I say, squinting at him slightly.

"Sorry. Non sequitur," he says. "My point is: maybe communication is different here. It could depend on each person. Maybe everyone else sounds like they're speaking English and all the signage is in English because that's the language we as individuals know best. But if we, as two people, both understand another language, that could exist here too."

"I'm not really following," I admit.

"Lemme just try something."

He swallows and takes a step closer to me. My body freezes.

"Me. Llamo. Caleb. Cómo. Estás?" he says, slow and loud like he's speaking to an old person with a hearing aid.

"Um, I'm . . . bueno?" I say with a confused laugh.

"You heard me in Spanish?" he asks with wide eyes.

"Yeah."

"Hm. Let me try something harder. Um . . . yo creo que el pan es mejor con butter."

When he says butter, his mouth weirdly looks like it's saying something else, like the sound coming out of his mouth is being dubbed over.

"You think . . . bread is better . . . with butter?" I ask.

"You heard *all* of that in Spanish?"

"Well, yeah, everything except 'butter.' You said that in English."

"No, I didn't!" he says, smiling like a madman.

"Now you're just messing with me," I say, beginning to turn away.

"Bea, seriously, I said it in Spanish. Do you know the Spanish word for *butter*?"

"No," I reluctantly admit.

"See! My theory is correct. Whatever you don't know automatically translates here. Now if, if I tell you *butter* is how you say *butter* in Spanish, does that—"

"*Butter* is how you say *butter*?" I ask, cocking my head.

"No," he corrects. "I just said *butter* . . ."

I give him a blank stare.

"Damn," he mumbles. "The flaw to the magical automatic translation is you can never learn any new words in other languages once you arrive. . . ."

"Sounds like you're onto something," I say, finally continuing to walk away.

"Hey, do you think anyone's ever escaped from here?" he asks, catching up to me. We're now approaching the food court again, making this our third loop around the airport.

"Yeah." I shrug. "People move on to Heaven all the time."

"No, I mean, like, escaped of their own accord."

"That's impossible."

"How do we know that the departing planes go to Heaven?" Caleb presses, his eyes going wild. "Are we totally sure this isn't just some really messed-up secret experiment being conducted by the government? We just arrived here randomly and are supposed to blindly trust that the process will work? What if they're downloading and storing our memories for some master database to use against us?"

"Do you want some red string?" I ask. "To tie all your conspiracy theories together?"

"Sorry," he mumbles, rubbing his eyes.

"I have briefly considered it, though. That this is some kind of Area 51 thing. Like, what would happen if we walked all the way to the end of the tarmac outside? What would we see?"

"Right! The end of the universe? Or just, like, a chain-link fence separating us from some random highway?"

"Really makes you think."

"We should find out for ourselves," Caleb says, a sudden purpose in his voice. "I'm going outside."

"Seriously?"

"Bea, I promised you we would go on an adventure. This is the adventure."

"I don't know—"

"What?" he asks, gently mocking. "Are you scared?"

I narrow my eyes.

"Of course I'm not scared."

"Okay, so then why don't you abuse your special agent privileges and take us out onto the tarmac?"

20

Todd is still manning the departures gate, although he's now half asleep.

"Good evening, Todd," I say.

He jolts awake.

"What do you want?" he asks, wiping drool from the corner of his mouth.

"My assignment, Caleb—you met him earlier, remember? He just had a major breakthrough. I don't know what it was, but something triggered his memory at lunch."

I turn and glare at Caleb. He begins nodding rapidly and unconvincingly.

"Yeah! You know, they say scent is very powerful when it comes to conjuring memories. Lunch was very, um, pungent."

"Were you eating together?" Todd presses.

"Y—" Caleb begins.

"No," I interject. "I mean, at separate tables, but we were eating in the food court at the same time. That's how Caleb here found me so easily. He asked if we could go out to the hangar ASAP. I hope that's okay?"

"Look, Beatrice," he says. "I don't let agents go out to the hangar for more than one session a day."

Todd pauses and quickly glances to his left and right.

"But you're a friend of Sadie's," he says, lowering his voice, "and I happen to know there is a free hangar right now because one of the other agents wrapped up early. Plus, conversion rates are really lagging these days and if I don't get more people moving out of the airport, the big guns are gonna come in and put the pressure on me.

"So," he says, sliding me a pair of keys. "Here. But just this once."

The corners of my mouth slowly turn up into a smile.

ONCE WE'RE OUTSIDE, I walk toward the fleet of golf carts.

"Oh no you don't," Caleb says. "We are doing this the old-fashioned way. We will *walk* to the end of the universe. Or whatever it turns out to be."

"But my feet are tired from all that aimless walking we already did!" I protest. "And I'm being forced against my will to wear these stupid shoes."

I stare down at my white patent-leather pumps and pine for the Converse high-tops I was wearing when I arrived.

"Do you need me to carry you on my back?" Caleb gripes.

"Uh, no," I say quickly, although the idea of him picking me up in his arms is not the grossest. This unfortunately seems to be the recurring theme with Caleb. The idea of him is consistently . . . *not* the grossest. So I force myself to remember: Driving under the influence. Blunt-force trauma. Internal bleeding. *Gross* is an understated way to even describe these things.

I pull my shoes off and walk barefoot. The smooth, black asphalt feels surprisingly squishy under my toes, almost pleasant.

"Let's go," I say.

We walk toward the impossible-seeming horizon line in the distance, illuminated by overheard lights. The cold night air makes the tiny hairs on my arms stand up.

"This will take forever," I mutter.

"I'll race you?" Caleb asks, raising his eyebrows.

"Mmm, no."

"Last one to the end of the universe is a rotten egg!" he exclaims, running off in his sandals.

I keep walking at a normal pace, resisting the pull to follow him. Plus, I hate running. The magical endorphins that everyone claims come after physical activity are basically nonexistent in my brain.

"I can smell you rotting from here," he calls back, mock-waving his hand in front of his nose.

"Whatever!"

Suddenly I notice a glow on the ground next to me. I turn around and look. An air traffic control guy with one of those giant glow-stick things is coming toward us. Maybe it's my fight-or-flight response kicking in, but I start running too.

"Nice of you to join me," Caleb says when I'm a foot behind him, panting and out of breath.

"Company," I say through pained breaths. "We've got . . . company. . . ."

He glances over his shoulder at the air traffic control guy.

"Ah," he says, slowing down his pace to a walk. "I don't want to get in trouble. We better head back."

"Are you kidding?" I say, speeding up. "We're nowhere close to the end. We need to see what's out there."

He hesitates while I begin to run past him.

"Who's the egg now?" I yell back.

"*Rotten* egg," he says, reluctantly beginning to run again.

"Same difference!"

And we're off. We run on and on and on and on. Somehow, the asphalt beneath my feet begins to feel like it doesn't exist. It's like I'm flying. Maybe these mythical endorphins do exist; they were just lying dormant inside me.

I think we might actually do it. We might actually make it to the end. The air traffic control guy is a distant memory. After a few minutes, our paces have evened out and Caleb and I jog side by side. If we were wearing actual exercise clothes, we'd look like one of those annoying couples who go for evening runs around the neighborhood together, flaunting that not only are they in love but they're also physically fitter than you.

I turn and look up at Caleb. He winks at me and begins to speed up again.

"You can't just wink at me and get away with it!" I yell after him.

But it's pointless. Because next thing I know, Caleb is gone. Not just ran-ahead-of-me gone. Gone as in his whole body has completely vanished into the ether.

21

"**Emmy!**" **I called,** out of breath as I approached her and Skyler's table in the cafeteria. "Something so weird just happened in Walsh's class."

"What?" she asked, turning to look at me.

Skyler crossed his arms and gave me the stink eye.

"Oh," I said. "Was I interrupting something?"

"No," Emmy said as Skyler nodded.

Things seemed tense between them lately and I had no idea why. I hoped it was just that Emmy was waking up to the fact that Skyler was a total try-hard.

Emmy and I had the same lunch period because she was a genius who was placed in a senior-level physics class that only fit into her schedule if she had lunch with us juniors instead of the sophomores. It was the same case for Skyler, but I wouldn't classify him as a genius. They had become close and started going out last year, when they were the only freshman in the junior-level biology class. Even though they were nerds, they had lots of friends, but none of them were juniors. I knew lots of juniors, but none of them were my friends. This meant the three of us all sat together.

"So you know that girl Taylor Fields? My enemy?"

"Of course," Emmy said. "One of your three thousand enemies."

"Well, she was going off about how abortion is bad and then was like . . ."

Emmy kept her eyes intently on me as Skyler ignored me and pulled two sandwiches for them out of a reusable plastic container. My stomach audibly grumbled at the sight of them even though I knew they were probably filled with something gross, like roasted cauliflower.

"Ugh, hold on. I'll tell you after I buy food. I wonder why I'm so hungry."

"Probably because your breakfast ended up down the front of some thug's shirt," Skyler mumbled.

"Don't use the word *thug*, Skyler," I said, rolling my eyes.

"What? Dominic is white. It's not offensive."

"Well, it's objectively offensive for you as a white person also to use the word *thug*."

At this point, Emmy would typically interject and tell us to stop arguing, but when I looked at her, I realized she was staring at her phone, her face frozen in a horrified expression.

"What is it, Emmy?" I asked.

It was like she didn't hear me.

"Em?"

Her phone dropped out of her hands, landing with a *thwack* on the linoleum floor.

"You okay, babe?" Skyler asked, leaning over to pick it up.

Ugh, he called her babe! Another thing I couldn't stand.

Emmy shook her head and pushed Skyler's arm away so he couldn't reach the phone. Tears pooled at the corners of her eyes.

"Emmy, seriously, what's wrong?" I pressed.

She closed her eyes and took a deep breath.

"Nothing."

"This doesn't seem like nothing," I said.

Skyler and I looked at each other with more than just our usual hostility for a moment. If Emmy was upset, it had to be either my or Skyler's fault.

"Is this because Bea made you late to school today?" he asked, putting an arm around her, but still looking at me. "I think it'd be a good idea if, from now on, you got a ride with me."

Emmy just ignored him. At that moment, his phone lit up where it sat on the table next to his lunch. He quickly glanced at it, then, noticing something that must've sparked his interest, picked it up and gave it his full attention.

"Emmy, what am I . . . looking . . . at?" he said, squinting at his screen.

"I . . . I'm sorry . . . I . . . have to get out of here," Emmy said through panicked breaths. She leaned over to pick up her phone, then, before I knew it, was sprinting away, leaving behind her backpack and a pile of textbooks.

"What happened?" I asked, turning to Skyler. "Did you do something?"

"No, I . . ."

I thought of Taylor's weird comment from earlier, *"Tell your sister that she shouldn't have ignored me on her way in."* I wasn't sure how all of this connected, but before Skyler could even finish his sentence, I was running after Emmy.

22

"**Caleb?**" **I cry** out as I come to a halt, panting and clutching my aching sides.

I stand up straight again and spin my body around, trying to look for him. This has to be some kind of practical joke. There is nothing and no one around except the glowing airport about a half mile behind us.

"This isn't funny," I say, and as the words come out of my mouth I realize who I've become: the girl in every horror movie who says "This isn't funny" as she realizes she's definitely about to die because she decided to go along with a plan made up by some stupid guy.

I should probably be happy that the person who killed me just got sucked up into thin air, but instead my heart pounds of out my chest and my body breaks out into a cold sweat.

"Caleb?" I say, louder this time even though I know it's pointless.

I inch forward, afraid that if I take a step too far, I'll end up wherever he is.

In the blink of an eye, I'm no longer outside in the cold dark night. I look to my right. Caleb is staring at me, mouth gaping, eyes wide. I jump away from him.

My heartbeat slows as I take in my surroundings. There are fluorescent lights beaming above my head, rows and rows of benches, an unappealing scent that reminds me of over-cooked broccoli in the air—I'm back in the waiting area of the airport.

"What . . . was that?" I say, still clutching my chest.

"I don't know," Caleb says, voice shaky.

We stand next to a concrete beam in the far corner of the room. No one sitting around or passing by has seemed to notice us materialize. Todd is still half asleep in his chair.

"I thought you'd totally vanished into the ether!" I say, putting my hands to my temples.

"I know! Me too!" he says, his eyes wide. "Maybe this means that if you try to escape the airport, you just get shot back inside using some sort of . . . wormhole?"

"So it's physically impossible to leave on your own?"

"Your guess is as good as mine."

Caleb purses his lips thoughtfully, then breaks out into a smile that dissolves into a laugh. It's contagious.

"That was amazing, though!"

"I know," I say, laughing too.

"See, when I promised an adventure, I wasn't lying."

"It appears you weren't," I admit. "But you would never have gotten out there without my help."

"We should try it again!"

"No way," I say, shaking my head once, remembering the Disciplinary Council. The surveillance cameras. *The surveillance cameras!* When did I become this stupid?

"C'mon! Just one more time," he says, grazing my arm with the back of his knuckles. "Are you scared?"

His touch makes my arm feel like it's on fire, in the best way possible. But so what? I need to remember where I am and who I'm with and why I should extract myself from this situation immediately.

"No," I say, pushing his hand away a little too forcefully, throwing a wet blanket on any bit of camaraderie between us. "That's enough adventure for me."

Caleb pulls his hand back and crosses his arms. He studies my face.

"Sorry. Yeah. I guess it's late. Maybe we can try again tomorrow. Or some other night."

"I'll see you tomorrow morning," I say. "We still have a lot of work to do."

THE NEXT DAY in the hangar, I worry that the mood feels too much like a classroom the day after you've run into your teacher out in the real world.

You see them at Walmart, a basket full of deodorant and laundry detergent and toilet paper, proof that their bodies betray them on a daily basis just as much as yours does. Or even worse, you see them letting loose with friends, getting buzzed from two and a half sangrias when you're just trying to enjoy your mediocre meal at a local fast-casual restaurant.

Except, in this case, I'm the teacher and Caleb is the student. I don't want him to humanize me. I don't want him to know too much.

Or do I?

Would telling him about my life make it all the more crushing when he eventually realizes he's the one who ended it?

He looks too comfortable strapped into his chair with the helmet on his head.

Maybe this familiarity can be a good thing. If he really trusts me, he'll reveal the worst depths of his mind to me.

"Did you have a girlfriend?" I blurt out, firing up the Memstractor 3000.

"I don't really get why that's a relevant question," he says with a nervous laugh.

"Everything is a relevant question here."

Caleb blows air out of his mouth and rolls his eyes.

"No," he says quietly.

"What's that?" I say, supporting my ear with my hand.

"The answer is no, I didn't have a girlfriend. I've never had a girlfriend," he mumbles.

"But not for lack of trying? Is that the vibe I'm getting?"

Caleb rolls his eyes, but then surrenders himself to a memory.

We're in a school cafeteria, standing near the pizza and chicken nuggets as they endure slow, painful deaths under heat lamps.

He stands in line for food and is about to grab a chicken patty sandwich wrapped in paper, but then a girl with long, glittery fingernails cuts in front of him and beats him to it.

"Hey!" Caleb protests.

"Snooze, you lose, Caleb," the girl says, smiling at him. He turns and looks at her. She has pink hair cut into a symmetrical bob. Her hair and makeup are truly on point, like how I wish

I looked if I weren't currently doomed to wearing smudged mascara for the next million years.

"Just kidding. You know I'm a vegetarian anyway," she says, plopping the sandwich onto his tray.

"Ha ha, Laura," he says. "So, library after school?"

"Sure, I mean, I would rather we just go to my house and watch Bob Ross on Netflix," she says, tugging on his arm, dare I say . . . flirtatiously?

"We can't. We have to finish editing each other's early decision applications," Caleb insists.

"Ugh! We can make time to watch him paint at least one majestic mountain landscape. He's so soothing. We deserve a break. Watching Bob Ross is, like, self-care, okay? In this increasingly high-pressure, late-capitalist society, it's important to take time for yourself."

"I don't have time for myself," Caleb deadpans.

"Fine."

"You said you'd give me feedback on my essay by now, Laura."

For a brief second, she gives him a disappointed look.

"I only ask," he adds, "because you know I think you're the only person around here who will honestly tell me if my essay is nonsense, even though I definitely think what you just said about Bob Ross is nonsense."

"All right. Library," she says, smirking. "But you're buying me McNuggets after."

"Those aren't vegetarian. . . ."

"So? Yes, I'm a vegetarian. Yes, I eat McNuggets. We do exist," she chants, backing out of the lunch line and waving goodbye.

"What were you thinking?" I yell at Present Caleb. "Laura is hot and clearly so much cooler than you—"

"You think I don't realize that now?" he mutters, glaring at me.

"I mean, I can't even believe you guys were friends, to be honest . . ." I continue.

"We were co–class presidents," he explains. "One person is automatically given the position for having the highest GPA in the class; the other is elected, well, out of popularity."

"Let me guess which one you were."

"Yeah," he says, rolling his eyes. "But Laura and I became really good friends. I definitely thought about us becoming, like, involved . . . romantically . . . but I don't know . . ."

"You don't know what?" I press.

"It just seemed impossible," he says.

"How? She was literally just begging you to come over to her house to Netflix and chill!"

"We were from two different worlds."

Caleb squints and looks away toward the large cafeteria windows with stunning views of a fountain shaded by oak trees. Typical Brentwood.

"What's that supposed to mean?" I ask. "I'm sure this wasn't some Romeo and Juliet thing. You went to the same school. She was comfortable acknowledging you in the middle of the cafeteria."

"She was cool and I wasn't!" he blurts out, turning back toward me. "It was as simple as that. It was acceptable to talk at school, but . . . Why am I even explaining this to you? You're my age. Don't you understand the ridiculous hierarchies of social behavior when you're trapped in high school?"

"Well, Laura was clearly *very* okay with you not being cool. Why didn't you make a move?"

"She just always asked me to hang out at the worst possible times, like the night before a test or right before our applications were due or . . ."

His memory changes again. Now we're in the school library. He's sitting across from Laura at a wooden table.

"So will you please just humor me and come on Friday night? How many times do I have to invite you to things? You never come when I ask you," she says, looking up from a laptop. "Pleeeeaseee."

Someone out of sight shushes her.

"*Shooosh*," Laura parodies, putting her manicured finger to her mouth. "Please?" she says, this time quieter, turning back to Caleb.

"I have . . . plans . . . every Friday afternoon, so I have to stay in Friday night. You know I'm taking the SAT on Saturday morning. I should be studying the night before."

"You can come out for a little bit! You know, studying the night before the SAT doesn't help you. If it's not lodged into your brain by then, you're screwed. And I'm sure, given that you seem to have started preparing for the SAT as soon as you came out of the womb, you'll be fine."

"I'm not big on parties," Caleb admits. "I hate being around drunk people."

"So why not get drunk too? You know, that's the only way you'll ever fit in," Laura says, smiling sarcastically. Caleb raises his eyebrows at her.

"I'm kidding! I'm just kidding," she continues. "Seriously, I understand. It's totally chill if you don't want to drink. Every-one always appreciates a designated driver."

I cluck my tongue at the irony of Caleb being a designated driver. I can't help it. He's too mortified watching his own memory to even notice anyway.

"C'mon, Caleb!" she says. "You're just saying no because you like making me beg, huh?"

Silently, I glare at Present Caleb and wave my hands palms up. He just rubs his eyes.

"Yeah, yeah. Maybe I'll stop by," he says to Laura, turning back to his clunky prep book.

The memory changes again.

Now we're sitting in the back seat of what I assume is his Range Rover, aka My Death Machine. His past self is sitting in the front seat of the parked car and his hand is drafting a text.

I lean forward and read over his shoulder in a way that would be too close for comfort if it were actually Caleb and not just a memory.

He's composing a text to Laura that says *Guess where I am* 😊. He backspaces the winky face and changes it to an exclamation point instead. Then he backspaces that again, leaves the text without punctuation, and just stares at it.

"Oh my god, send it already!" I yell in his completely obliv-ious ear.

"Can you please stop editorializing my memories?" Pres-ent Caleb says next to me, cowering in the back seat.

"Fine."

We follow Past Caleb as he gets out of the car and walks

up the driveway toward a beige ranch-style house on a quiet street.

He rings the doorbell, but no one answers. Instead there's just the sound of girls squealing and the thumping noises of an EDM remix of a Cardi B song. He jiggles the handle and the door's unlocked, so he lets himself in. As he walks through the formal dining room, which houses a table littered with red Solo cups, and then the kitchen littered with even more cups, people look up with a hopeful glint in their eyes at his face, then register that it's only him and immediately go back to their conversations.

It's a look I'm familiar with myself, that look that makes you feel totally irrelevant and unwanted when you walk into a room.

Caleb moves on through the whole first floor and past the sliding glass doors leading to the back patio, looking for Laura, I assume, but she's nowhere to be found. He walks back inside, tries the handle on what I guess to be the powder room, sees that it's locked, and walks up a carpeted staircase to another bathroom with the light on and the door slightly ajar. We follow him into the bathroom and he locks the door behind us. Even though our bodies are only illusions, the room feels too crowded with me, Present Caleb, and Past Caleb all inside.

Past Caleb looks at himself in the mirror and shakes his head, a shake that says, *Why did you even bother coming here?* Then he takes a deep breath and stands in front of the toilet, putting the seat up.

"Uh," I say, turning around to stare at the door. "Can you

skip this part, Caleb? I know I said that everything that happens in your memories stays here and you should be honest, but really, you don't need to go this far into detail."

"Hold on," Caleb says, a look of agony on his face. "This is, unfortunately, important."

Right as Past Caleb is about to unzip his pants to pee, he freezes at the sound of a girl giggling and then a boy going "Shush."

"*Shooosh*," the girl says, then giggles again.

Caleb turns and stares at the tacky seashell-print shower curtain for a moment, then shoves it open. Laura is sitting in the tub fully dressed, but the blond guy next to her has his pants down and she is clearly about to do something to him that would definitely get her sent to Hell, according to that one nun at Caleb's elementary school.

"Caleb?" she asks, squinting up at him.

"Uh. Sorry," he mumbles.

He pulls the shower curtain closed so forcefully that it rips off its hooks and falls onto Laura and the other guy.

A strangled noise comes out of Past Caleb's mouth.

We follow Past Caleb as he sprints out of the bathroom, down the stairs, and out the front door. Then the memory ends, though I'm guessing maybe he walked himself off a cliff out of embarrassment and there's been a mix-up with his passport and *that's* actually how he died.

"Is that enough for today?" Caleb asks as we float in blank darkness. He has the energy-zapped look of someone who has just run a marathon.

"Not so fast. What happened with you two after that?"

"Nothing," he says. "We never talked about it. I mean, I'd hoped that maybe Laura was drunk and hadn't even remembered I'd walked in on her, but I pretty much avoided her after that."

"Why didn't you say something?" I ask.

"What was I supposed to say? 'Sorry I walked in on you about to give Derek Carter a blow job'? 'I should've knocked even though the door was ajar'?"

"I mean, yeah?" I say.

"That would've been so weird! It's not like we were dating or that she even knew I liked her. She was free to hook up with whoever she wanted!"

"So why did you pull that shower curtain back? You knew you were going to find something you didn't want to see, didn't you?"

He says nothing and just pushes his hair back, then begins to slowly claw at it.

"You wanted to have an excuse to never talk to Laura again because that meant you'd never have to actually confront if you liked her or not. It was an easy out."

"That's a bold assessment," Caleb scoffs.

"Your SAT score, your grades, those are all things you can prepare for or quantify with numbers, but you can't quantify your feelings. Feelings are so fussy, so unpredictable. If you admitted you liked Laura, you could get hurt. It was something you couldn't control, huh?"

He stares up at me, his jaw slack.

"Damn," he whispers.

This is it.

The pain and the torment I've wanted him to feel all along.

"You're so good at this!" he blurts out, smiling. "That's, like, such a spot-on assessment. I never thought of it that way. Were you a therapist in your past life? Jeez."

I look up at the nonexistent ceiling and suppress a scream.

"So was that it?" he asks. "Was that the thing that's been holding me back from moving on to Heaven? My repressed feelings?"

"No, Caleb. You'll know when it happens," I say. "I'm pretty sure we're just getting started."

23

I'm brushing my teeth when Jenna comes into our tiny bathroom and sits down on the toilet directly behind me.

"Um," I say, my voice muffled by toothpaste. "Can you not?"

"What?" she says, the sound of her pee hitting the toilet bowl. "This is what roommates do!"

I spit out my toothpaste in disgust. Also out of necessity, but mostly disgust.

"No, they do not!" I yelp.

I wipe my mouth with the back of my hand and storm out without rinsing. At home, I would hardly give a second thought to Emmy using the toilet while I was brushing my teeth. Except for when she'd flush while I was in the shower and the water would go freezing cold.

"Have you ever thought about what would happen if you died while on your period?" she asks from behind the bathroom door, unfazed by my reaction. "Like, our bodies are frozen in time, so does that mean you'd have your period the whole entire time you're stuck here?"

I hear the toilet flush and the faucet turn on.

"This is kind of random, semi-related, but you know how

in *Twilight*, Edward says Bella's blood is like his own personal drug? So, like, what happens when she has *her* period? I feel like Stephenie Meyer never properly addressed this and I just think about it so, so much. . . ."

"Jenna," I say when she emerges from the bathroom. "We need to set some boundaries."

"What do you mean?"

"I mean, knock before entering and don't pee while I'm already in the bathroom and, most importantly, do not try to engage me in a conversation on the menstrual politics of the Mormon propaganda known as *Twilight*."

Jenna opens her mouth to speak but is interrupted by a knock at our door.

"Who is it?" she calls.

"It's Caleb," the voice behind the door answers.

"How does he know my room number?" I whisper to myself, my stomach doing a somersault.

"I gave it to him," Jenna says matter-of-factly. "I invited him over to hang out with us."

"And why would you do that?" I say, pulling her back inside the bathroom to muffle our conversation.

"I went around the airport today inviting basically everyone I saw who is our age to come hang out. I'm trying to start a support group slash social club. I thought about calling it the Minor Mixer, but that sounded too depressing, so I'm calling it the Gone Too Soon Club."

"Oh yeah, that's not a depressing name at all."

"I invited, like, ten people," she says. "But I guess Caleb is the only one who took me up on the invite."

"Jenna, this is what I'm saying. *Boundaries.* If you want to invite people to our room, you need to ask me first because I am your roommate and this is a shared space."

"Hello?" Caleb says, knocking at the door again.

I stare down at my orange pajamas I only just changed into.

"Pretend I'm out. I'll stay in here until he's gone."

"I don't get it. What are you so worried about, Bea? What do you have to lose?"

I put the lid down on the toilet seat and sit on it, hugging my knees to my chest.

"Ohhhhh. I get it. You *like* him, don't you? But he makes you nervous because you're not sure he likes you back. . . ."

I start to open my mouth in protest, but then I realize just letting her believe this interpretation is much easier than explaining the truth.

"Yeah," I say, looking down at the floor, fake bashful.

"Okay. You stay put here. I'll grill him and you can eavesdrop."

"Wait, Jenna, n—"

She ignores me and bursts out the door, slamming it behind her. Even though I'm not happy about this plan, that doesn't stop me from crawling on the floor and pressing my ear to the bathroom door.

"Hiiiiiiiiiiii," Jenna says, her voice high.

"Hey," Caleb says. "Sorry, am I early?"

"No, not at all. People have been . . . coming in and out."

"Cool," he says, but his voice is wary. "Is Bea around?"

"No. She's . . . in an emergency staff meeting."

I have to admit, I am pleasantly surprised by the efficiency and believability of this lie.

"Why?" Jenna presses. "Do you need to talk to her?"

"Oh, no," Caleb says quickly. "Just wondering. You know, since you guys are roommates."

"Of course."

It's silent for a moment. I can't see it to confirm, but I imagine it's awkward.

"Do you wanna come in?" Jenna asks.

"Uhhh . . . sure."

"Take a seat!"

I squint through the hinges of the door. Jenna is gesturing to the edge of my bed. Caleb sinks into it.

"So, how's . . . being Bea's roommate?" Caleb asks.

"Oh, it's great, for the most part."

Excuse me?

"What do you mean?" Caleb asks, his voice amused.

"She's just so *guarded*," Jenna says loudly. "I want her to *open up* to me. I mean, she knows everything about me, but I don't really know anything about her other than that she died in a car accident."

"She did?"

"Oh no," I mutter without thinking.

Caleb turns his head toward the bathroom. Jenna clears her throat, commanding his attention.

"Anyway, you spend more time with her than I do these days. Has she told you anything interesting?"

"Mmm. Not really. The only personal thing she's revealed is that she went to Bible camp once."

"That makes so much sense. Sometimes, I feel like she has a connection to the divine world. It's like, who knows what's going on in that mind of hers?"

I throw my hands up in the air, as if Jenna can see me.

"Yeah. I get that," Caleb says. "For the most part, I find her really easy to talk to. Like, easier to talk to than anyone. Then sometimes it's like she's somewhere else. She can be kind of . . . distant."

Well, if I knew this was going to be a roast, then I would've brought some marshmallows.

"Not in a bad way," he corrects quickly. "It's just, and please don't tell her I said this, it's like sometimes she can't stand the sight of me. Then other times, I get the sense that she's . . . flirting with me?"

"Well, do you *want* her to flirt with you?"

"If our roles were reversed, that'd be totally inappropriate. If it were *my* job to spend time with her, it'd be totally creepy if I were flirting with her. That's, like, workplace harassment."

With this, Caleb stands up and begins pacing, out of my line of vision.

"Yeah, but it's not *your* job," Jenna insists. "It's hers."

"I'm just saying things," he says with a nervous laugh. "Who knows what they mean? My sense of reality is pretty much nonexistent these days."

"So? You're still not answering my question, Caleb. Do you want her to flirt with you or not?"

As I wait for him to answer her, I get this weird feeling in my stomach, like it's filled with butterflies wielding tiny knives.

"I don't feel comfortable answering that question," he says finally. "Not to be rude."

"Oh my god, you totally want her to flirt with you! You like her! You *like* like her."

"Um, so when are more people arriving to this party?" Caleb says, his voice squeaky. "Can I use your bathroom?"

I hear his footsteps approaching the door. The knob begins to turn.

"*Wait!*" Jenna yells.

Under the door, I see his feet pause.

"Our toilet is clogged," Jenna elaborates. "Some Jell-O didn't sit right with Bea and . . . well, we're waiting on a maintenance person to come fix it."

"Oh. Okay. You know what? I'll just head back to my room then. I'm pretty tired anyway. Good night, Jenna."

"Night!"

I hear the hallway door open.

"Oh, and Jenna?" Caleb calls. "Please don't tell Bea anything we talked about tonight, if that's okay? I don't want to make her uncomfortable."

"Of course!"

I wait for the door to slam shut and then I count to thirty.

"First of all," I yell at Jenna, bursting out of the bathroom, "'some Jell-O didn't sit right' with me?"

Jenna reaches for Sprinkles and holds him up next to her face.

"We're sorry," she says in a baby voice, pouting.

"Save it."

I'M RUNNING OUT of ways to stall Caleb.

Today I've forced him to travel back and forth in his memory, extracting every embarrassing moment, every awkward run-in with a girl dating back to preschool, every time he's accidentally called a teacher "Mom." Yet he seems to have flatlined when it comes to being mortified. I need to up the ante.

"Have you ever done anything you're ashamed of?" I ask him.

"Of course," he says.

I remember his earlier, brief visions of the night we both died. I don't want him to think of them now. I can't let him remember that night yet.

"Something you're ashamed of that had no consequences," I clarify. "But still, it eats you up inside?"

"Well," Caleb says, swallowing once. "There was . . ."

Suddenly we're inside Caleb's car again. He's pulling into a Walmart parking lot at night. This isn't his part of town. This is *my* Walmart. The one where Monica buys Grayson's diapers and her corny pajamas. The one where people have gotten arrested for trying to buy and sell Oxycontin.

Past Caleb pulls his car into a spot in the far corner of the lot. Across from him, a tan sedan flashes its headlights twice. He gets out of his SUV and swallows hard, then walks over to the driver's side of the car.

The driver lowers his window. He's a nerdy-looking guy in his late twenties wearing glasses, a polo shirt, and a navy baseball cap with a mascot on it I can't place.

"Caleb?" the guy asks, his voice high and nasally.

Caleb nods at him once. The guy hands him a yellow manila envelope through the window. Caleb reaches into his jeans pocket, pulls out a wad of cash, and hands it over in return.

I always knew rich people sold drugs to each other, possibly even more than people who aren't rich. They just don't suffer the same consequences for it. The thing is, though, I never knew they could be so stupidly obvious when going about it.

The man waves goodbye to Caleb and drives off. Caleb clutches the envelope, returns to his car, opens it, and slides out the contents.

It's not drugs. It's the official answer key to this year's SAT.

"Oh, you have got to be kidding me," I groan.

Present Caleb shrinks next to me.

"How much money did you pay for that?"

"I don't want to say."

"Caleb. You have to be honest with me. It's part of the process."

He mumbles something inaudible.

"What's that?" I press.

He stares blankly into the distance at an old lady driving through the Walmart parking lot on a motor scooter.

"Fifteen hundred dollars," he says quietly.

I raise an eyebrow. On one hand, I have never seen that much money in my bank account, let alone as a stack of cash in real life. On the other, I know that's chump change for rich people who want to get their kids into fancy colleges.

"It was fake, wasn't it?" I ask.

He blinks at me twice.

"How did you know?"

"Fifteen hundred is way too cheap," I say. "If I had the answers to the SAT on my hands, I would sell them for at least $10K. Who even was that guy?"

"He was the cousin of a cousin of a guy on my lacrosse team. He worked at the College Board. Or at least, I thought he worked at the College Board. . . . I should've known it was too good to be true," he sighs.

I scoff at him.

"Look, Bea, I know. It's bad. I tried to cheat on the SAT—"

"It's not that," I explain. "Screw the SAT! I think standardized tests are evil. It's that you even had that kind of money to waste on trying to get ahead of everyone else."

"You're right," Caleb mumbles. "It wasn't fair. But you told me the more honest I am with my memories, the sooner we can get to the bottom of why I'm here. So that's what I'm doing. Is it really your place to pass so much judgment, Bea?"

I cross my arms and stare at the car floor. He's not wrong.

"So what was it?" I say, looking back up at him. "Why were you so obsessed with getting into college?"

"Isn't every American teenager obsessed with getting into college?"

"No!"

"What? You weren't?"

"Stop deflecting. Look, you're clearly not stupid—"

"Oh. *Thanks*," he says sarcastically.

"I mean, why did you need to cheat to get into college?" I elaborate. "Based on your other memories, it seems like you were prepared."

"Believe me, I was. . . ." he says, his memory shifting again. Now we're in an old Victorian-style house with books stacked up along the walls. Caleb sits at a long wooden table while an old professor-looking man sits across from him, pointing out mistakes on a practice test.

"There was weekly SAT prep tutoring for months . . ." he says. "The test key was just supposed to be a backup plan. Not to mention, my résumé of activities was stacked."

"You had a *résumé*?" I ask, blinking rapidly.

"Of course," Caleb says incredulously. "Model UN . . ."

We're transported to a school gym filled with tables. Caleb sits behind one with a placard that reads FINLAND.

"Isn't Finland ranked as, like, the 'happiest country' in the world?" I ask, making air quotes. "I can't imagine it was that hard to represent."

"No country is perfect, Bea," he says, and clenches his jaw. "Anyway, there was that, and I was editor in chief of the news-paper. . . ."

We move to a classroom where Caleb stands in front of a small handful of other students spread out among desks.

"Thank you everyone for your hard work on this issue. I'm all for having fun, but I just think given the state of our world, our cover story should be something a little more serious than . . ."

He flips up an issue from a stack on his desk. Its headline reads "BEST MEMES 2019!!!"

The other students start to boo him.

"Guys, c'mon . . ."

They ignore him.

"Anyway," Caleb says next to me, irritation in his voice. "I also ran cross-country . . ."

Now we're in a perfectly manicured field that smells of freshly cut grass, lined with trees with yellow and orange leaves. I recognize Caleb among a group of sweaty, hulking boys running past us in one terrifying mass.

"And played lacrosse . . ."

The trees turn green and the same boys are now wearing helmets and wielding nets on sticks. I can't identify Caleb out of any of them. Even though I'm technically invisible, I flinch and duck my body toward Present Caleb.

"Keep this montage moving, Max Fischer," I say. "A stampede of boys running with sticks is my nightmare!"

"Max who—like from *Rushmore*? You like Wes Anderson movies?" he asks, the corner of his mouth twitching.

"I wouldn't say I *like* them. I've just seen them," I explain loudly over the noise of screaming coaches and grunting boys. "My sister had a phase where she was obsessed with *Moonrise Kingdom* and checked out all his other movies from the library. I swear that's the only reason she dates her nerd boyfriend. Because he seems like he would be in one."

"You have a sister?" he asks.

"I got sidetracked," I say, shaking my head. "What else was on your résumé?"

"Why are you avoiding my question?" Caleb presses, eyebrows raised.

"Because we only get four hours a day to sort through *your* memories," I say, ducking away from two boys fighting for the ball with their nets, even though I know they theoretically can't hurt me. "I shouldn't waste this precious time talking about myself."

"I guess," he says, closing his eyes.

Next thing I know, it's quiet, save for a television playing a talk show on low volume. We're inside what feels like an extension of someone's grandma's living room. There's seafoam carpet and fake flower arrangements and a bunch of easy chairs lined up around mahogany tables. About a dozen elderly people sit playing board games. I follow Caleb's gaze to where he watches himself sitting directly across from a white-haired woman in a kaleidoscope-print muumuu.

"Ugh, I'm all out of options, Caleb!" the woman exclaims. "You really screwed me over when you got *quixotry*. Thanks a lot, you son of a—"

"Brenda!" another woman with reading glasses perched on the end of her nose calls from a table over. "Watch your mouth. That's my grandson you're speaking to!"

Even though her hair has gone completely gray, I recognize his abuela from his earliest memory.

"I organized a Scrabble club at my abuela's retirement home," Present Caleb says next to me as he looks at her with a glint in his eyes.

"Every Friday afternoon, I would set it up, keep tabs on everyone's scores, verify that words were real—that kind of thing. You'd be surprised at how some of these people behaved," he says, eyes dancing. "I caught Brenda stealing letter tiles on multiple occasions. She was almost banned."

"So this was your favorite thing that you did with your free time?" I ask, watching the past version of him walking around and offering a tin of butter cookies to each of the tables. The residents smile up at him like he's some kind of god.

"I don't know if it was my favorite," Present Caleb says with a dismissive shrug. "I liked all my hobbies equally."

"Really? This seems a lot more rewarding than lacrosse."

"It was. Don't get me wrong," he says. "It's just, Harvard wanted well-rounded applicants, so I did everything I could."

He gives a single bitter laugh and shakes his head.

"Harvard?" I choke out.

"What about it?"

"I didn't even realize actual people go to Harvard. I thought it was only for, like, the children of presidents or famous people."

"Regular people go to Harvard all the time," Caleb says, glowering at me.

"No regular people who I've ever known."

"You just said this isn't supposed to be about you."

"True. Thanks for keeping us on track," I say sarcastically. "So what were you planning on doing once you actually got to Harvard? Like, what was your passion? Shouldn't your activities in high school reflect what you want in the future—"

"I don't know!" he blurts out quickly, his face reddening. "What kind of question is that? What was *your* passion? Maybe I didn't have a passion, but I had a goal. Did *you* even have a goal, Beatrice?" he asks, spitting out my name.

I purse my lips for a minute and think it over. *Did* I have a passion? I spent most of my time being miserable and hating everyone around me. I liked hanging out with my sister and watching trashy TV and filling virtual shopping carts with clothes I couldn't afford and would never buy.

"My passion?"

"Yeah," Caleb says, indignant.

"Okay. You want to know my favorite thing to do? In the whole wide world?" I say at last, staring at the floor. "It was walking around the supermarket the hour before it closed. I love that feeling when no one else is there, except maybe some guy stocking the shelves, and soft rock is playing and it's peaceful. I can pretend that I'm not at the supermarket, but my very own postapocalyptic bunker, protected by a fortress of soup cans and sheet cakes. And everything's going to be okay because how could it not be when there's so much . . . I don't know . . . abundance . . . around me?"

I look up at Caleb. His face goes soft.

"Does that sound crazy?" I ask. "I know that makes me seem like some kind of doomsday prepper, but it's different than that and—"

"No," he says, staring at me like I've just appeared in front of him for the first time. "That doesn't sound crazy."

My cheeks start to burn. Why did I even say that? What am I even *doing*?

"Anyway, to answer your other question," I say, looking away from him. "I didn't have any goals. I was just getting by. The idea that you should know what you want for your whole life at age seventeen is ridiculous."

"No, it's not," he says, slipping his hands into his pockets and screwing up his face. "It's responsible."

"You know what? I'm wrong," I say. "You know what's truly ridiculous? Paying someone for the answers to the SAT because it might help you get into Harvard!"

"Well, what's the point of having this argument?" he asks. "Because responsible or not, look where we both ended up."

My body thrums with rage. If it weren't for him, I wouldn't be here.

"Can you just shut off the machine, please?" Caleb says quietly. "I think I've had enough of this for today."

I close my eyes and slam down the Memstractor's switch.

"I thought you would never ask."

24

"**Girls! Girls! Where** do you think you're going? You can't leave without a pass!" a hall aide yelled at me from her post at the cafeteria doors.

I turned and looked at her. She was wearing a Christmas-themed sweatshirt with a matching turtleneck embroidered with candy canes underneath, its cheeriness offset by her strict demeanor.

"My sister's having some kind of personal crisis, I think," I explained through panting breaths without stopping.

"Okay, well, are you also?" the aide pressed.

"Yeah. Maybe I am."

"Well, then I can give you a pass to the nurse's office. Just give me a second. . . ."

I ignored her and ran. Down the hall, the swinging door to the girls' room flew open and shut. I figured that was the only place Emmy could've gone. She was definitely not daring enough to straight up ditch.

When I got inside, I didn't see her, but several of the stall doors were shut.

"Emmy?" I called. No answer.

A ragged sob came from the handicapped stall at the end

of the row. I leaned down and caught a glimpse of Emmy's pink Vans.

"Em?" I said, quieter this time, walking toward the stall. "Please. Talk to me."

After a moment she finally opened the door and stared at me, her face already wet with tears.

"Would you be mad if I did something that was kind of a big deal?" she said, sniffling. "And I didn't tell you I did it, not because I don't trust you, but because I was scared it'd mean you'd do something to someone else?"

"What?"

Emmy was never this cagey with me. We told each other everything. Or at least that's what I thought.

She took in a sharp breath, pushed her hair back, and then pulled her phone out from the sleeve of her sweater. She unlocked it and handed it to me.

On the screen there was a photo. The resolution was blurry, but its contents were clear: it was Emmy, walking out of a Planned Parenthood clinic. I could tell by the logo on the door. The photo was candid, taken from across the street, as if Emmy were a celebrity and the paparazzi had been waiting for her.

"Oh . . . kay," I said. "So, you went to get birth control? Why didn't you ask me to come with you? You know I would've . . ."

Emmy shook her head at me and glared.

"Wait a second, who took this picture of you?"

"Bea, I don't know," she said impatiently. "But can you just think for a second about why I was really there? Why do people hate Planned Parenthood?"

I stared down at the picture again. Emmy's arms were

crossed tight to her chest. Her face was puffy like she'd been crying earlier, like how she would probably look again an hour after this.

"Oh. Emmy . . ." I said.

She started to cry all over again. I pulled her in for a hug.

Even though we're only a year apart, Emmy looked and felt so young to me in this moment. Like she was six, not sixteen.

"I'm going to kill Skyler," I said, holding her in my arms and talking into her hair. As the words came out of my mouth, I realized they were not a figure of speech. I wanted with every fiber of my being to run him over with my car. Twice.

Emmy had told me, much to my displeasure, about her and Skyler's first kiss. He'd invited her over to watch that documentary about the dark side of SeaWorld, and during a scene in which one of the trainers is attacked by an orca, Skyler leaned in and kissed Emmy, accidentally knocking into her teeth with his own. Obviously, I hadn't given much thought to their physical relationship beyond that, and I didn't really want to. But if they'd gotten serious, I imagined Emmy would have at least formally announced it to me.

"That's the thing," Emmy said, looking up at me, shaking her head. "Skyler and I have never, you know, done it."

25

I should be thrilled. Not only did I manage to embarrass Caleb and make him seriously question his life decisions, he even asked me to end the session early. At this rate, he'll blow through these thirty sessions without ever reaching a conclusion. He'll be forced back into the lottery, stuck here indefinitely.

Not like it matters, but he doesn't ask me to eat lunch and I don't see him at dinner, or around the rest of the airport, not even running around on one of his silly jogs. I think that maybe Caleb has totally given up when the clock strikes a quarter after eight the next morning and he still hasn't shown up to the departures counter.

It seems like everything is going according to plan, but somehow I'm left with an awful sinking feeling in my stomach.

"Sorry I'm late," Caleb says, breathless, when he finally shows up.

I just turn toward the exit onto the tarmac and he follows me. We ride the golf cart in silence.

"I was rude to you yesterday," he says at last when I park.

"Yeah," I say, staring ahead. "You were."

"I'm sorry."

"It's fine."

"And?" he asks.

"And what?"

"Well, aren't you going to apologize for being rude to *me*?"

"No. I'm not," I say, stepping out of the cart. "The only reason I was rude to you was because you were pressing me about my own life. That's not the point of these sessions."

"Fair enough. But you were being judgmental before that. About Harvard and the whole SAT answers thing. I know that was messed up, but I thought the point of these sessions was for me to be honest. And how am I supposed to be honest when I have to worry about what your reaction will be?"

He's right. I've let my guard down too far.

"I know I looked like a spoiled brat yesterday," Caleb says as we walk inside the hangar. "And maybe I was. But I didn't tell you exactly why I was so obsessed with getting into Harvard because . . . well . . . it's kind of a sore subject for me."

"All right," I say, settling into my seat. "Then show me."

Caleb takes a deep breath then flips down his helmet. I turn on the Memstractor and we're transported to a staircase lined with framed family photos.

"Those are my parents," he says, pointing to a photo on the wall of a couple laughing with each other on a picnic blanket, their textbooks spread out before them. It's the same woman from Caleb's earlier memory of his birthday party. His mom. She's sitting next to some football-player type with blond hair. His dad.

"They met at Harvard law school."

He stares at the photo for a few seconds, then looks at

another one. Suddenly we're transported to a college campus with redbrick buildings and a sprawling green lawn full of people sitting at round tables. Underneath a maroon-and-white balloon arch, toddler Caleb is getting his picture taken with his parents. They look perfect, like the photo could be used in a brochure promoting next year's reunion.

"You know, if I'm being honest," I say, looking around, "this place looked a whole lot nicer in *Legally Blonde*."

"That movie wasn't even filmed in Cambridge, Bea. It was filmed in Los Angeles."

"How do you know that?"

"Anyway," he says, drawing out the word and turning away from me. "My parents were super into alumni culture. They took me to their five-year reunion. They bought me little Harvard sweatshirts for Christmas. . . ."

Now we're inside his childhood living room. It's more modest than I was expecting, with a tabletop-size Christmas tree and only a handful of presents underneath. Past Caleb tears open a box, pulls the sweatshirt out, and holds it up to his chest. Caleb's dad puts his arm around his mom's shoulders and gives her a squeeze as they look on adoringly.

"I don't know," Present Caleb says. "It was just a given that I would go there and follow in their footsteps."

"So that's it?" I ask, unimpressed. "Your parents went to Harvard and had their happily ever after, so you had to go there too?"

Caleb scrunches up his face.

"That's the thing: they didn't have a happily ever after. My mom was a first-generation Mexican American who was going to school to become an immigration lawyer. My dad's ancestors came over on the *Mayflower* and my grandparents considered George and Barbara Bush to be, in their words, 'close personal friends.' Do I need to spell it out for you? They were doomed from the start. But I guess they were happy for a time. My dad had this progressive phase in college where he swore off his family, which was totally bogus because they were still paying his tuition. Then he met my mom and fell in love. She got pregnant with me the year after they graduated and they decided to keep me and get married."

"So then what?" I press. "His conservative supervillain genes were just too powerful and overtook his brain and he had to return to his old life?"

"Ehhh." He shrugs. "Kind of. His family cut him off and he freaked out about us having no money and became a corporate lawyer. That's when things fell apart and my mom realized she couldn't love him anymore. Now he's one of those people who identifies as 'socially liberal and fiscally conservative.' Whatever that means."

"Oh, so he thinks the problems that plague society are bad but their causes are fine?" I say sarcastically. "Because he can make a profit from them?"

Caleb looks at me slack-jawed.

"That's exactly how my mom would describe it to me," he says, blinking.

"I don't mean to totally trash my dad. All things considered, he was a good dad. He helped me with my homework. He'd buy me really, really nice Christmas and birthday presents. He went to all my soccer games."

His memories transport us through a montage of time

spent with his dad. They look like the stock footage that would appear if you searched "father and son bonding."

"You did a great job out there, buddy!" his dad calls, standing on the edge of a field, wearing a business suit.

"I lived with him in the summer and stayed with him on weekends, but . . ." He trails off.

"But what?"

"I don't know if you would get this, but, like . . . you know how companies will hire one person of color and then pat themselves on the back for being soooo diverse?"

"I've heard about it."

"Sometimes I felt like I was the diversity hire for my dad's . . . whole life. Or like I was just the holdover from some phase he had."

Now we're transported to a beach that's nearly empty except for a family clumped together near the water. It's Caleb's dad, a younger blond woman, a pair of blond toddlers, and Caleb awkwardly hunched next to them.

They're all wearing white button-downs and khaki pants. A photographer is taking their picture. It looks nearly identical in composition to the portrait that sat on my school principal's desk.

Who decided that wearing khakis on the beach was the ultimate way for the nuclear family to be immortalized?

"Who's that?" I ask, pointing to the woman. "Your stepmom?"

"Yeah. That's Cheryl and . . . *the twins.*"

She puts her arms tightly around the two of them, making Caleb stick out in the photo even more.

"I mean, she tried her best to include me, but . . ."

Now we're in a big, bright kitchen with granite counter-tops. The kind of kitchen people on *House Hunters* would go wild for.

"I made tacos, Caleb!" Cheryl says. "Your dad says they're your favorite."

She plops a platter in front of him. It's full of ground beef so gray and unseasoned that it resembles gravel. Past Caleb just makes a face at her that is half smile, half grimace.

"I've never told anyone this," Present Caleb says, looking over and gauging my face. "But I've always kind of felt guilty for being close with my dad."

"What? Why would you feel guilty for having a parent who cared about you?"

I think of my own dad and how he only did the bare minimum of keeping Emmy and I fed and bathed after our mom was killed. We really raised each other.

"Because my dad is everything *I* hate! My dad is *the* problem. He is a rich, entitled white guy who votes for the worst people. If he weren't a good dad, it would've been so much easier to take a stand and cut him out of my life and not let him buy me a stupid Range Rover with the money he made being a lawyer who thinks corporations are people."

"Oh yeah, that problem we all know so well," I say sarcasti-cally. "The turmoil of being gifted a luxury car."

Okay, well, my dad *did* give me that used 1999 Honda Civic under Monica's insistence.

"Bea. I'm serious. Do you know how guilty I felt just for having a relationship with him? I thought maybe it could be productive. Like, as his main connection to the non–Fox

News–watching world, it was my duty to change his mind, but then every time politics came up . . ."

Now we're back inside Caleb's dad's kitchen, where the family is eating dinner.

"Did you hear the news?" Cheryl asks. "They voted to keep the Affordable Care Act today."

"Yeah. Ridiculous," his dad says. "Healthcare should be a commodity, not a free-for-all."

Past Caleb takes a massive bite of his disgusting taco and chews aggressively for a very long moment, staring down at the table.

"It was like my body would shut down," Present Caleb concludes. "I knew why I didn't agree with him, but I could never just spit it out. I was such a coward. I've even wondered if that's why I ended up here. Because I had some moral obligation to change my dad's way of thinking and I didn't fulfill it."

He pauses and looks up and around.

"If you're hoping for the green light to start flashing right now," I say, "I don't think it will."

He waves a hand through his imaginary, pixelating hair.

"Look, Caleb," I continue. "I think God, or whoever or *whatever* is controlling all of this, is definitely petty, but that'd be straight up cruel to punish you, a child—"

"I'm *basically* eighteen," he interrupts.

"Whatever," I say, rolling my eyes. "It'd be petty to punish you, an almost-not-child, for your fully grown father's flaws."

"Well, what if I'm here because I wasted all the privileges I did have?"

"What do you mean?"

"Like, my mom grew up working her butt off so she could have a better life than her parents did. She didn't go to a fancy high school. She didn't have a personal tutor. She certainly didn't have fifteen hundred dollars to spend on a fake SAT answer key . . . and she still made it to Harvard. And now she uses what she learned there for good, to help people. What did I ever do to really help anyone?"

His memory switches again. We're back in the same small living room from his childhood. His mom is sitting at a table on her laptop, with stacks and stacks of files around her. She looks the same, but she has a single streak of gray in her long hair and wears thick-rimmed glasses now. Caleb walks through the front door.

"Hi, sweetie," his mom says without looking up from her work. "How was your father's?"

"Fine," Caleb says, taking off his backpack.

"Did you eat dinner?"

"Yeah."

"Did you actually eat dinner or did you just politely eat three bites of Cheryl's world-famous tacos again?"

"No," Caleb says, the corners of his mouth twitching. "I politely ate three bites of something called 'Mexican Lasagna.'"

His mom looks up and gasps.

"It was like lasagna, but with jarred salsa instead of marinara sauce," Caleb admits with a guilty smile.

"Oh, you have got to be kidding me!"

"She said she got the recipe on Pinterest. You know, I can text her and ask for the link if you're interested in making it, Mom . . ." he says with a sly smile.

"Oh yeah? Well, if I ever ask for one of Cheryl's recipes, please call 9-1-1 because that could only mean I'm having a stroke."

They start hysterically laughing. The two of them have the same exact laugh that kind of starts with a hissing noise through their teeth, and both sigh in unison when they're done.

It's a nice moment and, for some reason, maybe because I never really knew my mom and never got to make stupid jokes with her, it makes me want to cry.

I look to Present Caleb to my right and I realize that is exactly what he's doing.

"Your abuela came over and made us enchiladas last night," his mom says, turning back to her work. "There're some in the fridge if you want to heat them up."

"Thank god," Past Caleb says, heading toward the kitchen. "Is it cool if I eat in my room? I need to study."

"You're always studying," his mom says. "Look what I've done . . . raised a huge nerd."

Past Caleb stops and turns.

"Well, look at you," he says, gesturing to all the paperwork around her. "The apple doesn't fall far from the tree!"

"Have I set a bad example?" she asks with a touch of sarcasm, slumping over the table.

"No," he says, shaking his head. "No way. Good night, Mom."

"I didn't even ask her about her day or the cases she was working on," Present Caleb says next to me, tears streaming down his face. "All I could think about was me and Harvard, all the time. I thought that getting in would be this, like, big symbolic thing, and they could come together again and be proud of me."

"I mean . . ." I start. "Is it a bad idea to get obsessed with an elitist cultural institution that doesn't disclose to the public how they select from applicants? Yes. But can I kind of see why you were so obsessed now? Yeah. You just wanted to make your parents proud in their own ways."

And you did make them proud! I want to scream. *You'd have to be insane to not be proud of a son like you!*

But I can't.

Because I have to remember who it is I'm really talking to.

"So did you get in?" I blurt out ungracefully, throwing salt on his wound. "You mentioned before you were applying early decision. Did you find out?"

Caleb turns and stares at me and opens his mouth to speak, but before he can say anything, the Memstractor 3000 shuts down. There are no flashing lights, no alarms, no sounds over the PA system. We're back inside the airplane hangar, sitting across from each other in our helmets.

"That's so weird," I say. I turn and look at the machine switch.

Resting on it is a hand with long, mauve-colored fingernails.

Sadie.

26

"So what then?" I asked Emmy. "You were impregnated like the Virgin Mary?"

She winced and rolled her eyes at me.

"Why didn't you tell me this happened?" I continued. "I would've gone with you. I would've had your back."

"Because I didn't want anyone to know, okay? I just need you to stay calm for me."

"I'm being totally calm," I said in a high-pitched voice that was the opposite of calm. "Can you just tell me who did this to you?"

"What do you mean 'did this' to me?"

"What boy knocked you up and then didn't even have the guts to go with you? So I can go beat his ass."

"Nobody 'did' this to me, okay?" she said, finally, pulling out of my arms. "See, this is why I didn't . . . Do you remember how I got into that STEM scholarship competition at Penn State?"

Emmy had gone to the program during fall break, which sounded more generous in name than "two days off before a weekend in October." She'd designed a mock-up for an alarm system that saves children and pets from being left inside a too-hot car, because of course she did.

At the end, she won a scholarship that wouldn't pay for the entirety of college, but was significantly more than what our dad had put aside for us (i.e., exactly zero dollars and zero cents). I was so proud of her. And I was relieved she would have the few days to herself, independent from Skyler. At the time, she complained with a touch of self-consciousness that Skyler couldn't apply to the program with her because he was too rich and too male to qualify.

"Well, I lost my virginity to another boy in the program. I don't know. It just happened." She shrugged. "And then a few weeks later, I realized that I was . . . What was I supposed to do?"

"I'm not judging you, Emmy. You know that."

"Aren't you though?" she says, her voice cracking. "I didn't tell you because I know what you're capable of. You most definitely would've tracked this boy down and found some way to ruin his life."

She wasn't entirely wrong. As she was speaking the words "another boy in the program," I was speculating if that would be enough information to figure out his address.

"How did you even get there, Emmy? How did you even get home safely? I would've given you a ride!"

I couldn't believe this. My little sister got an abortion and she was too afraid to tell me, her best friend. I racked my brain, trying to think of any signs I'd missed of her crying out for help.

Was I really that selfish that I hadn't noticed her behaving differently? All those times I banged on the door to make her finish up in the bathroom, was she hunched over the toilet with morning sickness? Anxiously peeing over a drugstore pregnancy test? This was the type of thing that seemed impossible to hide from someone you not only shared a room but a bunk bed with. Emmy, who couldn't even sneak Oreos into our room without me instantly begging her to share them.

"I had Monica take me," she mumbled quickly, putting her head in her hands.

"Monica?" I yelled. "You trusted Monica over me?"

Somehow this was the part of the whole thing that shocked me the most.

"The thought of getting a mani-pedi with her is repulsive, let alone having her accompany you to your . . . your abortion. Ugh!"

"Shut up, Bea!" Emmy said, looking around self-consciously. "Can you just *shut up*? For once."

"Fine," I said. "Are you okay?"

"Well, I thought I was going to be, but then I got sent this creepy picture of myself from a number I didn't recognize. God knows who else got it! I mean, Skyler . . ."

Out of the corner of my eye, I noticed a nervous-looking freshman emerge from her stall and smile politely toward us, avoiding eye contact.

"No one has to know," I said to Emmy. "As far as Skyler's concerned, you had to go there for a cervical cancer screening. Or to get a urinary tract infection treated. Planned Parenthood offers a *plethora* of services."

By the end of my rant, I was practically yelling toward the unsuspecting girl just trying to wash her hands.

"I can't lie to him again, Bea," Emmy said quietly.

"Sure you can," I said. "This doesn't have to be any of his

business. Your secret is safe with me. C'mon, let's just take the rest of the day off and go home."

Emmy thoughtfully pursed her lips, like she might, for once, actually take me up on my proposition to cut class. But then her phone lit up again.

"Oh god," she said, staring at it. "It's from the same number."

Then her face went completely cold. Silently, she slid her phone over to show me the message.

Tell ur sis to back off or else I'm sending this pic to the whole school xoxo

27

"**What's up, Bea?**" Sadie says with a brilliant smile and unsettling, unblinking eyes.

"Nothing much," I say. "How are . . . you?"

"Well, I'm not in Heaven! That's for sure!" she says, then laughs for an uncomfortably long amount of time. "Sorry for interrupting you two. The day's almost over. Why don't I give you guys a ride back to the airport?"

She pushes up our helmets, both at once, making it a command more than a question.

"Sure," I say, glancing at Caleb.

"Oh, I'm sorry," Sadie says, reaching out her hand to him. "I'm Sadie. I feel like I know you from somewhere?"

"Uh, yeah, I've seen you around," he says.

She pulls back her hand before he can even return the shake, and starts impatiently walking out of the hangar. I push off my helmet and gesture for Caleb to do the same.

"What's going on?" I whisper to Sadie once I've caught up to her, Caleb trailing behind me. She ignores me and gets into the driver's seat of the golf cart.

"Bea, why don't you hop up here with me?" She pats the

seat next to her. I'm tempted to remind her that I'm the one who drove this cart out here in the first place, but I just get in.

Caleb sits in the back, facing the opposite direction. We've barely settled into our seats when Sadie speeds off.

"So what happened?" I ask.

"I don't know. You tell me, Bea," she says, hitting the gas pedal even harder. I hold tight to the dashboard.

"What are you talking about? Sadie, did you get kicked out of Heaven?"

"No. You can't get kicked out of a place you've never been."

I stare at her sideways.

"I got kicked off my *flight*," she elaborates.

"What? Why?"

"So 'apparently,'" she says, briefly taking her hands off the steering wheel and making air quotes, "'I.' 'Didn't.' 'Follow.' 'Protocol.'"

"And how is that my fault?"

"I'm not allowed to fly into Heaven until my successor has officially helped three souls move along in an efficient manner. You know, to prove that I've successfully trained you."

"I know. I did that."

"No! You didn't! Apparently, the first person didn't count because we moved her along together. She only counted for my quota, not yours."

"Wait, the pumpkin patch lady who killed a guy?"

"Todd conveniently forgot to inform me of this until I was all ready to board my flight and got turned away at the last second. Then got *detained* by the Disciplinary Council for allegedly trying to cheat the system."

"So this is Todd's fault! Not mine!"

Sadie blinks and ignores me.

"So now," she continues, "this a-hole back here is your *actual* third assignment."

"You know I can hear everything you're saying," Caleb pipes up from the back.

"Good!" Sadie growls. "Sorry. I'm sorry. This isn't your fault. It's just . . . they already cleaned my room out. They got rid of my treasures. They got rid of my *glitter*."

She hits the brake. Hard. We're back at the airport entrance.

"You've been working on his case for too long," she says, her face serious as she turns to me as Caleb walks away. "Something is up."

"It's only been a few days," I say.

"Yeah, but you were moving people along like rapid fire until you got to him."

"He's a complex case," I mumble, then purse my lips and look away toward the airport. "You said yourself that some people can take the whole thirty sessions to figure out what's holding them back."

"If you can't get him to move on soon, I'll get Todd to add five hundred more souls to your queue."

"What? Since when does Todd get to play God? This is his fault in the first place. That's so un—"

"Unfair? You've been stuck here for about a second. Do you know what's unfair, Beatrice? I have been dreaming of my Jacuzzi-filled mansion in the sky for decades now and I'm not going to let anything, or anyone, come between me and it ever again."

"Wha—"

"In the meantime," she silences me, "I'll be chaperoning your sessions with Caleb from tomorrow onward. To make sure I really have sufficiently trained you. And if things aren't going well, I'll have to step in and help until you're finally able to move another person along on your own."

"Chaperoning? You're not my dad!"

"You forget, Bea. I may look young, but I am very, *very* old! And, like, really wise."

I CAN'T SLEEP. I'm tossing and turning under the bed-spread that likely hasn't been washed in my lifetime. It's too hot when I lie under it, but too cold when I lie on top. All I can think about is Sadie catching on to my plan to punish Caleb for what he did to me. Well, that's not the only thing I can think about. Visions of Caleb watching his worst memories, looking sick and sad, dance behind my eyelids as I try to drift off.

Since when have I ever cared about someone's feelings so much? Let alone a someone who murdered me. And why do I keep having to remind myself of that fact every five minutes?

I need someone to talk to who won't judge me as harshly as I judge myself. I need a distraction.

"Jenna," I say aloud, a little louder than a whisper.

"Yeah?" she answers immediately.

"Are you awake?"

"Yep."

I roll over on my left side to look at her. I can see in the glow of the floodlight outside our window that she's lying flat on her back, staring at the ceiling, not one bit asleep.

"What are you thinking about?" I ask.

"My family," she says.

"What do you think they're doing right now?"

"Sleeping, I guess? I don't know if there's a time difference between here and Minnesota. I know this is really crazy, but I was thinking about my family *going to my funeral.*"

"That's not crazy," I say, realizing I haven't given much thought to my own. I hope that even if my sister hates me, she still made sure they didn't give my corpse awful funeral home makeup. I hope I was buried with a dignified smoky eye, but I know it's more likely I was laid to rest looking like an overgrown star of *Toddlers & Tiaras.*

"It was probably such a mess," Jenna elaborates. "I imagine my relatives brought a bunch of casseroles. All I can think about is everyone stuffing themselves with cheesy hash browns while my parents weep in the corner. But at the same time it's, like, what I wouldn't give to be eating some hot, delicious casserole right now, even if it meant I was at a funeral. My own funeral even."

I sit up in bed and turn to look at her.

"I know it's really awful to say," she continues, "but what if me dying was actually kind of a relief for my family? They'll save so much money not having to pay more hospital bills. My little sisters will probably get way more attention now as opposed to the zero attention they were getting before because I was sucking it all up. . . ."

She cringes and a tear falls down her cheek. It makes me uncomfortable to look at. I'm not exactly the most nurturing, but I take a deep breath and suck it up.

"Hey," I say, getting out of bed and moving on top of her covers. "It's okay."

I even manage to lightly touch her shoulder in a gesture of warmth. In turn, Jenna grabs on to both of my shoulders and sobs. Her snot falls onto my pajamas that are, thankfully, and mysteriously, collected and replaced once a week, like my uniforms.

"I'm sure your family misses you so, so much," I say awkwardly.

"I just want to know that they're okay," she says between sniffles. "I'm sick of waiting here. I want to move on to Heaven already so that I can look down on them and see that they're happy and even if they're not happy, that they're just . . . existing."

"I know how you feel," I admit.

"Really?" she asks. "Is there anyone you wish you could check in on?"

"My sister," I say without even thinking.

"I didn't even know you had a sister," Jenna says, her face brightening.

"Yeah. We were really close."

"I'm sure she misses you a lot."

"I don't know about that."

She frowns at me.

"We had this really big fight before my accident," I say. "It was the last time I ever saw her. I just never thought things would turn out like this. I always felt like what I had with my sister was the one good thing in my life. Like it kept me from ever truly spinning out of control and . . ."

Jenna stares at me patiently. I start to feel a lump forming in my throat.

This isn't me. I don't have heart-to-hearts. How do I expect Jenna to understand? She doesn't even really know me.

"I just wish things had gone differently," I say finally.

"You know, Bea," Jenna says. "Everything happens for a reason."

"How can you believe that?" I ask, sitting up and shrugging her off me. "You think you and I both died for a *reason*? That's just what people print on novelty coffee cups that they can sip out of while pretending to feel okay that their lives have turned out completely horrible."

"I don't know," Jenna says, her forehead puckering. "I believe it because it gives me some kind of peace. It keeps me from getting . . . mad."

"It's okay to let yourself be mad sometimes, Jenna," I say, slumping down against her pillows.

"Yeah, but if I do that, what if I never stop being mad? What if I just snowball into this big, angry monster? I don't want to lose who I really am just because something awful happened to me."

"You won't," I tell her. "Letting yourself feel angry doesn't make you an angry person. It just makes you a person who's honest with herself."

"Wow," Jenna says, smiling sadly. "Thanks. That's a really beautiful way to put it. They should be printing that on coffee cups instead."

She curls into my side and closes her eyes.

"Jenna," I say.

"Yeah?"

"While I recognize that we've both made ourselves vulnerable here tonight, we are definitely not at the stage where we can comfortably share a bed."

28

Of course Sadie has arrived at the departures counter before me. Knowing that Caleb moving on is the one thing separating her from Heaven, she's probably been camped out here all night in anticipation of today's session.

"I just wanted to apologize for my behavior yesterday," Sadie says cheerily after greeting me. "I behaved slightly unprofessionally in front of you and your assignment. And as agents, it is our duty to behave in a professional manner at all times."

She lowers her head toward me conspiratorially.

"Do you understand that? A professional manner, Beatrice," she repeats in a hushed tone.

"Yes?" I say, weaving my eyebrows together. "I don't know what you're getting at."

"Todd has made an observation, not an accusation, of course, that you and Caleb have been spending extra time together."

"Um, yeah," I scoff. "Extra time together *working*. To crack this case. Todd gave me the keys for an extra session because he told me himself that management is on him to move more people along. I don't know what you're implying, Sadie."

"You've checked Caleb's passport, right?" she asks, narrowing her eyes.

My stomach drops. I swallow hard. Has she seen it?

"Duh," I manage to spit out. "That's the first thing any agent should do. That's what you taught me."

"So you're familiar with the way that he died? Sometimes I find in cases where the person died in an unexpected or violent way, they have trouble conjuring up the memory of their death. It's repressed trauma. Who wants to think about that? Yikes. And, well, when they die in a violent or unexpected way, that's often the unresolved thing that's holding them back. So my point is . . . have you asked Caleb to remember the day that he died yet?"

"No," I say through gritted teeth.

"What? No wonder he's not moving. That's what we should start with today. Sound good?"

"I don't know," I say. "We were making such good progress yesterday. I think I should just pick up where we left off."

Sadie studies my face for a moment.

"Fine," she says. "But if it's not working, we go with my plan. Got it?"

I nod once.

"Let's make today a great one!" she says, suddenly smiling and raising her shoulders.

The clock above the counter strikes eight. Sadie crosses her arms anxiously. At 8:02, Caleb walks up to the counter.

"Hey, guys." He waves.

"Hi, Caleb! You're late," Sadie says, then turns to walk and motions us to follow her outside.

"How are you this morning, Bea?" Caleb asks me as we walk to the golf cart.

"Fine," I say, without looking at him.

We all get inside the golf cart and Sadie drives. There's no small talk.

"Take a seat," I instruct Caleb unnecessarily once we're inside the hangar, Sadie observing my every move.

As I lower the helmet onto his head, he gives me a confused look. Of course he knows he should take a seat. We've been doing this for a while now.

"So what is it I should remember today? The day my beloved pet fish died or what?" Caleb jokes as Sadie and I settle into our own helmets.

"Caleb," I say, all business. "Let's pick up where we left off yesterday."

"Sure," he says.

"I asked you if you got into Harvard," I remind him, switching on the Memstractor.

"And the short answer to that question is no," he says darkly. "I did not get in."

Immediately we're inside of Caleb's bedroom. I'm taken aback by how orderly and cozy it is. There's a plaid throw blanket folded at the edge of the neatly made bed and a tall bookshelf filled with hundreds of books in alphabetical order. I mean, there's even a potted plant in the corner that's positively thriving. The room looks like it belongs to someone in his forties, not to a seventeen-year-old boy.

Past Caleb sits at his desk, doing his homework. He's wearing the same outfit of basketball shorts and a T-shirt that he's wearing right now. His phone lights up with a text.

Sadie and I both lean over his shoulder to read it.

I note that the time display on his phone is 3:59 p.m. and the date is December 12, 2019.

The day that we both died.

Five and a half hours before the crash.

"Stop!" I say to Present Caleb.

"Is there a problem, Bea?" Sadie asks.

"I just want to see what his texts say. For clarity and insight," I elaborate, looking at Sadie.

"Great technique," she says.

Hi, Sweetie ☺ the text on his phone reads. It's from his mom. *Did you make it to Scrabble club?*

Nah, it got canceled this week. Didn't Abuela tell you? They have to set up the rec room for tonight's holiday party!

Oh wow, did you get an invite? Maybe you can meet a girlfriend! LOL

Thx mom smh

I let a laugh slip from my mouth. Caleb gives me a half smile and rolls his eyes.

"Ahem!" Sadie says. "Focus, please."

"Right, so . . ." he says. "That afternoon, after I got a text from my mom, is when things . . . went downhill . . ."

Now Caleb checks his email. The only new one has the subject line: "From the Harvard University Admissions."

He stares at it for a moment, then finally clicks on it. I only take in the words *Dear Mr. Smith, The Committee on*

Admissions has completed its Early Decision meetings and regrets to inform you before he slams his laptop shut. He stands, looking surprisingly calm, then proceeds to lie down on his bed and scream into his pillow.

Next to me, Present Caleb rubs his eyes, like he's trying to block out what he's seeing.

Past Caleb's phone buzzes on his desk. He ignores it, screaming even harder into the pillow. It vibrates a few more times in a row. Finally he picks it up. A few texts flash on the screen. All from the same contact. Laura.

ASHSJDLHGMNKFG NFSD I GOT IN WTF

Did you get in?

I'm assuming ur smart ass did

Sorry for this random text, I know it's been a min

Ur probs already celebrating, but i'm gonna have some ppl over later if u want to join ☺

Caleb????

He throws the phone onto the floor and lies down prostrate on his bed.

Now Caleb's memory moves as if it's being controlled with a fast-forward button. Outside his window, daylight turns to nighttime. He finally gets up.

Seconds later he's in the kitchen, taking a pint of cookie dough ice cream out of the freezer and then eating it straight from the carton.

After plowing through three fourths of the ice cream pint, Caleb decides he needs something stronger. That's when he makes his way to the fancy mahogany liquor cabinet he'd briefly remembered a few days ago.

My heart pounds as I watch the start of his stupid decision that ended both of our lives. The desire to laugh at him is completely absorbed by my rage.

Caleb takes out the fancy bottle of whiskey, then brings it back to the kitchen and pours a shot into a juice glass. He looks at it for another second, then fills it halfway. Based on the amount of hemming and hawing and staring at the glass, I wonder if this was his first alcoholic drink ever. Finally he brings it to his lips and swallows it in several long gulps. When he's finished, he gasps and clutches the countertop for strength. He picks up his phone again.

I walk over to where he's paused at the counter and look over his shoulder.

What time? he texts back to Laura.

8!!! she responds immediately.

See ya then 😊

He never actually answers her question of whether or not he got into Harvard.

Past Caleb puts his phone down again and pours another ridiculous shot of whiskey. Present Caleb cringes and I want to also, but I don't because I know that's not the professional thing to do with Sadie so close to me.

"It's stupid, right? That this was the worst thing to ever happen to me," Caleb scoffs, his face full of shame. "But I just freaked out."

I know how this ends, of course.

I die all because some brat is pissed off that he didn't get into his precious Ivy League university, so he decides to get drunk and go finally make a move on a girl he was too much of a baby to actually talk to sober.

Pathetic.

But if Laura goes to his school, then why was he driving all the way over in my town, at least a half hour outside of theirs?

Caleb picks up the second glass of whiskey and brings it to his lips, but before he can take a drink, he drops it, alcohol spilling across the granite. He clutches the countertop, gags, and hurls his body over to the fancy porcelain farmhouse sink where he vomits all over it, brown liquid and chunks of barely digested cookie dough flying everywhere. This time I can't conceal my cringe. I look over at Sadie. Her face is calm, bored even.

Past Caleb leans against the sink for a moment, then drinks cold water straight from the faucet. Finally he drags his body back to his bed and the memory fades out as he drifts off to sleep.

I'm . . . confused.

"What happened next?" I ask. "That's not how you died, right?"

"No," Caleb says. "Even though it looks like it, one pint of Ben & Jerry's and a shot of whiskey did not kill me."

A memory appears again. Now Past Caleb wakes to the noise of his phone ringing, but he fumbles around and can't find it. The ringing stops, and finally he unearths the phone from under his pillow.

Missed Call, Laura (1)

Laura: U cummin or what?

Laura: *coming sorry smh

Dad: Your cousin Sarah got her Harvard acceptance! Have you heard anything today?

Missed Call, Mom (3)

Mom: Caleb please call me. Abuela slipped and fell at the holiday party and had to be rushed to the ER.

Missed Call, Mom (1)

Caleb looks at the time. It's now 8:46 p.m.

"Shit," he mumbles to himself. "Shit, shit, shit!"

He shuffles out to the garage, pausing to put on his slides, not even grabbing a jacket even though it's the middle of December, and dials a number on his phone.

"Mom? Mom, I'm so, so sorry!" he says. "I got caught up with some homework and lost track of time. I'll be right over. Which hospital?"

He hops into his silver SUV and zooms out of the garage, down the driveway, and nearly hits his mailbox.

Present Caleb looks like he's about to claw his own face off.

"So you weren't . . . drunk?" I ask coolly.

He only drank a shot. And he threw up most of it. And then he fell asleep for a solid couple of hours. I'm not exactly sure how blood-alcohol stuff works, but I can guess the answer.

"No," he says quietly. "I was never drunk."

I was wrong about him.

Caleb didn't kill me because he was being an idiot drunk driver.

He's not the villain I thought he was.

But still he killed me, right? He's the reason I'm here. I mean, maybe he wasn't drunk, but why was he was driving on the wrong side of the road?

As if *my* head is the one conjuring memories, suddenly we're all in the back seat of Caleb's car as he's driving down the road where the accident happened. It flickers in and out.

"Caleb?" Sadie pipes up. "We need you to focus."

"I don't know," Caleb mumbles, clutching the car door. "I can't seem to remember exactly how—"

But before I realize what I'm even doing, I reach out and turn off the machine.

29

"Bea!" I hear Caleb call out to me once I'm way past the golf cart and nearly halfway back to the airport entrance.

I'm panting hard, the adrenaline of desperately needing to flee wearing off. Finally I force my body to stop and lean over with my hands on my knees. I've always prided myself on my steadfast refusal to participate in gym class, but in this moment I'm wishing I died just slightly more in shape. I don't feel any of the runner's high I felt the other night. I feel like I'm going to barf.

Caleb jogs up to me like it's nothing and puts his hand on the small of my back.

"You all right?"

I look up at him. His hair blows just slightly in the wind and his eyes are basically boring into my soul. It's too late to tell him the truth about who I am. If he finds out my secret, will he ever forgive me for holding him back from moving on?

I don't know how I should act toward him anymore, so I turn to my default mode for any situation in which my feelings confuse me: being a bitch.

"Yeah. I'm fine," I say as if it's the most obvious thing in the world, even though I'm still panting and sweat is dripping down my face. Wet, splotchy marks are beginning to form under my arms thanks to my grossly non-breathable polyester dress.

"That was horrible, what you had to watch back there. Sorry you had to see that. Definitely not my best. Definitely, like, my worst. Ever."

"It's whatever. A lot of people make bad decisions in their memories. I mean, not getting into Harvard? You *really* suffered. It's too bad that you only had one defining goal in life."

I stand up straight and tuck my hair behind my ears.

"You know," I continue, "maybe if you devoted all the time you spent studying for the SAT on cultivating an actual personality, you wouldn't be here."

Caleb looks like I've gagged him with a handful of sour candy.

"You're just another soul in my queue, Caleb. One of five thousand strangers I'm stuck dealing with."

"But I thought we were—"

"What? You thought we were *friends*?" I say mockingly as I cross my arms.

"Yes! I opened up to you. I showed you things I've never told anyone about before!"

"Yeah, because it's my job to get you to open up to me," I scoff. "I don't know what you expected."

He twists his mouth and looks like he's going to cry. But before a single tear can fall down his face, he sprints away, faster than I could ever manage to keep up with.

"What's going on?" Sadie calls, speeding up to me in the golf cart.

"I just needed some fresh air."

"In the middle of our session? Bea, do you not understand how important this is to me? This is the only thing holding me back. I'm so close, Bea. I'm so close to moving on."

Her eyes begin to water and she looks up and around the tarmac.

"I can't wait to get out of here," she continues, then pauses. "When I was getting ready to board that plane, it was like I was so close, I could taste it. My house in Heaven. I could *taste* my house. It tasted like shrimp cocktails and piña coladas. Every room has a different pastel-colored wall-to-wall carpet. And a Jacuzzi. Did I already mention that? And columns on the outside. And, oh my god, I even have my own phone line directly to my room."

I want to brush off this fantasy as stupid, but I get it. I miss my sister most of all, but I miss my phone too. And Internet access. And I miss changing clothes and putting on a fresh face of makeup every day. And I miss my mortality. I miss a lot of things.

I miss being normal.

I miss not constantly feeling the weight of the truth on my shoulders.

"That sounds really nice, Sadie," I admit, my voice catching in my throat.

"I really believe it will all be there waiting for me, Bea. I really do. But to finally get there, I just need you to push this one boy through. Just one boy! He's basically nobody."

"Yep," I say, gritting my teeth. "Basically nobody."

30

"**Ughhhhhhhh,**" **I groan** aloud when I return to my room and flop horizontally across my bed. I think I'm all alone, and then I hear the sound of the bathroom sink running. Jenna emerges in my peripheral.

"Rough day?" she asks.

"I've messed everything up," I say into the bedspread.

I feel Jenna sit down next to me and rub my back gently. The mattress slumps far too low to the ground under the weight of approximately one and a half teenage girls.

"I'm sure you didn't mess everything up," Jenna coos.

"No, like, I really, really did."

"What happened?

I turn my head so only my right cheek is pressed against the bed.

"You know how I said Caleb and I have a history together? It wasn't just because he tried to bribe me that first day I met him. I knew him before. Sort of."

"I'm not really following," Jenna admits gently.

"Caleb is the person who crashed into my car," I say quickly. "He's the reason I died."

Her eyes widen. "No! How do you know?"

I tell her about the passports. How I wanted to punish him. How getting assigned to him was the perfect revenge.

"But now that I've seen things from his point of view, I don't know if he deserves to suffer. Which is crazy because I usually think that when someone kills another person with their car, they deserve to suffer! Right? *Right?*"

By the time I'm done talking, I realize I'm half screaming, half hyperventilating. Jenna brings her sweat suit sleeve to her mouth and lightly rubs it against her top lip in contemplation.

"He doesn't deserve to suffer if it was an honest mistake," she says. "I mean, not more than the suffering he's probably already going through knowing that he's killed someone. If he's not a sociopath, then he's probably beating himself up inside over it. And he's probably not a sociopath, because he wasn't sent to Hell."

I roll over and sit up to face Jenna.

How is she suddenly so *logical*?

"The thing is, I don't think he even knows he killed a person. So he definitely doesn't know that I'm the person he killed. He was too hurt himself to find out what happened, which makes me think that that must be what's holding him back from moving on. But when we go through his memories, I always find a way to stop him before he can think about the crash itself. I . . . I have to figure out a way to get him to move on to Heaven without exposing the truth I've been withholding from him."

But why is there part of me that doesn't want that to happen? It's the part of me that just likes . . . being near him.

"No," Jenna says firmly. "You have to come clean. It would be unfair of you to keep Caleb here for any longer."

"But I—"

She puts her hand up for me to stop speaking.

"You can't play God, Bea. It's not your choice whether or not he's able to move on to Heaven. That's up to Caleb to figure out. To take that away from him is the worst thing you can do to someone."

"Is it really?" I press. "Is it worse than murder?"

Jenna looks at me impatiently.

"You know I'm trying to make the best of being here, Bea, but I'd do anything to move on and know how my family is doing. If someone tried to sabotage that for me, I don't even know what I would do. You have to tell him that you know."

"But that means I have to admit I was wrong," I say, weeping. "I hate admitting that I'm wrong."

"So? You need to get over it and be the bigger person."

"I hate that phrase, Jenna. I feel like I've never heard anyone say it outside of reality TV."

"Okay, okay! Maybe it's not being 'the bigger person.' Maybe it's just doing the decent thing."

I turn over on the bed again and make another loud whining noise. Jenna yanks me up by my shoulders.

"You need to go find him and tell him the truth," she says, staring into my eyes. "Now. Or, in a few minutes, when you're done blowing snot bubbles."

I know she's right. And that just makes me cry even more.

— ✈ —

FINDING CALEB IS harder than I thought it would be.

I don't know his room number, so I pace up and down all the terminals, poking my head in every store and every waiting area. I even linger in the food court, sitting near the Home Cooking counter, watching people pile their plates with whatever mess du jour is on the menu, anxiously hoping that he'll be one of them. But dinner comes and goes and he never appears.

In a last-ditch effort, I loop around the terminals once more. It's quiet, save for the sound of someone vacuuming in the distance. I pause in front of the only place I hadn't stopped to look: the bar with the neon IT'S FIVE O'CLOCK ANYWHERE! sign. I go inside.

There's something kind of nice about it. Red light bulbs give off a warm glow on the multicolored bottles lining the bar. A bossa nova version of "Hey, Soul Sister" plays from the speakers, which is definitely the most tolerable of all the cover styles. Even the shiny orange booths and stools look inviting. If I were on Earth, or the mortal realm or wherever I'm not right now, I could imagine hip, annoying adults in their twenties hanging out here.

I've never actually been inside a bar, at least one that's not just a fixture inside of a chain restaurant. I wonder if the bartender will ask to check my passport, and, if they do, will they count my age from the day of my birth to the day that I died? Or at some point, will I be technically twenty-one here and allowed to drink? Is there even a drinking age here?

I look around for Caleb, but the place is nearly empty. There's a booth of old ladies laughing together. A few men sitting alone. Defeated, I take a seat at the bar.

"What can I get for you?" a middle-aged woman with an updo and a Southern accent asks me from behind the counter.

My brain blanks. I try to think of a cocktail. Any cocktail.

"Martini. Dry, please," I say, feeling like I'm doing an impression of a movie character instead of acting like I order this all the time.

"I'm sorry, ma'am. We don't serve alcohol here," the bartender explains.

"But you're a bar!"

"It's airport policy that no alcohol is served on the premises."

"To anyone?"

"Anyone," she says, shaking her head emphatically.

"So what can you serve me?"

"Well, I can pour some ice water in a martini glass and throw an olive in it for you."

I squint at her.

"It's actually quite a popular drink around here," she insists.

"I'll just have a Shirley Temple," I say.

While I sit and watch her prepare the drink, I feel a tap on my shoulder.

"Caleb," I gasp, turning to see him standing behind me. He looks sweaty, but under the reddish lights, he kind of . . . glistens. "Have you been running?" I ask, stupidly.

"Yeah. I had to clear my head, think some things over. But then I was running because I was looking all over for you."

"For me?"

"I need to apologize to you, Bea."

"To *me*?"

The bartender slides me my Shirley Temple.

"Anything for the handsome gentleman?" she asks, turning to Caleb.

"No, thank you," he says, even though he's panting and clearly thirsty.

"You sure?" the bartender presses.

"That's okay."

"All right." The bartender shrugs, then leans up against the bar, staring at us.

I give her a look.

"What?" she says defensively. "There's nothing else going on. Thought I might watch y'all's lovers' quarrel."

"This is not—" I begin to say to her.

"I'll have the most complicated drink on the menu," Caleb interrupts, turning to her with a smile.

The woman walks away with a grunt.

"Look, Bea," he continues. "I realize why you were so cold to me earlier, but not in your usual way. I could tell you were upset."

I raise my eyebrows.

"What do you mean my *usual way*?"

"Maybe 'cold' is the wrong way to put it. You're honest. You call things like you see them and don't put up with any bullshit. I . . . admire that about you. Looking at all my memories, I wish I'd been more like that."

He pauses and takes a deep breath.

"Watching the final hours of my life today was rough. I'm sorry you had to see me like that. I could tell it upset you."

"You don't have to apolo—"

"No, Bea. I do. Look, I want to make it up to you. I was

thinking we should go back to the hangar. I want to show you something."

This has to be a cruel joke, right? He probably remembered the accident. He figured out my plan. Now he wants me to watch myself die as punishment.

But I know it's not.

Because now I know Caleb.

And I know he would never do that.

"We can keep going over your memories in the morning. Right now I need to say—"

"It's not a memory that I want to show you," he interrupts. "Not exactly. It's a dream."

WHEN WE GET to the departures counter, we find that it's closed for the night.

"Of course," Caleb says, running a hand through his hair. "Sorry. I got carried away and didn't think of the time."

The look of disappointment on his face gets to me. He's had to relive so much sadness and pain today, he doesn't deserve this obstacle to whatever his plan is, on top of everything else.

"Hold on," I say, eyeing the empty counter.

Todd keeps the keys to the golf carts and the hangars locked in a safe underneath it. I look around the waiting room. It's deserted, save for a few people staring blankly ahead, lost in their thoughts, and a man snoozing, his whole body spread across three seats. I walk behind the counter and kneel down once I get to the safe. It has a keypad covered in letters, not numbers.

It's *password* protected.

I close my eyes and try to remember the last staff room password Todd shared with the team. At the time, I thought it was a little lazy on his part . . . that he was probably too bummed by Sadie's departure to think of anything as over-the-top as he usually goes for. . . . It was so obvious. . . .

Frantically, I begin typing, my chest pounding and my arms vibrating:

T-o-d-d-i-s-r-e-a-l-l-y-g-o-o-d-a-t-m-a-k-i-n-g-u-p-p-a-s-s-w-o-r-d-s

I swallow hard and pull at the safe.

It gives.

I grab a pair of keys and lift my hand up in triumph.

"Quick, Caleb," I say, jumping up. "Let's go!"

— ✈ —

"CLOSE YOUR EYES," Caleb says as we sit down at the Memstractor. "Then turn on the machine."

Normally, I'd remind him that I'm the boss in this situation, but I do as he says.

"Okay," he breathes. "Open."

Fluorescent light beams down into my eyes. Soft rock music fills my ears. I look around and see endless shelves, stocked neatly with boxes of all different colors.

"A supermarket?" I ask, a slow smile spreading across my face. "This is your dream?"

"Remember when you were describing how browsing the supermarket the hour before it closes is your favorite thing to do?" Caleb says, walking down the aisle full of boxes of cereal. "And you asked me if it made you sound crazy? And I said no?"

"Of course I do."

"That's because I've had this recurring dream for years that I'm stuck inside a grocery store after hours and I'm the only one shopping. Whenever I tried to describe this to anyone—my friends, my parents—they all looked at me like something was seriously wrong. They thought it sounded like a nightmare."

We come to the back of the grocery store, where all the cuts of meat are wrapped up in shiny plastic, and turn to the next aisle, full of frozen food.

"But the thing is? I love it. It's my favorite dream."

I stop in my tracks.

"Whenever I'm feeling anxious, I just visualize myself roaming around an empty supermarket, and it calms me down. I don't mean to sound like some kind of quack," Caleb continues, "but I think it means something. That we have this in common."

"Like what?" I ask.

"I don't know exactly, but I think there's a reason we both ended up here at the same time."

He peers into my eyes. I look away and stare at my own reflection in the shiny glass doors protecting all the ice cream and frozen waffles.

There *is* one reason.

"Anyway," Caleb says. "Sorry if this is weird. Or disappointing. I just thought it would be . . ."

"It's nice," I say, turning around. I notice a box of Hot Pockets in the freezer behind him and smile to myself. "It feels like home."

Over the store radio, some synth-pop song that sounds like it could be on the soundtrack to a John Hughes movie starts to pick up tempo. Caleb looks toward the ceiling and raises his eyebrows.

"Do you want to dance?" he asks me.

"Um," I say, peering around. "I don't dance."

"We're the only ones here, Bea."

"I don't dance," I repeat.

"What? Are you worried about looking stupid?" he asks, beginning to sway his body from side to side. "Because as the only other person here, I can assure you . . ."

He stiffly waves his arms back and forth.

"You will not be the most stupid-looking dancer present."

I give him a hard stare and breathe out of my nose. Then I begin swaying from side to side just the tiniest bit, without moving my arms.

"See!" Caleb says, a smug grin on his face. "I knew you could dance."

"You think you know everything," I say with an eye roll, moving my hips a little more.

"I don't know *everything*." He takes a step closer to me. "There's still so much I don't know about you."

"Oh yeah? Well, what *do* you know?"

Caleb draws his bottom lip between his teeth and thinks it over for a second.

"Here's all that I know about you, Beatrice Fox," he says, looking up and peering into my eyes.

"Your favorite color is holographic lavender, which apparently exists. You have a sister. Your favorite food is salt-and-vinegar potato chips. You went to Bible camp once, but retained absolutely nothing you learned there. You hate infinity symbols, or really, I'm guessing, anything vaguely sentimental in nature. So you'll probably be super annoyed when I tell you that, um . . ."

He slows his dancing and takes a deep breath.

"That I think you're really beautiful."

Slowly, he leans forward.

My heart pounds in my chest.

Our lips are about to touch when his body becomes pixelated against mine.

Because this isn't real.

It's just an illusion.

31

After staring down at her phone for what felt like the longest minute of my life, Emmy slammed the bathroom stall door in my face.

"Em, please!" I cried out. "I can explain. I swear."

I heard her take several deep breaths, then step from the toilet to the door. She unlocked it and opened it halfway just to glare at me.

"I think I know who sent the pic," I said. "It was Taylor Fields."

Emmy squinted and cocked her head to the side.

"How would she have even gotten that picture? Or taken it?"

"I think sometimes she protests or something outside . . ." I glanced up, noticing another girl enter the bathroom. ". . . the place . . . you went to. For religious reasons or whatever," I finished, rolling my eyes.

"She probably recognized you and took your picture, but then didn't do anything with it because she had no reason to, until now," I said, shaking my head. "What an evil bitch."

"I don't understand. Why would Taylor Fields want to expose me like that?" Emmy said, finally letting me inside the stall. "I don't even know her."

She sat down on the toilet seat and put her hands near her temples.

"You don't know her, but I do. And she hates me and wanted to get back at me for something I did to her."

"What did you do?" Emmy asked.

I looked around the walls of the bathroom stall for a moment, searching as if somewhere among all the illicit graffiti and hearts around couples' names there would be a better answer than the one I was about to deliver.

"We got into an argument today that involved me insulting her by saying she can't even hold down a job at Chili's. But, also, I am sort of the reason she got fired from her job at Chili's," I mumbled. The words felt so deeply and profoundly stupid as they fell out of my mouth.

Emmy looked up at me and her whole body froze.

"Why?" she asked.

"Because Taylor had some really insensitive views on birth control in health class."

"What do you mean?"

"They were just, like, totally ignorant and harmful."

Emmy started to speak and stopped several times, like her body was malfunctioning.

"So . . . you got her fired from Chili's for . . . being pro-life?" she finally sputtered.

"No. I mean, that was my intention, but it's not really a fireable offense, so, um, I tried to see if she said anything similarly ignorant, but fireable, like, you know, racist or something. But she didn't, so ultimately . . . I got her fired from Chili's because she tweeted about hating Chili's. Like, several times. I mean, I was really doing them a big favor."

Emmy's face became more and more clouded with sadness with each part of my pathetic explanation.

"You don't actually care about changing the things you get so upset at people about," she said finally.

"What do you mean?"

"Inequality, all the school rules you call 'fascist,' racism, sexism . . . all of it. You don't actually *do* anything to stop these things or help anyone they affect. You just love getting mad at people you see as morally inferior to you and ruining their lives to prove a point, but I don't know what your point is."

"I mean . . . that's . . . not . . ."

My stomach dropped. I couldn't be that superficial. Or so I thought.

"Maybe it's that you think you're smarter than everyone *and* that you can outsmart everyone? You think no one can ever get back at you, but there's collateral damage now, Bea. Skyler knows my secret and I'm going to have to clean up the mess and explain myself. You took my chance to tell him one day on my own terms."

"Well, technically, *Taylor* took your chance. Regardless, Emmy, you shouldn't be ashamed of—"

"There's no way Skyler will want to still be with me after this. I made one stupid mistake and I figured everyone makes stupid mistakes, but now this one will haunt me forever. All of the plans Skyler and I had . . . our future together . . . It's just over. My life is *over* and it's all your fault, Bea! But you'll never just apologize, will you?"

"What do you mean your 'future together'?" I asked, squinting.

"We were going to go to college together and then get married and maybe even grow up to have a wonderful, *normal* family!"

"You guys are only sixteen. It's fine. You were probably going to break up at some point anyway. Your life is most certainly not 'over.' You can't blame me for what happened. Skyler would've probably found out eventually. You know, good relationships shouldn't be built on lies. Or so I've heard."

Emmy shook her head at me.

"I'm hurting right now and you can't even apologize. All you can do is blame everything on everyone else."

She twisted her mouth up like she had more to say but was trying desperately to keep it in.

"You know, Bea, you're a heartless bitch," she gasped at last.

"What?"

Her words didn't sound so much like an attack, but a realization. These were the kind of laughable insults that would usually roll right off my back, but coming from Emmy, they made me feel like someone had pulled out the ground beneath me. She was never one to curse or say anything bad about anyone, so when she did, I knew she meant it. And she had every right to mean it.

"You don't understand what it's like to love someone," she said. "You've built too many walls around yourself and you never let anyone in."

"That's not true," I mumbled, the first inklings of tears forming in the corners of my eyes. The first tears I'd cried in what must have been years.

"All you do is focus on yourself and being better than everyone else all the time," she continued, her voice cracking. "But one day you're going to be alone. I'm not going to be around to be your only friend just because I'm your sister."

"That's not true," I repeated. "We're not just friends because you're my sister. We're friends because we love each oth—"

"I wish that one day were right now. If we didn't have to live in the same house and share a stupid bunk bed, I would never see you again."

32

—

I reach my hand out and turn off the machine, bringing Caleb and me back to reality.

We're not dancing in his dream, about to kiss.

We're sitting two feet apart in an ugly, empty airplane hangar.

Caleb's face is completely red, then in an instant loses all color.

"I should . . . go," he mumbles, pushing his helmet off and limply waving a hand goodbye without making eye contact with me.

I don't even bother asking him if he wants a ride back to the airport.

I sit in the hangar for a few more minutes, replaying what just happened over and over in my head.

Here's the thing: I'm smiling.

I'm giggling alone like someone who's lost control of themselves.

Honestly, I think I have.

Kissing Caleb—well, almost kissing Caleb—felt *nice*. And *fun*. Two simple things I haven't felt in what seems like forever.

I want to run back to my room to wake Jenna and tell her all about it. But even though opening up to her is all she's ever wanted from me, I know she'll also remind me that I actually failed in my mission to come clean. That I've only made a bigger mess out of things by almost kissing Caleb instead of apologizing to him.

I slump against the Memstractor and put my head in my hands. My high from the night wears off immediately. I collect my train case, lock up the hangar, and drive back toward the airport.

When I get inside, the waiting room is empty except for three people standing in a group in front of the departures counter.

Todd.

A tall Asian guy in a suit who I've never seen before.

And Caleb.

His back is to me, but the guy in the suit looks up. We lock eyes, and Todd and Caleb turn their heads.

"Beatrice!" Todd calls, cupping his hands around his mouth as if I wouldn't be able to hear him from this distance. "Come over here for a minute."

"What's going on?" I ask, locking eyes with Caleb. He scratches the back of his neck and gives me a sheepish look.

"This is Wayne," Todd says.

"A pleasure to meet you," the man says, giving me intense, direct eye contact. Everything from his outfit to his complexion to his haircut is almost unsettlingly flawless.

"Uh . . ." Todd begins, sliding his hands into the pockets of his orange vest. "Wayne is a member of the Disciplinary Council and, technically, my boss."

"Cool," I say, my face betraying nothing, even though this revelation makes the hairs on my arms stand up.

"Yes," Wayne says with a crooked smile. "Very cool indeed. We were just talking to Caleb here. You two know each other? Is that correct?"

"Sure," I say without looking at him. "He's my assignment right now."

"Well, it seems he's gone rogue," Wayne says with a humorless laugh. "See, when someone opens the doors leading onto the tarmac after the departures counter has closed for the day, an alarm sounds up in the control tower. So I came down here to check with Todd and see what was going on and then we ran into him."

"I tried to sneak out," Caleb says, looking at me. "I'm sorry for going behind your back, Bea. I just wanted to get a look at my memories . . . alone."

"Which is a punishable offense," Wayne interjects.

"Yeah!" Todd chirps. "No one is allowed outside without the assistance of an agent."

I stare between him and Wayne. If I thought Todd was a joke of a boss before, he looks even more so now, with his rumpled uniform and grease-covered glasses.

"We're going to have to take you before the council, Caleb," Wayne says. "Beatrice, you will be reassigned a new soul tomorrow morning."

Caleb stares at the ground while Wayne places his perfect, veinless hand on his back, forcing him away.

A week ago I couldn't have imagined a better outcome.

But now?

"Wait!" I cry out. "He didn't do anything."

Wayne pauses and turns to look at me.

"It was my idea. I forced him to come out into the hangar with me. I wanted us to make some extra progress so he could move on as soon as possible and I could get to my next soul."

He considers this.

"But he turned around and ran back to the airport when he realized we were breaking the rules," I continue. "He's just being nice because he doesn't want me to get in trouble. He's a good person. I've seen it for myself."

"Fascinating," Wayne mumbles. "Is that true, Caleb?"

Caleb stares at me for a second then nods once.

"Don't punish him," I say. "Punish me."

"Well," Wayne says. "I must admit I do admire your commitment to your duty here, Beatrice. But the most important part of your duty is a commitment to the rules."

He removes his hand from Caleb's back.

"Consider this a warning: you are under watch. Never let something like this happen again."

—— ✈ ——

WHEN I GET back to my room, the lights are out and Jenna is sound asleep. I quietly shut the door behind me, go to the bathroom, change into my pajamas, and throw cold water on my face. I rub at the permanent remnants of makeup even though I know they'll never budge. I slide into bed, but I can't turn my brain off.

Have I made things with Caleb better or worse? I had the chance to get rid of my problem. To get assigned to someone else and have Caleb taken out of the lottery. And I didn't take it.

Why?

Because he told me I was beautiful and almost kissed me in a virtual-reality version of a freezer aisle?

I squeeze my eyes shut, but the image of Sadie suddenly pops into my head, an angel on my shoulder nagging me to do the right thing.

The one piece of information that I want to keep buried, that Caleb killed me, is the thing that will free her to live her destiny. When he realizes the truth, he will be ready to move on, and so can she. Even if her destiny is something as silly as re-creating a Barbie Dreamhouse, it's still hers.

Panic pokes at my chest.

There's no way I'll get any rest tonight.

Emmy used to tell me that if I couldn't fall asleep, I should get out of bed and do something else until I tired out again so my brain wouldn't start associating being awake with being physically in bed, thus making me unable to fall asleep in it every night after. She'd heard the tip on some bogus wellness podcast and I'd blown it off, but now feels like as good a time as any to try it.

Hopping out of bed, I wonder if it's inappropriate to go walking around in my pajamas. Maybe it's not inappropriate, but the more apt question is: Do I want anyone to *see* me walking around in my pajamas?

Instead I change into the cropped fuzzy black sweater and jeans I arrived in. I've been storing them in the empty dresser under our TV, which serves no real purpose other than being the place where I sometimes hide Jenna's stuffed poodle when she's not in the room and it's freaking me out. Since it's the middle of the night, I figure I won't get in trouble for being out of uniform.

I walk down the hall to the elevator bank, and when I mash the up button, an elevator arrives in seconds. It's empty, so I press the button for the very top level and sit down on the floor, clutching my knees to my chest, hoping that the up-and-down motion will eventually make me sleepy again.

The elevator keeps going and going, until it stops at the twenty-second floor. The two orange doors split open, revealing Caleb like he's a game-show prize.

"Bea?" he says, raising his eyebrows. "What are you doing down there?"

I stare up at him from the elevator floor and blink several times.

"I couldn't sleep."

A smile tugs at his lips. I try to keep my face stoic, but I can't help but smile back.

"What are you doing up there?" I say from my spot.

"Couldn't sleep either."

As the doors are about to close, he clutches one with his hand to stop it and steps inside. He sits down next to me. The elevator continues going up.

"You're wearing normal clothes," Caleb says.

"You're very observant," I say with a sidelong glance.

We sit in awkward silence as we pass two more floors. The energy between us isn't as easy as when we were in the imaginary supermarket.

"You know how it sucks that you died wearing basketball

shorts and socks with sandals because you never actually really wore them?" I say at last. "Or so you claim."

"Yeah."

"Well, I get what that must feel like. These are my least favorite jeans. I died on laundry day, wearing the pair of pants that I hate the most. It sucks."

Caleb chuckles.

"They look nice, though," he says shyly.

"They make me look like someone's mom."

"I mean, do moms even wear 'mom jeans' anymore?" he asks. "I feel like their culture has been appropriated by hot teenage girls."

I turn and stare at him incredulously.

"Are you implying that you think I'm a 'hot teenage girl'?"

He gulps once. "Yeah," he says.

"Hm. Interesting."

"Sorry. Is that weird?"

"No, it's okay. You're allowed to think that I'm hot."

"Oh, well, in that case, thank you for your permission."

I smile at the elevator doors in front of me.

"Hey, thanks for bailing me out earlier," he says, tapping my arm with his knuckles.

"You were trying to cover for me, so . . ."

"Well, it *was* my idea to sneak into the hangar in the first place."

"True," I say.

The air feels heavy between us, and all I can hear is the rattle of the elevator climbing its way up.

"Caleb, can I ask you something?"

"Sure. Anything."

That "anything" gets me. He's too trusting. He doesn't deserve this.

"Do you . . . um . . ."

Do you remember if you hit someone with your car the night you died? Do you remember who it was? More specifically, do you remember that it was me?

He holds my gaze. His eyes are like two sparkling brown gemstones. Or probably not. I don't know. They're probably just two normal eyeballs. Surely the only way to explain that I'm even capable of thinking of a metaphor like that is I've had a brain transplant of which I was unaware. Maybe at the hospital where I was pronounced dead, my brain was swapped with that of a horny romance novelist.

"Do you wanna make out?" I blurt.

"Yes."

This time I make the first move. I lean toward Caleb's face and he closes his eyes and I just . . . go for it. First, it's weird, like my lips are two rubber erasers mashing up against another pair of rubber erasers. I don't how else to describe it.

Then the kiss just turns good weird. New and strange, but I want to keep going. And going. Then it just feels so good that my brain shuts down and I stop analyzing how it feels at all.

And after what feels at once like a really long but way too short amount of time, Caleb pulls back.

"I, um, I . . ." he stammers.

I place my pointer finger on his lips to signify that he should be quiet. He smiles beneath it.

Our lips meet again, but now they just feel like they're made of soft petals (really, where is this coming from?) and move in rhythm. I reach up for Caleb's neck, then he tentatively puts his hands around my waist, where my sweater crops. He pauses and opens his eyes, startled that he's touching skin and not the sweater.

"Is this okay?" he whispers.

"Yeah," I say impatiently, then go back to kissing him.

I slip my tongue inside his mouth. It tastes like industrial-grade mouthwash. But somehow combined with the natural taste of his mouth, it's not just the same mouthwash I use in my hotel bathroom. It's delicious. Better tasting than anything I've eaten since I arrived here. I kiss him urgently, like I can't get enough.

I tug at his T-shirt, exposing his perfectly average abs, and pull him closer toward me and he complies, pushing me closer to the elevator wall in turn. He groans, low and soft. *He actually groans*. I feel like I'm screaming internally.

This is so ridiculous.

This is absurd.

This is not a thing that happens to me.

Caleb's hands travel up my back, under my shirt, and suddenly he's near my bra. He touches the back straps gently and pauses.

"Is this okay?" he whispers again.

"Yeah," I say, this time slightly nervous.

I try to remember what bra I died in and fail, even though I've been wearing it under my uniform for weeks now. I hope it was a cute one. I'd always imagined the inaugural time my boobs would be touched to be different. For one thing, I wouldn't have eternally unwashed hair and smeared makeup.

I wouldn't be wearing my least favorite jeans. And I wouldn't be sitting in a stale-smelling elevator. And I'd be alive.

Then again, what does it even matter?

But before Caleb can move his hands any farther, the elevators doors open with a loud *ding!* and we quickly pull our intertwined bodies apart.

Standing before us is an old woman in a tattered night-gown and long, matted gray hair down to her waist. Gladys.

She makes one sustained wailing noise like an alarm and doesn't pause to take a breath. I could not pick a more effective sound to pull me out of this moment of passion if I tried.

"Uh, um, uhhh," Caleb mumbles, suddenly crossing his arms over his basketball shorts.

Oh my god. *Oh my god.*

My heart sinks. My body's elusive flight-or-fight response activates again. It chooses flight.

"I have to go," I blurt, my voice throaty.

Just as the doors are about to close, I stand and push myself into the hallway. Caleb calls out after me, but then the doors cut him off and, for the second time in twenty-four hours, I'm running away from him, and my problems.

33

Back in bed, I'm exhausted. Again. And the prospect of falling asleep seems even more impossible than before. On top of everything I was already feeling, now I'm full of even more shame and regret and guilt. I watch the sunrise through the hotel room window and think about how if Gladys hadn't interrupted us, maybe Caleb and I would've kept kissing all night, until now, and we could've watched this sunrise together like two incredibly insufferable, yet totally normal, seventeen-year-olds. Maybe it wasn't even Gladys's fault that we stopped. Maybe she was just a physical embodiment of my own guilty conscience.

Before my alarm clock even goes off, I get up and change out of my real-life clothes, folding the jeans with a newfound gentleness like they're a beloved family heirloom. I slip back into my orange uniform and look over at Jenna, still sleeping soundly in bed just as I'd left her the night before.

On my way to breakfast, I pause by the elevator bank, but choose to take the stairs instead. It's really what I should be doing anyway since my room is only on the third floor. And maybe part of me wants to preserve my memory of last night, even if it ended up being super embarrassing. Like if I never ride that elevator again, then the doors will seal shut and an alternate reality where Caleb and I keep making out will exist forever.

Since it's still so early, the food court is deserted. Breakfast isn't set out yet, save for a massive tray of coffee cubes. I scoop up a bowlful and take a seat near the window, staring outside and bracing myself for what lies ahead of me.

Today is the day I come clean to Caleb.

I swear.

I swear.

"BEA?" I HEAR a voice ask.

I open my eyes and look up at Caleb in front of me, out of breath like he ran here. My cheek is on the plastic tabletop and I can feel a pool of drool next to my mouth. I look around. Food is being served and people are sitting at tables all around us. I had to have been out for over an hour.

"You all right?" he asks.

"I still couldn't sleep." I sit up and wipe the spit off my face with the back of my glove. "So then I came down here and, I guess, finally fell asleep."

"I couldn't either," Caleb says with a small smile. "I went to your room just now, looking for you, but Jenna said she hadn't seen you all night."

"Look, Caleb. Last night was . . . fun," I say. His eyes brighten. "But . . ."

"But . . ." he echoes, his face falling.

"We need to focus on your memories right now. No distractions."

"That's exactly why I came looking for you," he says, a pained look flashing across his face. "Don't get me wrong. I thought last night was amazing. Even with the interruptions from the suit guy who lives in the air traffic control tower and the old lady screaming at us. But the reason I came looking for you this morning is because, well, I think I just had some kind of epiphany. I remembered something about the night I died. I need to show you as soon as we can get out to the hangar."

I stare up at the clock hanging over the center of the food court. It's 7:45. Fifteen minutes before the lottery. Todd and Sadie are in the morning staff meeting. She's still supposed to be monitoring my sessions with Caleb, but I don't know if I can handle an audience during what I suspect he's about to show me.

I reach for my train case and look inside. The keys I stole last night are still in there. After all that, Todd didn't even remember to collect them from me.

"Let's go," I say, grabbing his hand. "Right now."

CALEB AND I run straight to the hangar, without even pausing for a golf cart. I know I can't put this off much longer. I squeeze his hand one last time, knowing that after what he's about to realize, he won't ever want to touch me again.

When we get inside Caleb's memory, we're in his car and ahead of us is an expanse of road, surrounded by trees, where his headlights are the only source of light.

"So I'd left my dad's house," he explains, "and I was driving to the hospital in Northwood where they'd rushed my grandma after she fell."

My heart sinks at the mention of Northwood.

That's my town.

"And then, this is the thing I just remembered. There was this group of boys . . . and I think . . . I might've hurt . . ."

Suddenly, in the road, as Caleb drives down a hill, a small group of kids who look about thirteen or fourteen appears. One boy has his shirt off even though it's December and another is drinking out of a gallon-size plastic bottle of iced tea. They look so stupidly fearless, yet so vulnerable. I wish I could reach out and just shake their stupid pubescent bodies and scream at them to not be so confident, especially in the middle of the road.

They begin to scatter and move toward the trees at the sight of Caleb's headlights, but the boy with the iced tea just takes another swig from the bottle, casually standing in the middle of the street.

To avoid hitting him, Caleb has no choice but to swerve into the other lane. But he loses control, the road wet from melting snow, and nearly hits a pine tree, so to avoid it, he swerves again. And again. And again. A stupid luxury SUV-shaped bowling pin sliding down a slippery road. And this is when he swerves right into the middle of the intersection of Huntingdon Pike and Susquehanna Road, where I happen to be driving.

It was an accident, in the truest sense of the word.

I have always believed the concept of an out-of-body

experience to be complete nonsense, but here, watching myself from the perspective of the driver who killed me, I finally get it. The girl in the car opposite Caleb is me, there's no doubt about it, but it's like looking at an unflattering candid photo of yourself that you didn't know someone had taken. It makes you question everything you thought you knew. Like, I'd always assumed I was an ugly crier. But seeing myself behind the steering wheel, weeping over Emmy, not knowing I'm about to die, my face is the spitting image of a newborn baby.

I wince into my shoulder, because I know what's to come.

My head will make its way through the window and, eventually, I will die.

Yet, when I see Caleb go headfirst into his own steering wheel, his fancy car's airbags nowhere to be found, hear the sound of him moaning in pain, I'm not prepared. Not at all.

I don't understand how I watched myself die and yet this sight is just as gut-wrenching.

Even though I knew it to be true, I think a tiny part of me was still secretly holding on to the hope that this was all just a mere coincidence. I look around, desperate for a third, unknown driver who we could project the blame onto, but there's no one else around.

I turn toward Caleb. He's clawing at his mouth with his hand and tears are streaming down his face. He looks like he might be in as much pain as he is in the memory.

"No" is all he says.

I open my mouth to say something, but no words come out.

"No. This doesn't make sense. I must be getting my memories confused," Caleb manages to choke out. "Why would you be . . ."

He blinks back tears and his memory moves in reverse.

There I am again.

Past Me, right across from us, my eyes widening at the sight of Caleb's headlights, staring straight into his eyes and, possibly, his soul.

34

Emmy bolted out of the bathroom as soon as the bell rang. I guess she wouldn't even let the most devastating of personal crises mess up her perfect attendance record. Or, more likely, she just couldn't stand to look at me for a second longer.

I started to run after her, but I knew it was pointless. Out of the probably thousands of times I'd pissed her off in her lifetime, she would always end up forgiving me. This time, when she told me she wished she could never see me again, I knew she meant it.

In the hallway, everyone was staring at her as they walked past. A quiet chorus of whispers traveled along with them.

At the end of the hallway, Emmy practically ran into Skyler's arms, but he crossed them before she could. He just stared up at the ceiling, refusing to even make eye contact. She tried to explain, but he just kept on walking. Asshole.

"Emmy!" I yelled futilely for what felt like the millionth time.

I thought maybe she would come around then. That she'd realize I was right about Skyler all along and that this whole thing would blow over and she would be okay. We would go home, but not before stopping at the store to buy cheese puffs and sour gummies and all the other nutritionally deficient foods we would fill ourselves with when we were sad. Even though they had no vitamins, they would have made her stronger and she would have recovered from this. Everything would go back to normal as soon someone else's shiny new personal scandal made its way through the school.

But Emmy didn't come around. She just turned, looked at me, and shook her head one last time, vanishing toward the science wing.

I didn't run after her a third time. She needed space from me. Maybe for forever.

So I stormed off, back into the cafeteria, where I'd left my backpack with my keys inside it, and then I ran outside, too determined for any hall aide or security guard to stop me. I got into my car, but I couldn't make myself drive.

I just sat there all day, until school let out. Until everyone leisurely got into their cars, laughing and joking with one another, not a care in the world as they blared bad Top 40 songs out of their stereo systems and sped out of the parking lot to go home or to get their nails done before the dance or to just go loiter in a different parking lot.

By the time I snapped out of it, the sky was turning dark and there were no cars left. I realized what I was doing; I was waiting for Emmy to meet me after school, like always. One teeny, tiny piece of my heart truly believed that at the end of the day, she'd show up. But she didn't. So I put my keys in the ignition and drove off into the night, with no idea of where I was headed.

35

"It was you?" Caleb says breathlessly, closing his eyes.

I reach to turn the machine off so we don't have to look at the wreck a second more, but it goes off on its own as Caleb's helmet flashes green.

He stands up from the chair and reaches out like he wants to do something but he's not sure what. He puts his hand to his forehead and paces back and forth, gasping for air.

"Bea, I'm so sorry. I had no idea. I can't believe this," he says, the words flying out of his mouth. "I'm just . . . so, so sorry."

He thinks what I just witnessed is news to me. I stare at him blankly, then turn and look at the floor.

"Why aren't you freaking out?" he asks. "You should be punching me in the face right now. Did you not just see what I saw?"

"I already knew," I say quietly.

"What?"

"Do you remember when I found your passport? Your time and place of death were the same as mine, and I knew the crash wasn't my fault, so I figured—"

"You knew this whole time and you didn't tell me?"

I nod once.

"You knew I killed you and yet you just sat through all my memories. Why would you do that?"

"I don't know!" I blurt, tears forming at the corners of my eyes. "I mean . . . I do know. I wanted to waste all thirty of your sessions so you wouldn't make a breakthrough and would have to be stuck here, like me. And I guess I thought if I forced you to relive all your worst moments, revisiting all the pain, it'd be like some kind of satisfying revenge for what you did to me, but—"

"But you became my friend. You hung out with me. I showed you my dream. I mean, we *kissed*, Bea," he interrupts. "How could you make out with your . . . your . . . killer?"

He spits the last word out, disgusted. But I can't tell if it's disgust pointed at me or himself.

"I don't know," I say flatly. "I guess it's because I'm just some kind of freak."

"I actually started to have second thoughts about leaving here," he says, shaking his head. "You made me think for a minute that it'd actually be better to stay here with you than move on to Heaven. The whole reason I asked you if you could help get my lottery number called that first day was because I was so desperate to move on and see how my abuela was doing in the hospital. God, I'm so . . ."

He pauses, a look of realization crossing his face.

"Was that all part of your plan to put one over on me?" he continues. "Make me fall in love with you, then reveal that I killed you so I'd feel like even more of a monster?"

"Make you what?" I say with a humorless laugh. My organs feel like broken glass at the sound of *fall in love with you*.

He stares into my eyes and he doesn't look angry anymore, just sad. So devastatingly sad. Like his whole body could just crumple onto the floor.

"Never mind," he mumbles.

"The stuff with your memories was on purpose, but I didn't plan anything else," I say, raising my voice. "And you were the one who kissed *me* first, even if it was just in your dreams. You were also the one who killed me, okay? *I'm* the one who gets to be mad! *I* get to be confused about what this all means!"

I cross my arms and it's like I can visualize every bit of feeling I had for Caleb shrivel up inside my chest.

Caleb looks at me and swallows hard.

"I'm sorry about the accident," he says with finality.

"Okay then," I say, suddenly taking on a coldly professional tone. "Congratulations, Caleb. We've successfully figured out what was holding you back from Heaven. I think it's time for you to move on."

36

Caleb follows me back to the airport in silence, keeping about a foot of distance between us. I walk slowly, my body drained of all energy. I wish I could lie down right on the asphalt of the tarmac and become one with it, just letting airplanes roll off my back forever instead of having to make sense of my stupid feelings.

When we reach the departures counter, Sadie and Todd are standing beside it, staring me down.

"You," Todd says, pointing a finger at me. "You're in big trouble, young lady."

"Why?" I ask, moving my eyes between them. "Is this because I went out there without you, Sadie? Look, don't worry about it. Caleb's done."

Out of the corner of my eye, I see Caleb's mouth twitch slightly.

"Wait, really? You did it? He's moving on? That's amazing! Oh, Bea, I can't thank you enough."

Suddenly she grabs me by my shoulders and hugs me, lifting me about a half inch off the ground.

"No problem," I say, wiggling out of her grasp. "Glad to help."

"I'm going to Heaven!" she exclaims, reaching out for a high five. I reciprocate half-heartedly.

"*We're* going to Heaven!" she says, turning to Caleb and offering him a high five as well.

He gives her a sad smile and extends his hand in an even less enthused manner than I did. It doesn't matter, though. Sadie is too blissfully unaware to notice that my and Caleb's faces look like we've just returned from war.

"Well, all right then," she says, taking a deep breath to calm down. "Bea, you'll just have to fill out the discharge forms, and Caleb, in a few days the next flight will be taking off."

"A few days?" Caleb asks through his teeth. "But I'm ready to go now."

"Hold your horses," Sadie says, raising her palms. "Some of us have been waiting for this moment for *years*, okay? You can handle a few more days. Just relax. Say goodbye to the friends you've made. It'll be fine."

Caleb's winces at the mention of "friends."

Todd loudly clears his throat behind her.

"This still doesn't absolve her of her crimes, Sadie."

"What crimes?" I ask.

"Toddyyyyy," Sadie cries. "Let her off the hook. Her methods were unconventional. So what? They worked!"

"Can you please just tell me what the hell you two are talking about?" I ask.

They give each other a look.

"Wayne from the Disciplinary Council has requested to see you," Todd says. "Now."

They drag me away, leaving Caleb behind. I turn my head to look at him, but he's already moving in the opposite direction. I stare at the back of his neck and wonder if it's the last time I'll ever see him.

IT'S NOT. NOT technically, because, here in the Memory Experience office, right before my eyes is black-and-white surveillance footage of Caleb and me making out in the elevator.

"Jeans? I can't believe you would go out without your uniform on, Beatrice," Sadie scoffs.

"This was a mistake," I say to them. "I should've never kissed him, okay? It only happened once and it will never happen again."

"Only once?" Wayne presses. He adjusts the film in the projector and the footage on the wall changes to Caleb knocking on my hotel room door.

"I swear my roommate was having a party that night. I was in the bathroom the whole time."

"A party?" Wayne asks mockingly. "Then how come the footage shows that this boy was the only one who showed up?"

"I didn't say it was a well-attended party."

"And what about that first night you two went out to the hangar after hours?"

The footage changes again to two small figures darting across the tarmac, like it was taken from a high distance.

"How do you even know that's us?" I protest.

He switches the footage again. Caleb and I appear out of thin air in the waiting room, just seconds after each other. I slump in my chair.

"Todd, you gave us the keys to go out there," I say, looking at him.

Todd crosses his arms. "I cannot confirm or deny. But I can confirm that every choice I make is done with the goal of raising conversion rates. Sir."

"I don't get it," I say, looking at Wayne. "What's the problem here? Sadie told me that it wasn't against the rules to be close to the people I'm assigned to, just a bad idea, for me, emotionally . . ."

"The problem is," Wayne says, shutting off the projector and walking toward the front of the room, where the rest of us sit, "precisely that: you were close to Caleb. Because you knew him before you arrived, didn't you?"

My mouth falls open. I say nothing. I can feel Sadie's eyes on me.

"After our run-in last night, I requested copies of your individual passports from the processing department," Wayne continues, reaching into his suit jacket and pulling out two thin orange books. "When I looked at them, I was stunned to learn that you and Caleb Smith died just a moment apart in the same location."

He leans down so that we're at eye level, and scrutinizes my face. My cheeks flush.

"You should have spoken up," he says in a surprisingly gentle tone. "But I understand why you didn't. You're very young, not just in age, but in your role. Your supervisor, on the other hand . . ."

Wayne stands up straight and looks at Todd.

"It's part of protocol as supervisor to check an agent's

passport before assigning them to someone. You're supposed to be making sure that there are no glaring similarities. Even dying in the same town, let alone the same spot or time, is a conflict of interest and should be cause to reassign the agent to someone else."

"Well . . . I mean . . ." Todd sputters, raising his hands in the air. "What are the chances?"

"Apparently, very likely," Sadie exclaims, reaching across where I sit between them and swatting his hands down.

"The Disciplinary Council will prepare an investigation of your recent leadership, Todd, to determine if more time needs to be added to your sentence of employment."

"I've already been here for *forty-five years,* man!" Todd says, a vein bursting in his neck. "C'mon, I've only got five left."

Wayne gives him a hard stare and he shrinks back down into his seat.

"I'm sorry you had to endure this mix-up, Beatrice," Wayne says, turning back to me, "but it's time for you to get back to work."

I'm off the hook, but that doesn't mean I feel good.

In fact, I feel positively like garbage.

— ✈ —

"BEA, WAIT UP!" Sadie calls after me as I leave the office.

"Can't. I'm late. Lottery numbers have already been called and I have 4,997 souls to get to," I say without looking back.

"Please."

Reluctantly, I slow my steps and turn around. She looks at

me with puppy eyes. Puppy eyes that are caked with blue eye shadow.

"What?" I ask.

"I wanted to thank you for moving Caleb along today."

"I was just doing my job." I shrug.

"I realize I put a lot of pressure on you. Of course you wouldn't have spoken up and told me that you knew him in your past life. I feel like I failed you. I should've been this, like, big-sister figure, but instead I was so focused on getting out of here—"

"Hey," I say, putting my hand up. "Failing at being a big sister is kind of my specialty."

She raises her eyebrows.

"It's a long story," I elaborate. "But just know you didn't."

Sadie reaches her arms out for a hug and this time, I hug her back. With feeling.

"So are you and Todd over?" I ask, pulling back.

"Yeah," she says. "We had already said our farewells before I got on my initial flight. So it was awkward when I got kicked off the plane. Then it was even more awkward when I found out that it was his fault. Now we're definitely over. He's not the man I thought he was."

She stares wistfully off into the distance for a moment.

"It's okay, though. I'm counting on there being a significant number of hotties in Heaven."

WHEN I GET to the departures counter, there's only one person left who hasn't been assigned an agent.

And isn't it just my luck that that person happens to be Gladys.

"Good morning," I say, plastering on a smile in spite of the complete disaster of a morning I've already endured. "How are you today?"

She just stares at my feet in silence. It's so unsettling, it almost makes me pine for her usual screaming.

In the hangar, she ambles over to the Memstractor, her house slippers squeaking against the floor, like she's done this a million times. She flips her helmet over her tangled hair and I take a seat.

"Before we begin," I say, "I just want you to know that I've heard about you. The other agents say that you don't show them anything. That you refuse to open up. That this will be a big waste of my time. Of course I don't want to waste my time. I want to get out of here. But I thought you should know . . . I totally get it."

Gladys shifts in her seat but still doesn't look at me.

"Keeping your guard up is easy. It's better to scare people away than let them in. Especially when you've never really had someone around to teach you how to. So you go through your life thinking that when you let someone in, they can only hurt you, right? And you become this unapproachable bitch because you think it will keep you safe. And maybe it does. Until it inevitably doesn't."

My eyes well up.

"And what if you were so focused on protecting yourself that you never stopped to consider everyone else around you? And how you were unintentionally hurting them?" I say, my voice catching. "So maybe the point is that keeping your guard up is useless because any of us could get hurt at any time so you might as well . . . let other people in. While you can."

Gladys looks into my eyes, which are now streaming with tears.

"Sorry," I say, wiping my face with the back of my glove. "I don't really know where I was going with—"

"All right, all right," she squawks. Her voice has a throaty twang to it. "Save your crocodile tears, honey. I get it. And, frankly, I'm getting tired of the food here anyway. So what the hell? Let's see what's going on in that head of mine. Turn on the damn machine!"

I break out into a smile and, for once, everything doesn't feel totally hopeless.

37

A scratchy noise comes out of the PA system as I'm walking back to my room. I didn't move Gladys along today, but we're making progress, and that's more than any other agent who's dealt with her can say. Without thinking, I find myself holding my breath and clenching my fists, silently praying that the announcement won't be "Now boarding."

Even when I realize it's just the non-news that a sweater was found in a terminal bathroom and can be recovered at the lost and found, I'm still uneasy (and a little annoyed that the lost and found is finally functioning when I have no use for it). Caleb could be taking off any day now, and the thought of him leaving just like that, the way we left things, feels wrong.

When I open the door to our room, Jenna is sprawled on my bed, sprinkling glitter on a piece of paper.

"Where'd you get that?" I ask, realizing its close resemblance to the glitter on the sign Sadie was holding my first day here.

"I found it in the trash. In the hotel basement."

"And you were looking in the trash because . . ."

"I needed supplies. I'm making decorations for the mixer," she says cheerfully without looking up.

"What 'mixer'?"

"I'm trying to make my social club happen again. I won't let one defeat get me down. Attendance was only low because my strategy was weak. There aren't many people our age around. I figured out everyone here is sixteen or older. I think they, whoever *they* might be, determined the minimum age in accordance with the driving age. Which is so unfair. We're not old enough to drink or vote, but we're old enough to be sent to purgatory? It sucks that there aren't that many of us. Well, I mean, I guess it's technically good that there aren't that many dead sixteen- to eighteen-year-olds, but you know . . ."

She stops and looks up at me. I realize my eyes have glazed over while she was speaking.

"Hey, you okay?"

"No, Jenna, I'm not okay," I say, sitting on my bed. "We should just determine from here on out that I am never going to be okay."

"Why?" she says, putting down her glitter. "Oh. Of course. How did coming clean to Caleb go?"

So much has happened since Jenna and I last spoke. Too much.

"It . . . happened" is all I can manage to get out.

"What happened, specifically?"

I tell her everything. The fake kiss. The real kiss. The big reveal.

She absentmindedly puts her glitter-covered fingers to her mouth and bites her nails.

"Anyway, the worst part of it all is that he said he's in love with me. Or was, rather."

She gasps, briefly inhaling the glitter then coughing it back up.

"That's amazing, Bea!" she says hoarsely, clutching her chest.

"No, it is not amazing. It is profoundly messed up."

"Oh, come on! You have to at least see the bright side in all of this."

"Jenna, there is no bright side!" I snap, pushing myself off the bed and walking across the room. "We're dead," I say, gesturing between us. "I'm stuck here. For probably decades. Caleb just gets to move on, while I'm going to become a bitter old woman in the body of a teenage girl. If that's not Hell, then I don't know what is."

"But it's not too late for you to change things," Jenna says.

"Yes, it is. I can't go back and undo the things that I've done."

"At least you got to do things!" Jenna snaps back, throwing the glitter across her bed. "Even if you regret them, so what? You still had experiences. Hell, you even got to have this sordid airport romance. It's not fair!"

"What are you talking about?" I mumble.

"Do you know what happens to girls like me? Girls who have a terminal illness?" she says, quietly this time. "Nothing, okay? Absolutely nothing. My life was all hospitals and homeschool and living my life vicariously through people in books and movies. Do you know how many crappy cancer girl narratives there are out there? They are literally all about finding love right before death. There are none about how deeply boring and uneventful dying young can be. It's so frustrating!"

I stare at the floor and take in this truth.

"And yeah, now I'm dead. That also sucks, but you know what? At least here, I'm not sick anymore. My body is frozen and the cancer can't spread, so I can actually try to make a life for myself for the time being. I can move on from who I was. Isn't that the whole point of this place? Forgiveness?"

She gestures around at the pile of glitter and the ugly bedspread as if they've taken on some profound meaning.

"I suggest you make a life for yourself too. Instead of obsessing over what an awful person you are, or were, because, frankly, Bea, it's not a cute look for you. I know you're not as cool and tough as you act like you are. I've known that since I met you. You know how I know?"

"How?" I ask, arching an eyebrow.

"Because no one who has mascara tears permanently stuck to their face is actually heartless."

I look up and stare at Jenna for a long moment, then I smirk at her.

"What?" she asks, breathless from her rant.

"It's just . . . you're finally letting yourself be mad about something! You're not curbing your emotions to make other people comfortable. You're laying it all out there. This is good, Jenna. I'm proud of you."

She threads her eyebrows together in contemplation, then a look of realization washes over her face.

"Yeah. I guess you're right. I *am* finally letting myself be mad about something!" Jenna says, smiling back. "But stop deflecting, Bea. We need to return to the matter at hand. Do you have feelings for Caleb or not?"

"Since when was that the matter at hand?"

"Since I said it was."

"He hates me now and—"

"I didn't ask if he hates you," she interrupts. "I asked if you have feelings for him."

I ignore her question and lie back down on my bed.

"Fine, I'll stop trying to squeeze an answer out of you," Jenna says.

"I don't really know how I feel," I say finally. "I don't really know anything anymore."

"All right, but if there's one thing I've learned from watching too many romcoms, it's that if you love someone, you should always tell them before it's too late."

"That doesn't apply to real life."

"Well, this isn't real life, Bea. We're dead!"

FINDING CALEB IS easy this time. I spot him from afar, waiting in the departures terminal in one of the long rows of plastic seats. His knees are curled up in his chair and he's wrapped his arms around them. When he sees me walking toward him, he quickly unwraps them, sits up, and crosses his arms. I can't read the expression on his face. It's totally neutral.

"Hi," I say.

"Hey," Caleb replies, the word sounding heavy.

We stare at each other uncomfortably.

"Are you busy right now?" I ask.

He looks around at all the potential passengers waiting half asleep in their chairs as if they might need him. They obviously don't.

"Can you come with me out to the hangar?" I ask. "There's something, well, lots of things, I want to show you."

He scrunches up his face and looks away from me.

"I think we've made enough trouble for each other already," he says. "It's probably better, for the both of us, if I just stay put."

"Do you really believe that?"

"Yes."

"But do you wish it weren't true?" I press.

He nods once.

"Then just get over yourself and come with me," I say, reaching out my hand.

Reluctantly, he takes it.

38

"**I made you** show me the worst moment of your life," I say, settling myself into my helmet for what feels like the millionth time today. "So I thought it would only be fair if I show you mine."

So I take him through the final day of my life.

He doesn't ask questions. The whole time, Caleb's face is completely captivated by what he sees, but I can't tell if that's a good thing. Maybe my memories, like a trashy reality show, are so bad that you can't look away.

The corners of his lips turn up just slightly at the sight of me burrowed into the bottom bunk, refusing to get up for school. He laughs when I throw my food on Dominic. His eyes go wide when I talk back to the principal. They go even wider when I talk back to Taylor Fields. He cringes as I argue with Emmy in the bathroom. When we get to the part where I'm in my car, arguing with Siri, his face is in his hands.

I stop and turn off the machine before I can remember the crash itself. I think watching it once was enough.

"Do you have any questions?" I ask. "They don't have to be of the superficial variety."

He sits quietly for a minute.

"I don't get it," he says at last. "Why didn't you tell me? If I were you, I wouldn't have been able to even look me in the eye."

"What was I supposed to do? Say 'Hi. I'm Bea. I think you might've killed me with your car'?"

"Well, okay . . . I didn't mean like that. . . ."

"What would you have done?" I blurt out. "If the roles were reversed. If you knew I killed you but I didn't know it."

He thinks it over and sighs.

"I probably would have tried to avoid you at all costs and pretend it never happened, while quietly stewing in my own anger the whole time."

"See?" I shrug. "Being passive-aggressive isn't really my thing. Pure aggression is. Or was. But you made me rethink everything. You made me understand that people can screw up but I can still care about them."

Caleb flashes his eyes at me.

"You care about me?" he asks.

"I'm sorry," I say, avoiding his question. "I was just in too deep. I knew things would change between us if I revealed that I knew what happened and had been keeping it from you on purpose. And I think part of me was actually scared of you finding out the truth because that meant you'd have to apologize and move on to Heaven."

"What would be wrong with that?"

"Because then that would leave me here. Without you."

Saying it aloud, I realize that this is the first time I'm actually being completely honest with myself.

"You don't have to be sorry, though," Caleb says, standing up and walking over to where I sit. "Yeah, you lied to me, but, at the end of the day, I'm the reason you're here, even if it was an accident. I just feel like I can't say it enough. . . . I'm sorry."

"You don't have to say it anymore."

"Why? Am I being annoying?"

"No, Caleb. Because I forgive you."

He stares at me, taken aback.

"Cool," he says.

"Cool?" I ask, squinting.

"Sorry. I probably shouldn't say something so casual. I'm new to situations like this."

"You mean situations like apologizing to someone you accidentally murdered and then having them forgive you for it?"

"Uh. Yes."

"Me too."

We both stare at the floor.

"You said something this morning that I've been thinking about. A lot," I say.

"What?"

"You said I made you fall in love with me. Is that true?"

Caleb looks at me, then back at the floor, then back at me again.

"Yes," he says, swallowing.

"Well, I thought I should tell you, you made me fall in love with you too."

Somehow, saying those words feels natural. Good, even. We lean in toward each other and kiss, slowly.

I'm shocked how it feels even nicer than when we kissed before. I'm shocked that kissing someone you love actually lives up to the hype. I'm shocked that in this land of extreme mediocrity, we are managing to feel something extraordinary.

— ✈ —

"DO YOU THINK we would've ever met in real life?" I ask.

Caleb and I are lying on the concrete floor of the hangar, peacefully staring up at the ceiling as if the crisscrossed steel beams were constellations.

"Sure," he says, twirling my hair with his finger.

"How do you think we would've met?"

I turn on my side, propping my head on my elbow to face him.

"Hmm," Caleb contemplates. "Maybe road conditions were just slightly different and we both survived the accident, but you sued the hell out of me because you broke your, I don't know, arm."

"What?"

"Hear me out," he says, sitting up. "We meet in court. You don't even have a lawyer because you're so good at arguing your own case. You win. I owe you millions of dollars. Fast-forward a few months later. Life is lonely in your new mansion. You think, *You know, honestly, that boy I took to court? He was pretty cute. Maybe I should ask if he wants to come over sometime.*"

"Realistically, I would probably just win thousands of dollars and I'd have a McMansion. I'd be nouveau riche and probably have bad taste in houses."

"Out of that whole thing, that's the part you have a problem with? But also . . . good point."

Caleb stares at me for a moment.

"All right," he says finally. "How about this? We meet in college, like normal people."

"That wouldn't happen," I say. "I don't have the grades to get into Harvard."

"Well, as you saw, apparently neither did I."

"I don't even know if I had the grades to get into *a* college, period," I protest. "So then where do we meet?"

"Penn State," he says. "I settled. You finally got your act together and embraced the fact that you're really smart—"

"Wow, thank you so much."

"And actually started doing your homework to bring your grades up and applied."

"Hm."

"But the thing is, we both hate it," Caleb continues. "College is the worst. All the football games and those stupid frat parties. Just everyone behaving like absolute sheeple."

"Sheeple?" I giggle.

"Yes, sheep peop—"

"I know what sheeple are. You just said I'm really smart. Of course I know what sheeple are."

Caleb tilts his head back in frustration, but he keeps going.

"So it's freshman fall and we both happen to be at one of those stupid parties and you go outside to get some air because your roommate has abandoned you . . ."

"To talk to some guy whose face *and* personality closely resemble a package of bacon," I add. "This hypothetical roommate has horrible taste in guys."

"Exactly," Caleb says. "It's all a bit much. Then I come outside because I'm feeling the same way. And I make some stupid comment that I instantly regret like, 'Glad it's not raining, huh?' And you just stare at me like, 'Who is this idiot?' and I go, 'Name's Caleb. I think we live on the same floor?' Even though we probably don't, but I just want to make some kind of excuse."

"Then I just nod vaguely at you and say, 'I'm Beatrice,'" I interject. "There's an awkward silence, but then you actually say something extremely thoughtful and observational, and I turn and look at you like, 'Who *is* this idiot?'"

Caleb gives me a sad smile.

"You really didn't want to go to college?"

"Well, no," I say. "But now, after that beautiful fan fiction we've just written, I think I do."

"Did you really have no hopes and dreams in life?" he asks with a sidelong glance.

"It was my sister's thing to have hopes and dreams. My thing was always being convinced that, like, sea levels would rise too high or a nuclear bomb would hit before I could achieve anything."

Caleb shakes his head.

"I mean, but I was proven right! Although, I guess your Range Rover was slightly less powerful than a nuclear bomb."

"Jesus, Bea!"

"Too soon?"

We look at each other and smile.

I want it to be real.

I want to wake up from this dream we're in and have our fantasy of a completely run-of-the-mill encounter come true.

But before we can continue the fantasy, we're interrupted by the crackling noise of the PA system.

"Attention, guests," a voice blares. "The next departing flight is now boarding. All ticketed passengers should make their way to the departures terminal immediately."

39

"I'm not leaving," Caleb says, sitting up. "I'll stay here with you until you've helped enough people move on. Until we can travel to Heaven together."

The expression on his face is dead serious.

"It's going to be years before I'll be allowed to leave this place, Caleb."

"I don't care. As long as I'm with you, it doesn't matter where I am."

"But we're talking about this dump versus Heaven."

"What's the point of Heaven if you're not there?"

I can feel the ghost of the old me cringe at how much Caleb's words sound like they're the lyrics to some generic boy band hit. But the new me has gone soft. She feels her heart break at the sound of them.

"You have to move on, Caleb," I say, putting both of my hands on his cheeks. "You have to see how your family is doing. You don't deserve to be here a moment longer. You made an honest mistake. You apologized for it. You're a good person. I hurt people on purpose, and I need to stay behind until I've made up for everything I've done."

A tear trickles down his cheek. I wipe it away with the pad of my thumb.

"Remember when you tried to mansplain the concept of 'liminal spaces' to me the first time we met?" I ask.

The corner of his mouth turns up in a smile.

"It's like you said then," I continue. "This place isn't made for people to stay a long time. It was built to be left behind."

He swallows hard.

"But I don't want to leave you. What if nothing I feel there compares to the way I feel now? What if Heaven really isn't all it's cracked up to be? Then what? What if eternity is really underwhelming?"

"Maybe it will be," I say. "But there's only one way for you to find out."

"Do you think we're even allowed to *kiss* in Heaven?" Caleb asks.

"I don't know," I say. "Hopefully, yes."

"Maybe we won't even want to kiss. Maybe in Heaven you don't even feel human attraction anymore. Maybe the only thing you can be attracted to is, like, some abstract ball of light. Maybe you *are* some abstract ball of light. What if you lose your entire physical being? You don't even have lips—"

I put my finger to his mouth to make him stop talking.

"Then we should probably kiss now, while we still have lips," I suggest.

And so we do. I don't need to explain the mechanics of kissing again, but know that this kiss is happy and sad at the same time.

There are things I feel and do now that I never thought I would before.

Running out of ways to describe a kiss is one of them. Even knowing what a kiss feels like is another.

I pull back from the kiss, knowing that if we don't stop now, there's a low chance we ever will, and Caleb will certainly miss his plane. He keeps his eyes closed for a second longer than I do.

"C'mon," I say, pulling him by the hand. "It's time for you to get out of here."

OUTSIDE THE HANGAR, it's dark, but the overhead lights are blinding. They spotlight a plane boarding across the tarmac. I guard my eyes with my hand and squint into the distance. I can see people walking up the temporary flight of stairs leading to the plane. Some of them are even cheering and whooping like they're about to board a roller coaster, thrilled to be moving on.

Most of me is happy for them, but a tiny part of me wishes they would just shut up. I guess old habits die hard.

I focus harder and realize that the person leading all the cheering is Sadie. I lift a hand to wave at her, catching her eye right before she boards.

She pauses on the stairs and winks at me.

"I won't forget you, Bea," Caleb says, taking both of my hands into his. "We'll be together again one day. I know it."

"That's if I don't find another airport boyfriend to keep me company," I joke.

Caleb rolls his eyes and smiles.

"I won't forget you either," I say, serious. "I'll see you around, Caleb."

"I'll see you around, Bea."

He turns and walks off toward the plane at a regular pace, but as he gets closer, he switches to one of those awkward half jogs that dads do when they cross the road. I can't help but laugh.

Caleb walks up the steps of the plane, but before he boards, he turns and looks at me one last time. I smile at him and suddenly my laugh dissolves into a rush of tears.

I stand there on the tarmac, as still as an ice sculpture but just as fragile, until the stair car drives away, until the airplane is all boarded, until an air traffic control employee motions with his oversize glow stick for me to move. I don't move. I stand there and let the wind whip my hair as I watch the airplane take off and carry the boy I love to a whole other dimension.

40

As I walk back inside, I can feel a fresh batch of tears forming behind my eyes like dark clouds before a storm. Like my story with Caleb began, I can feel it ending with me ugly crying. This is just who I am now.

A Crier.

I will myself to hold them in until I get back to my room, where I can collapse onto my bed in private and just let them rip.

I'm only human.

I guess that's what I've learned from this whole thing. Whatever this whole thing is.

But when I turn down my hallway, the usual silence is punctuated by the sound of . . . a banjo?

As I walk down to my room, I realize the music is coming from behind my door.

I push it open, and when I do, I feel about a dozen pairs of eyes turn and look at me.

"You made it!" I hear Jenna's voice squeal. "You're just in time. We're about to play a get-to-know-you game."

Sitting on the edge of my bed is a blond boy around our age, wearing overalls and strumming away on a banjo. A group of other teenagers stands around him. Two girls have their arms interlocked and are twirling in a circle, doing some kind of jokey square dance, but everyone else is just hanging out, leaning on our dresser or sitting on the beds.

Jenna has somehow managed to cover the walls in glitter. She's draped orange napkins that she probably stole from the food court over all of our lights for some pseudo mood lighting. I have to admit, it does make the room feel pretty cozy if you don't stare at each individual element too closely.

"I told you I could make it happen!" Jenna exclaims as she stands to greet me.

"What's up with the banjo guy?"

"Oh, that's Beau," she explains. "Hey, you two almost have the same name! Isn't he so cute?"

She leans in toward my ear.

"He died while he was playing the banjo at a county fair," Jenna whispers. "Some freak accident where a Ferris wheel car flew off and right onto the stage where he was performing. Anyway, he says playing it helps him heal, so just be nice."

My eyes widen just slightly.

"Guys, this is Bea!" Jenna says loudly. "This is her room too."

"Hi, Bea!" the room says back.

"Bea, this is everybody."

I stare at them uncomfortably for a second. I know, if I chose to, I could retreat into the bathroom right now, curl my body into the fetal position inside the shower, and cry my eyes out until the party ends. I could lean in fully to being some half-widowed car crash victim who fell in love with the boy

who accidentally killed her. I could shut myself off to everyone and suffer in silence today and maybe for the thousands
of other days I'll be stuck here alone.

But that's the thing. I'm not alone.

"Hi, everybody," I say.

"Now that you're here," Jenna says to the room, "we're
going to play Two Truths and a Lie. Like the name says, everyone tells two truths about themselves and one lie, and we all
have to guess which one is the lie. Got it?"

No one really moves.

"This will be so fun!" she exclaims.

Jenna motions for everyone to sit down in a semicircle,
and I swallow back the urge to shoo them all off my bed.

"Bea, since you arrived last, you have to go first."

"Um, okay." I swallow. "I'm really grateful that Jenna is my
roommate. Uh . . . I would be absolutely thrilled if I never had
to look at any form of Jell-O again. And . . ."

I mull over my answer for a minute.

"I'm an awful person who doesn't deserve to be happy,"
I say.

The room sits around contemplating my answers, but
Jenna smiles back at me.

"Well, duh, the lie is obviously the last one," the boy with
the banjo says in a thick Southern accent. "Because Jenna's
great."

He winks at her and she blushes.

"And I think I speak for all of us when I say that nobody
wants to see any form of Jell-O again," he continues.

Everyone nods and murmurs quietly.

"*And,*" Jenna butts in, "you are *not* an awful person and you *do* deserve happiness. Is that why you included that? Because you wanted someone to say that to you?"

A smile tugs at my lips.

"I mean, no. But now that you've said it . . . it's nice to hear."

MIRACULOUSLY, THE PARTY goes on until the wee hours of the morning. I should have never underestimated Jenna.

Beau is the last to leave. I watch Jenna hug him goodbye, shut the door, and flop onto her bed. She clutches her pillow to her chest dreamily.

"I don't want to jinx things, but I think he's, like, in love with me."

I look at the clock on the nightstand. It's 5:12 a.m.

"Hey, Jenna," I say, pulling the cover off my bed. "Are you tired?"

"Yeah." She yawns. "Now that you mention it."

"Well, you better stay awake."

"Why?"

"Because," I say, looking toward the door. "I have an idea."

"ARE YOU SURE we should be doing this?" Jenna asks, clinging to the sides of the stair car as it drives us over to the airplane hangar. "Couldn't we have just waited for it to park and then climbed up?"

"No. This is all part of the experience," I explain.

She looks at me warily as wind blows in her face. Finally the car comes to a halt.

"Thank you!" I call over the side to the driver. "I owe you one."

I hoist the bedspread I'm carrying over my shoulder.

"Let's go!" I say. I lead us up the temporary staircase and onto the roof of the hangar.

"Okay, so, we're on a roof?" Jenna observes after climbing up and dusting her hands off on the back of her sweat suit.

I unfurl the blanket and sit down in the middle of it, gesturing for her to join me.

"Jenna, you said that your real Make-A-Wish, your non–Disney World Make-A-Wish, was to camp out at the Grand Canyon and watch the sunrise."

"Right."

"So I thought that since I can't get you to the Grand Canyon, I could do the next best thing."

I point out into the expanse of nothingness before us. The sky has turned the color of cotton candy, a gradient of pink and lavender and baby blue, and the sun has just begun to rise, its glow emanating from behind a patch of clouds. The way we sit, we can't see the airport or the air traffic control tower or anything else. We're not just sitting on the roof of some glorified giant shed. It's like we're sitting on the edge of the world.

Jenna looks out into the distance. Her face is blank and she says nothing.

"Well, maybe it's, like, the next, next, next times a thousand best thing, but—"

"It's perfect," Jenna says, tears forming at the corners of

her eyes. She puts her arm around my shoulders and I put mine around hers.

Before I know it, I'm crying too. I am what you might even call weeping.

"You okay?" Jenna asks after a moment of hushed observation.

"It's just, I don't feel like I'm staring into the sun," I say. "It's like I'm staring into the void. And the thing is? The void? It's, like, really beautiful."

"It really is."

And so, we look out, staring into the void, together.

ACKNOWLEDGMENTS

THANK YOU TO everyone who made this book possible:

My iconic editor Alex Sanchez who once knocked on my door and asked, "What do you think of purgatory?" It has been a joy to work with someone who so totally gets me, but also knows when to politely ask what the heck I am doing.

Marissa Grossman and Jess Almon for your amazing brains without which this book would literally not exist.

My publisher, Casey McIntyre, and the entire team at Razorbill.

My agent, Dana Murphy, for your calming presence, over the phone and IRL. This is just the start of our long, beautiful businesswoman lifestyle.

My publicist, Vanessa DeJesús, for spreading the word that this exists.

Kelley Brady, for designing such a beautiful cover, and Jeff Rogers, for making illustration magic.

My copyeditors Marinda Valenti and Kaitlin Severini, for saving me from calling Chili's menu items by their incorrect names, among other things.

My proofreaders Maddy Newquist and Krista Ahlberg.

My first reader Haley Mlotek, for your genius observations

and ability to make online shopping and airing petty complaints feel like a meaningful part of my artistic method.

America's Nicest Young Man, Brendan O'Hare for your constant emotional support, encouragement, and, yes folks, ability to make me laugh even when I am having a day where I think my writing is trash. I love you!

Rachel Porter, for your thoughtful insights and feedback that made this book so much better.

My family, Bill, Alicia, and Lydia Noone, for always believing in me.

My friends, roommates, and/or coworkers who always lent me their ears and a steady supply of memes throughout the writing process: Lola Pellegrino, Hazel Cills, Brittany Spanos, Estelle Tang, Marie Lodi, Anna Fitzpatrick, Krista Burton, Brodie Lancaster, Allegra Millrod, Joey Vincennie, Eloise Giegerich, Rika Mady, Erin Kelly, Julia Panek, Kyle Hide, Claire Salinda, and probably many more, as I am really popular!